'Hang on a minute!' Peace called out in sudden alarm as full understanding of his new predicament came to him.

He was on board the warship which had drawn his attention earlier – the unusual activity surrounding it had been an indication that it was preparing for blast-off – and soon he would be on his way to do battle against the Martian invaders. It was true that he had been praying to escape the dreariness of his life in Manchester – but not like this! Even if the ageing pile of metal did manage to get into space intact, the Martian weaponry was bound to annihilate it in the first instants of the engagement . . .

'What am I saying?' Peace demanded of himself. 'There *aren't* any Martians. Or are there? I'll bet the whole solar system is knee deep in them. *Help! Help!*'

Driven by fresh panic, he began pounding on the side of the crate with his fists. The sound was drowned out by a blaring of klaxons which in turn was obliterated by the growing thunder of rockets. Vibrations shook the crate and its contents as the rocket exhaust swelled far beyond mere thunder, becoming a mind-numbing, heart-stopping tumult which seemed to tear reality itself apart.

Peace slowly sank to his knees, giving way to despair and the accelerative in

BOB SHAW
DIMENSIONS

VGSF

First published in Great Britain 1993
by Victor Gollancz Ltd
under the title *Warren Peace*

First VGSF edition published 1994
by Victor Gollancz
A Division of the Cassell group
Villiers House, 41/47 Strand, London WC2N 5JE

A catalogue record for this book is
available from the British Library.

ISBN 0 575 05719 X

Printed and bound in Great Britain
by Cox & Wyman Ltd, Reading, Berks

To Charlotte and the rest of the Alabama branch of the Jophan family

Chapter 1

Warren Peace was *bored*.

It was the eighth day of the Oscar Galactic Jamboree, and he was supposed to be having the time of his life – but the malaise of a bleak, grey, sterile discontent had entered his soul.

There was nothing really new about his having a fit of the blues. In the past, back in the days when he was a human being, he had quite often found himself plunged into a mood of depression. The difference between then and now was that in the old days a number of remedies had been available to him. Depending on his frame of mind, he could dose himself up with vitamin-rich foods; or drown his sorrows in the company of a few congenial boozers; or uplift his spirits by venturing on an exciting new love affair.

Now, however, those paths to happiness were barred to him – for the simple reason that, as an Oscar, he had no need for food, drink or sex.

This is terrible, he thought, glancing down in resentment at his gleaming body. It was more than two metres tall and resembled a golden statue of a perfectly developed man. It was also naked – partly because Oscars were impervious to even the most extreme weather, partly because there were no embarrassing protuberances in the region of the groin. When Peace had found himself ensconced in the splendid, indestructible body almost a year earlier he had been delighted, but of late he had come to regard it as a prison.

And it was a prison from which there could be no escape.

'Hey, Warren!' The familiar subetheric voice belonged to Ozzy Drabble, one of Peace's oldest friends among the Oscars. 'Why are you skulking around here by yourself? Why aren't you joining in the fun?'

'What fun?' Peace said gloomily, turning to face the approaching figure. To human eyes Drabble would have looked exactly like any other Oscar – a bald-headed, ruby-eyed golden giant – but Peace's superacute vision was able to pick out distinctive lineaments in his face.

'Are you kidding me?' Drabble was unable to repress a laugh as he gestured towards a group of Oscars who were sitting around a campfire a few hundred metres away in the deepening twilight. 'Those characters are still at it! They passed the four-thousand mark a while ago – and they're *still* going strong! It's the funniest thing you ever heard, Warren.'

'Is it?' On the first night of the jamboree, eight days earlier, the Oscars by the fire had begun a rousing subetheric chorus of 'One man went to mow . . .' – and they had been singing ever since. Peace had eventually managed to tune them out of his consciousness, but Drabble's remarks were weakening his mental defences. Suddenly the joyously combined voices came flooding into his mind.

. . . 4460 men, 4459 men, 4458 men, 4457 men, 4456 men . . .

'Old Harry Kurtzle got his numbers all mixed up last night, and they nearly had to start the song all over again,' Drabble said with an enthusiastic chortle. 'You should have heard him, Warren. I thought I was going to *die!*'

'That seems an appropriate reaction,' Peace commented.

'Aw, don't be like that, Warren.' A concerned expression appeared on Drabble's smooth-cast features. 'You should be joining in the fun. There must be *something* going on that you can enjoy. How about going back into the relay race?'

Peace shook his head. The jamboree was being held on the planet Mildor IV, a smallish uninhabited world whose surface was entirely covered with rocky desert. On the day he arrived Peace had been persuaded to take part in the relay race, in which members of competing teams had to run all the way round the equator to get back to the starting point and hand over the baton. It had taken Peace three days to complete one circuit of the globe – three days of utter stultification as he

8

pounded across a featureless landscape – and on getting back to the camp he had promptly resigned from the team.

'Well, how about the pitching competition?' Drabble went on. 'You were doing great there, Warren.'

Peace glanced towards another campfire, where a dozen or so Oscars were engaged in hurling pebbles in a generally eastern direction. They had been similarly occupied since the jamboree had begun and, as Oscars never had to sleep, had kept going even during the hours of darkness. The object of the competition was to see who could propel the largest pebble into low orbit. Peace had found the activity almost as dull as the relay race, the single spark of excitement coming when Joby Lorenz had been struck in the back of the neck by a big pebble descending from a freakishly accurate single orbit. Joby had somersaulted for more than a hundred metres across the desert floor before coming to rest, and his companions were still chuckling over the comical expression he had worn when rejoining the group.

'I'm sorry,' Peace said. 'I just can't work up any kind of interest in chucking rocks into the sky.'

'At least you could sit by the fire with Hec Magill and me,' Drabble persisted. 'We're roasting wienies and mallows and yarning about the old days.'

'For God's sake, *Ozzy*!' Peace cried, losing his temper. 'What's the point in roasting wienies and mallows when you can't even eat the flaming things?'

Drabble looked hurt. 'It's traditional, Warren. It creates a nice atmosphere.'

'That's another point! This is an airless planet – so there's no atmosphere of any kind, nice or otherwise. Even your campfires are running on bottled gas! And why the hell would anybody in his right mind want to talk about the old days? All that happened to us in the old days was that the Legion kept us half-starved and shipped us to every hellhole in the galaxy and did its best to get us killed!'

'Those were hard times,' Drabble conceded. 'But talking about them reminds you of what a great life you have now.'

'Great life!' Peace was no longer able to keep his feelings in

9

check. 'You call *this* a life! I'd have been better off if you and Hec had left me to die that day I got hit by the van. I'm sorry I ever became an Oscar.'

'Warren!' Drabble took a step backwards, the ruby lenses of his eyes widening in shock. 'That's a terrible thing to say – you must be sick!'

'Oscars don't get sick, you dummy.'

'I forgot,' Drabble said. 'But there must be *something* wrong with you, Warren – nobody else has ever had any complaints.' Drabble paused, corrugations appearing on the brazen skin of his forehead. 'Maybe the throwrug we put over you was sick.'

Peace considered the new idea for a moment. The throwrugs were an alien life form which had been encountered in the forests of the planet Aspatria. Their name was derived from their blanket-like body form, which had vivid patterns on the upper surface. The underside, consisting of millions of quivering blood-red feelers, had far less aesthetic appeal. The throwrugs lived in the branches of tall trees, and had the disconcerting habit of dropping on any human who was unwary enough to walk directly below. At first it was thought that any legionary engulfed by one of the bizarre aliens was simply digested by it, but it later transpired that the throwrugs were not killers. What a throwrug did when it swaddled a man was to enter a symbiotic relationship with him – and the outcome was an Oscar.

Peace had been badly mangled when knocked down by a van, and Drabble and Magill had rushed him to Aspatria. He had been on the point of death when his friends had taken the extreme measure of draping a throwrug over him, thereby saving his life. That had been almost a year ago, and during that time Peace had seemed to be just like any other Oscar – an invincible golden giant, immune to all human weaknesses, dedicated to fighting crime and corruption throughout the galaxy. Now, however, the honeymoon was definitely over.

'Look, I'm sorry about this, but I have to get out of here,' Peace said. 'I'm going to slip away on the quiet for a while. I'm going to go gafia.'

'Gafia?' Drabble looked puzzled. 'What does that mean?'

'It's a new acronym I've just made up.' The Oscars had a strange predilection for inventing words which outsiders could not understand, and for reasons Peace could not explain he had a longing to be the originator of at least one in-group expression. 'It stands for Getting Away From It All, and I hope it becomes part of Oscar-speak.'

'There isn't much chance of that,' Drabble said. 'It's a direct contradiction of Oscaring Is A Way Of Life – which we usually shorten to oiawol.'

'That's a *useless* word,' Peace protested. 'It makes you sound like you've got sinus trouble.'

'Oscars don't have sinuses.'

'I forgot,' Peace mumbled. 'And I still don't like it.'

'Never mind that,' Drabble said. 'Where are you going to go? What will you do with yourself?'

Peace glanced up into the sky, which had turned completely black during the brief conversation, and let his gaze drift from star to star. 'I'll go back on duty. There must be somebody out there who needs help, and I feel better when I keep myself busy.'

'Brown Owl isn't going to be too happy about this,' Drabble said. 'He likes everybody to show solidarity.'

'Brown Owl will just have to put up with it,' Peace said carelessly. He had not spent much time with his commander-in-chief, but – even though Oscars were without gender – he was slightly unhappy about serving under a former male who had chosen himself such an odd title.

'You'll be on your own if you get into a jam,' Drabble warned. 'The jamboree has another six days to run, and the guys won't want to tear themselves away before the fun is all over.'

'I won't get into a jam,' Peace said confidently. 'I'm the first to admit that I'm slightly accident prone, but I know I can stay out of trouble for a mere six days. I can do that standing on my head, for heaven's sake! Six days! Huh!'

He gave Drabble the Oscar salute – circled forefingers and thumbs pressed to the eyes to symbolize vigilance – then turned and strode off towards where he had left his spaceship. The parking lot resembled an industrial estate filled with ugly, prefabricated buildings – which reminded Peace about another of his grievances against life in general. The romantic side of him demanded that a spaceship, especially one dedicated to the fight against evil, should be an aesthetically gleaming spire with a needle prow pointing at the stars.

By contrast, the standard space cruiser was a low-lying metallic rectangle made of coarsely welded steel sheets, 200 metres long and with a small tower at each end. One tower housed a matter transmitter, and the other a matter receiver, and the ship progressed by transmitting itself forward and receiving itself millions of times a second. In that way it could travel at huge multiples of the speed of light without violating any of the laws of relativity.

There was no doubt that the design was superbly efficient. It was also very safe because, as no ship could be regarded as being in one place or another at any given instant, it was impossible for it to be in a collision. The main trouble, as far as Peace was concerned, was that he had dreamed of crusading through the galaxy, in one piece, in a beautiful silver ship – not of being wafted from star to star as a cloud of particles inside a crude steel lunchbox.

He had no trouble locating his own vessel among dozens of identical shape, because his was the only one with shabby and blistered paintwork. Perhaps his first indication that he was not cut out for the life of an Oscar had come when he noticed he did not share their compulsive need to keep everything gleaming like new, no matter how much boring and repetitive drudgery it took.

He entered the ship by the door in the forward tower, activated all its systems and took off at a leisurely speed. The desert, with its sprinkling of orange and yellow fires, sank in the view screens. Although he had escaped the oppressive tedium of the jamboree he was still suffering from ennui and, just to occupy his mind, he decided to try departing Mildor IV along the centre of its conical shadow without using astrogational instruments. He studied the image of the planet, which was mostly in sunlight from his point of view, then directed the ship sideways until all he could see was a vast black disk imposed on fields of stars. When he judged himself to be in the right position he nudged the ship into what ought to be a perpendicular course, then he switched off the drive and allowed it to coast. If his aim had been good he would eventually be rewarded by the sight of an even corona appearing around the planet as its apparent size shrank to less than that of the sun.

'It's not as good as that wonderful moment when a beautiful woman first locks eyes with you over the candle flame at dinner,' he told himself. 'It's not even as good as when the waiter is coming towards you with a bottle of decent wine cradled in his arm. It's not even as good as slipping your fingers under a well-built burger – but it sure as hell beats sitting around a fire with a bunch of overgrown boy scouts.'

Peace incautiously allowed his long-range supersenses to focus on the group who were singing the roundelay and a wisp of unmelodic song drifted into his mind: . . . *3824 men, 3823 men, 3822 men, 3821 men . . .*

He shuddered, tuned the relentless phrasing out of his thoughts, and settled down to watch the aft view screen. An hour dragged by, then another and another, during which the view on the screen scarcely altered. Peace was beginning to think that his newly invented pastime hardly deserved its generic name when, with shocking suddenness, a voice echoed silently within his skull.

Wimpole! What are you doing with your helmet off?

A moment later came a reply: *My head was sweating, boss. These lead helmets is murder. I swear my brains was beginning to cook.*

The strength with which the words registered on Peace's telepathic faculties told him, much to his surprise, that the speakers were quite close. Their proximity was unexpected because a starship's radio and tachyon beacons normally advertised its presence in any given region of space – and all of Peace's detectors had remained quiet. He concentrated on trying to glean more information.

Your brains can boil over and spill out through your ears for

13

all I care, the first speaker stated. *This is my last warning to you, Wimpole – keep your helmet on!*

But the Oscars ain't likely to pick us up at this range – and, anyways, you ain't wearing your helmet.

That's only because I have trained myself not to think when I'm on a mission like this.

There wasn't no need to train yourself, boss.

Are you trying to be funny, Wimpole? Put your helmet back on and get ready to release the meteorite.

There followed a long silence which suggested to Peace that the men on whom he had eavesdropped had again screened off their brain emanations by means of lead-lined helmets. But on the last word of the exchange, because telepathic communication often went beyond the verbal level, he had picked up a peculiar mental image. It was of an egg-shaped boulder which seemed to emit a shifting purple glow.

Frowning, he bent his mind to the task of interpreting the stray fragment of conversation. It seemed obvious that criminals were sneaking up on the Eighth Galactic Jamboree with the intention of launching an attack. In one respect the plan was a good one, because all the Oscars in the galaxy were supposed to be conveniently gathered into one small area of Mildor IV. That, however, was where the merits of the attack plan ended. It was impossible to kill an Oscar, and any misguided attempt to do so would only result in a battalion of enraged golden supermen descending on the aggressors. Peace did not like to dwell on the outcome, because the strength of Oscars was such that, even when they were doing their best to exercise only reasonable force, wrongdoers tended to come apart in their hands.

Puzzled by the naivety of the unseen attackers, Peace went to the ship's control console and switched on its full range of detector systems. There was nothing to indicate the proximity of another ship, but that was hardly surprising considering that cheap anti-detection devices were available at Dixons electronic stores on most civilized worlds. Peace turned the instruments up to maximum sensitivity and was rewarded when one of the screens began to register a small body which

14

was travelling towards Mildor IV at 40 km/sec. When he processed the data he found that the speeding body was slightly more than a metre in its major dimension and had a density greater than that of pure uranium.

It was clear that the criminals had launched their weapon towards the assembly of Oscars, but Peace was still unable to make sense out of the operation. No matter what kind of explosion the projectile might cause the Oscars would survive it, and would set off in pursuit in their –

That's it! Peace thought, feeling the same kind of exultation he usually got on solving a difficult crossword puzzle. *Although the Oscars will be unharmed, all their spaceships could be destroyed! The Oscars could be marooned on a backwater planet . . . it might be a year before they were discovered and rescued . . . and the forces of organized crime could achieve many of their evil ambitions in only a year or so . . .*

'Not while I'm on the scene!' Peace snarled aloud, all his sense of a purpose in life returning with full force. He interrogated the ship's main computer, then instructed it to put him alongside the missile which was plunging towards the Oscars' camp site. The operation took less than a minute, thanks to the fact that the ship's auto-transceiver system of propulsion was not plagued by the age-old problems, such as inertia, associated with Newtonian physics.

He slid aside the door in the forward tower section and saw, less than a metre away, and set against a starry background, a purple-glowing ovoid of chipped and pockmarked rock. Its strange luminescence aside, the object looked just like any other chunk of celestial debris. It was gradually sliding forward with regard to the ship because of a slight mismatch in velocities.

Peace took a firm grip on the doorframe, extended one leg and placed his foot against the rock. At the instant of contact a curious icy tingle ran up his leg and through his body, causing a momentary blurring of his vision, but the effect was too slight to command much attention. Even if the rock proved to be highly radioactive, which was a possibility, it would do no harm to his superhuman constitution.

15

There are times, he told himself, *when being an Oscar is no bad thing*.

Gathering all his strength, he drove his leg out straight and propelled the luminous ovoid away from the spaceship. It departed immediately with considerable speed, tumbling as it shrank in apparent size, and within a matter of seconds had dwindled to a point resembling a fading star. Peace waited until it had passed beyond even his long-range perceptions, then went back to the control console and told his computers to advise him of the rock's current status. The answer was highly satisfactory: the glowing boulder had been guided into a new path which would take it clear of Mildor IV, and from there, with gravitational slingshot assistance, directly into the local sun.

It had been his intention to disappear into the depths of the galaxy, and perhaps live like a hermit until he felt like rejoining the mainstream of life – no matter what the damage to his standing among his fellow Oscars. Now, however, he had a personal triumph to report to Brown Owl, and the prospect of a great deal of egoboo was almost enough to make him change his mind. (Egoboo, an abbreviation of ego boost, was a term which had been invented by the Oscars to describe the great satisfaction that a member of their fraternity derived from seeing his name favourably mentioned in their group publications.) After a moment's thought, realizing he was beyond normal telepathic range, he switched on the ship's subetheric communicator and got through to Ozzy Drabble on the special Oscar band.

'Hello, my old buddy,' he said cheerfully. 'This is Warren calling. How are things going?'

'Things are going great,' Drabble replied, sounding a little cautious, undoubtedly wondering why Peace had taken the trouble to call him. In the background Peace could hear . . . *4133 men . . . 4132 men . . . 4131 men . . .* and was suddenly tempted to break the connection, but his craving for egoboo won the day.

'Ozzy,' he said, 'have you mentioned anything yet to Brown Owl about my taking off on my own?'

16

'No. He's having so much fun in the tunnel-digging competition that I didn't like to interrupt.'

'Well, when you do speak to him,' Peace said nonchalantly, 'perhaps you could let him know that I have just foiled an attack on the games.'

'What?'

'It's true! I overheard a couple of characters who were steering a boulder into a path which would have dropped it in your lap. I couldn't trace their ship, but I went after the rock and kicked it off course. It's now heading into the sun.'

'You did well, Warren.' Drabble sounded impressed, gratifyingly so. 'But I wonder why anybody would have been stupid enough to lob a piece of rock at us.'

'That baffled me as well,' Peace said. 'All I know is that there was this glowing boulder, and I . . .' He paused as the subetheric waves underwent a sudden distortion which, had the communication been verbal, might have indicated that someone was choking on a hot chestnut. 'Are you feeling all right, Ozzy?'

When Drabble spoke again he sounded tense. 'Did you say the boulder was glowing?'

'That's what I said.'

'Oh Gawd! Warren, it wasn't glowing *purple*, was it?'

'As a matter of fact, it was.'

'Oh Gawd! But it wasn't a kind of shifting, unsteady purple glow, was it?'

'As a matter of fact, it *was* a shifting, unsteady purple glow.'

'Oh Gawd! But, Warren, when you said you kicked the rock into a new direction you actually meant that you had nudged it with your ship, didn't you? You didn't mean that you actually *kicked* it with your foot, did you?'

'I meant that I actually kicked it with my foot.'

'Oh Gawd!'

'Will you stop saying that?' Peace snarled impatiently, feeling a sudden nervous tension develop in his chest. 'Are you sure you're all right?'

'More to the point, Warren,' Drabble replied in disturbingly sombre tones, 'are you sure that *you* are all right?'

'What a dumb question!' Peace cried in exasperation. 'How can I *not* be all right if I'm an Oscar?'

'That's the burning question,' Drabble said, now sounding positively ominous. 'You have put your finger on it.'

'Funny I don't feel any heat in my finger,' Peace cracked and, as was his unfortunate tendency, went on to overdo the rather feeble joke. 'If I had put my finger on a burning question I would have expected – '

He broke off, shocked, as he realized that what he had taken to be a mere jangling of the nerves in his chest had developed into a genuine pain, a manifestation of physical distress. He looked down at himself and was appalled to see that his golden skin had become wrinkled and had developed numerous scaly brown patches. As if that were not bad enough, holes had appeared at the centre of some of the patches, and protruding from the holes were thin, wavering, pink tendrils.

'Aaarrgghh!' Peace retched. 'Where's the Germolene? I must have the Germolene!'

He tried to go towards the ship's medical cabinet, in which were plentiful supplies of the ubiquitous pink ointment which had originated on Earth early in the twentieth century and had since became a universal panacea. It should have been easy for him to reach the cabinet, especially in the zero gravity conditions which prevailed in the ship, but he found himself floundering helplessly, unable to control his arms and legs. There was a roaring sound in his ears, bright-rimmed dots were sizzling across his vision, and the agony in his chest was becoming unbearable.

Oh God! he thought, stunned by sudden revelation. *On top of everything else that's happening to me, I'm bloody well suffocating!*

He had existed as an Oscar for less than a year, but that had been sufficient time for him to forget that virtually all living beings depended on a continuous supply of oxygen. His own spaceship was a standard model, and therefore was fitted out with air generators, but he had long ago switched them off in protest against the unpleasant burping sounds they tended to produce. And, even if they had been operating, their life-giving

18

gases would have been dissipated into the void because of his sloppy habit of flying the ship with its doors open.

I've got to activate all the life-support systems, he told himself as, with arms and legs twitching, he drifted uncertainly around the control room. *Then I must seal the ship. Or would it be better to close the doors first and then . . . ?*

The planning of his immediate future came to an end as he lapsed into unconsciousness. He sank into a fluttery, murmurous darkness, appalled by the realization that he was about to die.

Chapter 2

'Pryktonite,' said the ruby-eyed, golden giant who was gazing down at Peace. 'It was definitely pryktonite.'

Even though he had a devastating headache and his senses were strangely muzzy, Peace made the effort to speak. 'Prick what?'

'*Pryktonite.*' The Oscar carefully spelled the word out for Peace's benefit. 'It used to be quite plentiful in the neighbourhood of Rigel before we had it swept up and dumped into the sun. As far as we know, it's part of the residue of a planet which blew up a long time ago. We thought we had got rid of all of it, but obviously we were wrong. I'm so sorry, Warren – I can't apologize enough.'

Peace tried to focus clearly on the smooth-gleaming face and realized he was talking to Ozzy Drabble. The look of concern on Drabble's glistening features abruptly reminded him of how awful he had felt just before losing consciousness. His mind was suddenly invaded by grim and icy premonitions.

'Ozzy,' he whispered feebly. 'Is this the end for me?'

For an answer, Drabble lowered his head and covered his face with his hands.

'But what about the Germolene?' Peace knew he was clutching at straws, but he was young and it was hard for him to relinquish his claim to life. 'Am I so far gone that ... even Germolene can't help?'

Drabble did not raise his head. 'I'm sorry, Warren.'

'So this is it,' Peace said in hollow tones. 'I didn't expect this moment to come so soon, but now that it's here I want to die with dignity.'

'Die?' Drabble looked up with a startled expression. 'You're not going to die, Warren.'

Peace gazed blankly into the ruby eyes. 'Then what's all the fuss about?'

'I don't know how to break this to you,' Drabble said, 'but the fact that you have come into contact with pryktonite means . . . well, it means . . .'

'It means what? Is it a fate *worse* than death?'

'It means . . .' Drabble hesitated, obviously trying to contain a deep anguish. 'It means that you have reverted to being human!'

'*Human!*' Peace resisted an urge to spring to his feet and dance around the control room. 'Are you telling me that I'll have to endure emotions and desires again? That I'll feel cravings for steaks and real ale and game pie and crisp white wine and mulligatawny soup and French brandy and home-made apple pie with custard? Are you telling me that I'll again be irresistibly drawn to beautiful women? That I'll have to go to all kinds of trouble and expense just to win their favours?'

'I had to give it to you straight, Warren,' Drabble said with a catch in his voice.

'I appreciate you letting me have it like that. Man to man . . . I mean Oscar to man . . .' Peace sat up on what he now realized was one of the ship's slumber couches – a small bed provided with enough artificial gravity to enable a person to sleep in reasonably natural conditions even when in free fall. He gazed around him in wonderment, noting the presence of other Oscars in the ship's long midsection. He looked down at himself and, for the first time in almost a year, saw a pale-skinned and reasonably muscular human body which was equipped with certain attributes which unarguably established it as being male.

'You aren't a symbiont any more,' Drabble commented.

'I can see that,' Peace said. 'But what happened to me? One minute I was feeling perfectly normal; the next . . .'

'You came in contact with pryktonite,' Drabble explained. 'The radiation from it was deadly to the throwrug part of your constitution . . . the throwrug died . . . and your body promptly rejected it. You turned back into a human. We got here just in

21

time to save you from dying from lack of air. You weren't a pretty sight, Warren.'

'I believe you.' Peace, suddenly struck by a highly unpleasant thought, sat up straighter and looked around his immediate vicinity, fearful of seeing drifting fragments of loathsome organic debris which had once been part of his body.

'It's all right,' Drabble reassured him. 'We scooped up all the bits, especially the ones that were still wriggling and twitching and squirming, and dumped them into space.'

'Thanks,' Peace breathed. 'I'm nearly sure that makes me feel better.'

'It was the least we could do.' Drabble glanced over his broad shoulder at the other Oscars, who had positioned themselves near by and were obviously absorbed in the conversation. 'If that meteorite had struck the ground near us we would all have been showered with pryktonite particles – and every one of us would have experienced the same terrible fate as you. We would all have been turned into human beings again, Warren. It doesn't bear thinking about.'

'In that case, don't think about it.' Peace, for his part, was having no trouble in directing his thoughts on to more beguiling subjects. The first thing was to go as quickly as possible to a civilized world, head for its best bar, and in the first hour knock back five or six pints of a quality real ale, just to take the edge off his thirst. All the while he would be blasting through packs of Woodbine, Lucky Strike or Passing Cloud cigarettes – all guaranteed to replicate the original twentieth-century blend – while getting his stomach into the mood for a cholesterol-rich banquet which would be washed down with well-chosen wines. Then, and *only* then, would he allow his imagination to wander in the direction of silken dalliance.

Just to make sure that he was in good enough physical condition for a prolonged bout of riotous living, he eased himself up off the bed and flexed his limbs. He was amazed at how small and puny he seemed when compared to the bulky forms of the Oscars, but in human terms he was in remarkably good shape. It appeared that the throwrugs, in spite of some disgusting features, looked after their hosts' bodies well while they were in residence.

'It looks as though everything has worked out nicely: I saved you, then you saved me, so we're all square.' Peace took a deep, pleasurable breath. 'And now, my old buddies, I must ask you to leave. It's been nice knowing you, but I have a date with a barstool.'

He propelled himself at the door of the fore control room in what should have been a graceful zero-gravity trajectory, but its symmetry was spoiled when an Oscar positioned himself directly in the way. Peace, taken by surprise, was brought to a halt by dint of his nose colliding with the Oscar's steel-hard chest. He was quickly reminded of another sensual experience that had been absent during his brief term as a golden superbeing – intense pain.

'You berk!' he accused, his voice somewhat muffled by the fingers he had clamped over his damaged nose as he rebounded into the ship's midsection. 'Why did you do a fool thing like that? I was planning a night on the town, and now . . .'

'You don't understand the situation,' Ozzy Drabble said quickly from nearby, raising his hands in a placating gesture. 'Warren, it simply isn't safe for you to leave our company – not in human form anyway.'

Peace gaped at him for a moment, then his brow cleared. 'Is it because I'm naked? That's no problem, Ozzy. All I have to do is put down near the edge of some city, get on the radio and have some clothes delivered to the ship. Wait a minute! I see the problem now? I haven't any cash or credit! How am I going to get cash or credit, Ozzy? Nobody warned me about . . .'

'The problem has nothing to do with finances,' Drabble cut in. 'Try to calm down a bit, Warren. You're babbling like a human being.'

'I *am* a human being,' Peace gritted.

'Yes, but you won't be one for long,' Drabble said. 'In fact you won't be *anything* for long unless we take special measures to protect you. You see, Warren, you have crossed swords with . . . Jeeves.'

'Jeeves?' Peace could find no significance in the name. 'Who's Jeeves when he's at home?'

Drabble glanced around his companions before replying. 'Jeeves is the most wanted, the most feared, the most evil criminal in the galaxy. He's the only one who could have obtained enough pryktonite to launch the attack you headed off. His intelligence network is everywhere, so he'll soon be able to find out exactly who it was that crossed him – and when he finds out you're just an ordinary human he'll come after you, Warren.'

'Let him come,' Peace said unconcernedly. 'The galaxy's a big place, and I'm a good runner.'

'You're not taking this seriously enough, Warren. I tell you, you're in terrible danger.'

Peace began to feel irritated. 'If this Jeeves character is so evil and deadly, why has nobody mentioned him before?'

'We were hoping he had stabilized in the good side of his character, and that the evil Jeeves would never appear again. It looks as though we were wrong.'

'You make him sound like a split personality,' Peace said with a grin.

'He *is* a dual personality. That's why we have never been able to bring him to justice,' Drabble said. 'Every time we get him dead to rights his evil side goes into retreat, his good side becomes dominant, and he turns into just about the kindest and nicest guy who ever lived.'

'Is this some kind of a joke?' Peace scanned the gleaming faces. 'Do you seriously expect me to believe that the Oscars have a sworn arch-enemy ... the embodiment of evil ... a galactic super-villain ... but he only does the job part-time?'

'It's no joke,' one of the other Oscars, named Kermody Masson, replied. 'For your own good, Warren, we have to rush you to Aspatria immediately.'

'Aspatria?' Peace began to feel dark suspicions. 'What's the good of going to Aspatria?'

'Throwrugs,' Masson said, confirming Peace's misgivings. 'We'll find a good healthy specimen, drape it over you, and in

24

no time at all you'll be an Oscar again – and you'll be safe from Jeeves.'

'No way!' Peace cried, cowering away from the impassive golden giants. 'Now that I'm human again I'm forking well going to stay human and there's nothing you can do about it.'

'You don't know what you're saying, Warren,' Drabble put in, sounding both anxious and hurt. 'You won't last more than a matter of hours as a human. Jeeves will hunt you down for sure.'

'I'm prepared to take my chances,' Peace said firmly. 'And now, gentlemen, I would appreciate it if you would kindly vacate my ship. I want to hit the nearest town and do something about this thirst.' A smile spread across his face as he realized what he had just said. 'Did you hear that? I've got a *thirst*! A real honest-to-God thirst! Ozzy, it's the most beautiful feeling in all the universe. I'm going to get a big jug of beer, then I'm going to look through it for a while just to appreciate the colour, then I'm going to inhale the aroma just to get my tastebuds sitting up and begging, then I'm going to trickle the golden nectar over my tongue and let it wash around my palate and go foaming and tingling down my throat and into my—'

'Tripe,' Drabble said abruptly.

'That's hardly the word a gourmet would have chosen,' Peace reproved, 'but if you mean the lining of my stomach . . .'

'I mean that you're *talking* tripe, Warren,' Drabble cut in. 'We, the Oscars, can't let you go anywhere near an inhabited world. Even if we gave you a twenty-strong bodyguard, Jeeves would find a way to get through to you – and think of the remorse we would feel if you were killed. You protected us, Warren, and now it is our duty to protect you.'

'Forget it! Think nothing of it! All in the day's work! Grist to the mill! Or, as they say in the air-conditioning business, mist to the grille! The carpenter to his last! The ploughman homeward plods . . .' Realizing he was becoming incoherent, Peace spread his arms in defeat, accepting that for the time being the wall of massive golden statues was completely impenetrable. His well-meaning allies were determined to put him into some kind of boring sanctuary, but eventually he would devise a way of escaping, and in the meantime there was the delightful prospect of satisfying his newly regained human appetites. Things might not be too bad for a while – in fact things could be quite enjoyable – were he to be given certain facilities, certain inalienable human rights . . .

'We gotta look after you, Warren,' Masson said, drawing nods of agreement from his companions.

'Fair enough,' Peace said, making himself sound reasonable. 'But now that I'm human again I'm going to need some sustenance. I can't last very long without something to drink, so one of you will have to go for supplies immediately. You'd better get me six cases of beer and two cases of wine and a few bottles of brandy – French, of course – and now that I think of it I could probably use some gin and some rum and some . . .' Peace's voice faded away as he saw that, as one, the entire group of Oscars had begun to shake their heads.

'OK,' he said, 'never mind the rum. It always did give me a bit of a hangover, anyway. I'll just have the beer and the wine and the . . .' His voice dried up once more as the Oscars continued to shake their heads, and this time he began to feel a grim premonition.

'We'd be failing in our duty to you if we allowed you to poison your frail system with alcohol,' Drabble said.

'Just the beer then,' Peace pleaded. 'One case.'

'No.'

'One tube?'

'Get a grip on yourself, Warren,' Drabble said, beginning to show some signs of impatience. 'You're talking like a human weakling.'

'I *am* a forking human weakling,' Peace cried. 'It was bad enough thinking about booze when I was an Oscar, but now that I'm normal again, and haven't had a decent drink for nearly a year, I can't bear the thought of living on plain water.'

'Nobody is expecting you to live on water,' Drabble said magnanimously. 'We'll get you loads of tomato juice, and carrot juice, and tea. Camomile, of course.'

'Great!' Peace scowled for a moment, then his stomach

reminded him that life still offered considerable gastronomic pleasures. 'And to eat I'll need a supply of quail, plover eggs, partridge breasts cooked in red wine, lobster ...' His voice dwindled once again as he saw that the Oscars were showing signs of disapproval.

'Warren, do you want to kill yourself before Jeeves even gets a shot at you?' Drabble said. 'We can't allow you to ruin your stomach and clog up your arteries with stuff like that. No, we'll put you on a good, sensible vegetarian diet – one that'll keep you slim and healthy.'

Appalled, Peace suddenly became aware of another craving. 'Cigarettes help me keep my weight down. I don't suppose ...'

'You must be joking!'

'Yes ... joking,' Peace said gloomily. 'Ha, ha, ha.' A vision of a dark grey, monastic future was opening up before him like prison gates. What if he never managed to get away from the Oscars? He had daydreamed of becoming human again, but the whole point of being prey to desires and temptations lay in yielding to them. The new prospect of eking out his years under permanent and close surveillance by the puritanical supermen was so utterly depressing that he could almost consider submitting to the throwrugs.

Peace shuddered at the very notion, and glanced up at his guardians with dispirited eyes. 'Does anybody here play cribbage?'

The boredom was worse than Peace could have imagined, so bad that he would have made a break for freedom had not vital parts of his spaceship's drive been confiscated.

He spent the remaining days of the jamboree locked up in the ship, gagging on its artificial atmosphere and watching the games on the view screens. Unfortunately, the Oscars' favourite activities could hardly be described as spectator sports. There was little to see in equatorial relay races; the hurling of stones into low orbit was repetitious in the extreme; and the other big favourite, long-distance mole tunnelling, was a total non-event when there was no means of following the competitors' progress through the rocky soil.

To make matters worse, the Oscars had thoughtfully rigged up and installed in Peace's ship a subetheric speech converter. The device not only enabled him to listen in on what was happening – it *forced* him to do so. By the end of the games the group at the nearest bottle-fed campfire had got up to 7658 men going to mow a meadow, and Peace was about ready to go with them. He had become pale, and wild of eye, and had taken to punching the walls of his ship every time a whoop of subetheric laughter swamped his senses. Had he still been an Oscar this violent behaviour would have caused serious damage to the ship; as it was, Peace ended up with knuckles so red and swollen that even Germolene gave them little ease.

Four days after his transformation he was dozing in bed, dreaming that nude women were plying him with roast beef sandwiches and beer, when his dream-self became aware of distant music. The tune was uninspiring – permutations of only four whole notes – but as it grew louder he recognized it as the Oscar anthem. Alluring though the dream scenario was, it quickly faded away as he realized its significance . . .

The jamboree was ending!

Peace jumped out of bed, ran the length of the ship and back in his excitement. He put on some of the clothing which had been brought in with his food supplies, then sat down on the edge of his bed to await developments. His future as a ward of the Oscars promised to be dull in the extreme, but *anything* had to be a big improvement on his present miserable exist-ence. No matter how remote and stultifying the planet of his incarceration proved to be, he would at least be able to walk in the fresh air. There was bound to be animal life, in which case he would find a way to hunt without being noticed; there was bound to be some form of fruit or edible grass, in which case, with the aid of wild yeasts, he would also learn to produce his own booze in a way which would not draw the attention of the golden nannies. It was even possible that he would find some palatable weed to smoke, perhaps a variety which would yield headier pleasures than ordinary tobacco. Things no longer looked so bad. In fact, if one adopted the proper philosophical viewpoint, things were looking pretty good.

A few minutes later there came the sounds of the airlock doors being operated. Peace stood up, smoothed his clothing, and advanced to meet the three Oscars who entered the middle section of the ship. The trio was made up of Brown Owl, Magill and Drabble.

'Ready when you are, Browners,' Peace said, rubbing his hands. 'Where are we off to next?'

'Nowhere,' Brown Owl replied, also rubbing his hands.

'I . . . I don't get you.' Peace wondered if Brown Owl, who was inclined towards self-importance, could be punishing him for having used an overly familiar form of address.

'There's nothing to get,' Brown Owl said. 'We aren't going anywhere. Jeeves will be expecting us to rush you off to a hideout on some distant and really out-of-the-way planet, but we're going to fool him by keeping you right here on Mildor IV. We're going to set up permanent headquarters here. It's a great idea because nobody would ever think of looking for you right at our centre of operations.

'And, after all . . .' Brown Owl gestured towards the ship's view screens '. . . why should we leave all this?'

Peace gaped in dismay at the vistas of airless and rock-strewn desert which had been churned up by the Oscars during their games. 'But . . . I can't stay here,' he said weakly.

Brown Owl's brazen countenance inclined towards him, the ruby eyes pulsing. 'Why not?'

'Because there's nothing for me to *do*.'

'Oh, I've already solved that problem,' Brown Owl said. 'You're going to be my personal assistant. As soon as we set up our new communications network, urgent calls for help will be coming in from all over the galaxy. Your job will be to re-route the calls to the Oscars who are best placed to deal with them. It won't be as fulfilling as actually *being* an Oscar, but it'll be the next best thing.'

'Thanks a lot,' Peace mumbled, his dispirited gaze travelling from one impassive golden countenance to the other. 'Does anybody here play cribbage?'

*

Peace had always had a low threshold of boredom, therefore it was quite in keeping with his character that, on the tenth day of his new job, he decided to commit suicide.

The Oscar GHQ was nothing more than a single spaceship parked on the desolate plains of an airless planet, and if Peace had been on his own there would have been no hindrance to his escape from life. He could, for example, have gone outside without benefit of a spacesuit. But Brown Owl was never more than a few paces away, was ever vigilant, and would have been able to haul Peace back indoors before a decent amount of damage was done to his cardiovascular system.

Being dead isn't everything in life, Peace thought, trying to console himself, but it was all to no avail. There was no escaping the fact that it was pretty humiliating to have one's major ambition thwarted by an animated statue. *I won't put up with this*, Peace vowed. *I'm determined to kill myself – even if it's the last thing I do*.

Accordingly, he went quietly to the front end of the ship and peered into the control room, where Brown Owl was taking his turn at directing operations. As the giant's subetheric voice was directly linked to the pan-galactic communications equipment, he appeared to be doing nothing. Oscars never had any need to sit down and rest their legs, so Brown Owl was standing in the centre of the control room with the brassy dome of his head tilted to one side while he dealt with the flow of messages.

Peace nodded in satisfaction, knowing that Brown Owl's telepathic faculty was saturated to the point where he would have little awareness of what was going on in the immediate vicinity. He backed away a few silent paces, then turned and walked quickly to his own private quarters in the rear tower of the ship. Moving with a steady and doleful precision, he extricated a chair from its floor sockets and positioned it in the centre of the room, directly underneath a major utilities conduit. He took a roll of unbreakable insulation tape from a locker, got up on the chair and by lapping the tape around the conduit and his own neck prepared himself for a painful but certain death.

To hesitate now would be fatal, he thought, as the part of his mind which retained some sanity began to protest at what he was doing. *I'll die if I don't succeed in killing myself.*

Allowing himself no more time to think, he kicked the chair out from under his feet.

He fell a short distance, then the improvised noose snapped tight around his neck. *Here we go*, he thought in a kind of ecstatic terror. *A few seconds in which to repent for all my mistakes and sins, then the plunge into Nothingness. Mercifully, it will all be over quickly. They say your whole life flashes before your eyes when you know you're going to die – say in a falling elevator – but I won't have time for that. I'm going to lose consciousness almost immediately. I won't even have time to fret about that night when Rita Hogle invited me up to her apartment and I didn't go because I was ashamed of the holes in my socks; I won't even have time to brood about that day a gang of us went to Kolk's Arcturian restaurant in Seattle and, against all advice, I ordered the multipede mousse and I got such a small serving that I was finished in two minutes while all the rest, who had stuck to things like snail steaks, got enough to keep them eating for about an hour; I won't even have time to regret that day in Sunday school when I let Rocky Barnes bluff me out of a big pot with only a pair of threes when I had a running . . .*

Wait a minute! Peace's eyes widened in anxiety. *What's going on here? This is the slowest sudden death I've ever heard of!*

Abruptly it came to him that, instead of suffocating, he was merely dangling – admittedly with some discomfort – at the end of the plastic ligature.

Mildor IV is a low-gravity world! The revelation that he was not heavy enough to be choked by his own weight caused Peace to groan aloud. He tried to free himself by peeling away bits of insulation tape, thus weakening the noose, but tension had drawn the layers into an indivisible rope. After a moment's consideration he pulled himself hand over hand up the rope until his head was level with the supporting conduit, then he released his grip. The wrench at the end of the longer drop was extremely painful, but came nowhere near to breaking his neck, and he found himself bouncing and swirling at the end of his tether, all the while emitting strangulated screams and curses.

It was at that moment that Brown Owl chose to enter the room. He froze for several seconds, the ruby cabochons of his eyes taking in the bizarre scene.

'Warren,' he said eventually, his subetheric voice echoing from nearby speakers, 'what do you think you're doing?'

'Isn't it obvious?' Peace croaked. 'I'm pretending to be a teabag. Get me down from here, you useless great lump of non-ferrous scrap.'

Brown Owl reached up, effortlessly snapped the plastic strands and lowered Peace to the floor. 'Tell me the truth, Warren,' he said. 'Were you trying to kill yourself?'

The unexpected note of kindliness and sympathy in Brown Owl's voice brought a lump to Peace's throat, an unfortunate piece of timing in view of the already distressed state of his larynx and epiglottis.

'Brown Owl,' he husked. 'I . . . I can't really pour my heart out to somebody called Brown Owl. May I call you B. O. for short?'

'B. O.?' Brown Owl mused for a moment. 'Yes, that has a certain air to it. I like it. All right, go ahead.'

'OK, B. O.,' Peace said. 'I have to tell you that I just can't go on like this. Now that I'm human again I've got to *live* as a human – otherwise I'd rather be dead. I would dearly love to go on working with the Oscars, because I truly believe in all the Oscar ideals, but there is nothing I can do that an Oscar couldn't do a hundred times better, so I am only a useless encumbrance to you.

'At this point you can do only two things for me. You can turn me loose; or you can personally grant me an instantaneous death. I would prefer the former, but . . .'

Peace fell silent as Brown Owl tilted his head and raised a hand to indicate that he was receiving a subetheric communication from another part of the galaxy. He nodded a couple of times, his glistening features fluxing in a way which indicated emotional stress, then his gaze again steadied on Peace.

'Sorry about that,' he said. 'I was turning down a call for help – and I just *hate* having to say no to anybody who's in trouble.'

In spite of his inner turmoil, Peace felt a flicker of interest. 'I didn't realize there were jobs the Oscars can't tackle.'

'It doesn't happen very often, but I'm afraid that's the way it is.'

Peace struggled with the notion that the golden giants were not totally invincible. 'What was the call about? Is some poor guy falling into a black hole?'

'Oh, nothing like that,' Brown Owl said. 'It's a fairly simple policing job, actually – but we can't touch it because it's on the planet Golborne.'

'Never heard of the place. What's the big problem?'

Brown Owl's ruby eyes dulled for an instant in the equivalent of a sigh. 'Golborne is a water world – and, as you know, Oscars can't swim.'

Of course! Peace thought, remembering the time in his previous human incarnation when he had escaped from Drabble and Magill by dumping them in the sea. The body of an Oscar was so dense that no amount of flailing and beating at the water would keep it afloat. With the possible exception of hang-gliding, aquatics was the only branch of sport in which humans naturally excelled over Oscars.

'I see,' Peace said, his interest still caught. 'But if the planet is completely covered with water why does anybody live or work there? I mean, the galaxy isn't exactly short of fish.'

'Golborne doesn't export fish. Did you ever hear of a drug called glum?'

Peace thought for a moment, shaking his head. 'No, but my memory got wiped out when I joined the Space Legion, and huge chunks of it are still missing. What's so special about glum?'

'It's just about the most expensive narcotic in the whole galaxy, that's all.'

'I don't suppose you've confiscated any of the stuff and have

33

a bag or two tucked away around here,' Peace said hopefully. 'It's got a funny name, but it must give you one hell of a high.'

'On the contrary!' Brown Owl sounded as though he hated to discuss the drug, as though the very fact of mentioning it would contaminate him in some way. 'Glum makes those who use it feel utterly miserable. It gives them the ultimate *low*.'

Peace was unable to prevent his jaw from sagging. 'But that doesn't make sense. Who would want to pay for something which makes them depressed?'

'Poets,' Brown Owl replied. 'You see, over the last few hundred years so much has been done to improve the human condition that there's no need for anybody to be miserable and despairing any more – and that has made things difficult for people who need to be in a real black mood before they can write. Poets are the main users of glum, especially in Golden Tropicana.'

'Where's that?'

'On Earth. It's a region that roughly corresponds to the old Central Europe and Russia. I've heard life used to be pretty gloomy in those parts before the climate and economic conditions perked up and they renamed the whole area. Now the ordinary people are so happy there that before glum came along no poet worthy of the name could write a word.'

'My memory must be in worse shape than I realized,' Peace murmured abstractedly as an idea took shape in his mind. 'Is glum Golborne's principal export?'

'It's Golborne's *only* export,' Brown Owl said. 'It's extracted from a kind of water lily that grows on the surface of the sea.'

'What's to stop you flitting around the place in powerboats or helicopters?'

'They churn the water up too much. The glum lily is so delicate that it comes apart and dies when the water is even slightly disturbed.'

'I see.' Peace cleared his throat and made his voice firm and businesslike. 'I've got a proposition for you, Browners.'

'Yes?'

'You can't keep me here against my will. Not only is it

unethical – it's futile. Eventually I would find a way to kill myself, and you would have that on your conscience. So I propose that I be allowed to go on working with the Oscars as a special kind of one-man task force. A force that can be sent all over the galaxy to deal with problems that the ordinary Oscars find unusually difficult or maybe impossible.'

'You?' Brown Owl's gleaming visage reflected doubt as he scanned Peace's comparatively puny body from head to foot. 'A *force*?'

'At least I can swim,' Peace said huffily. 'I've got a school certificate for swimming five lengths. All you can manage is a depth.'

'There's no need to be sarcastic.'

'Well, send me to Golborne! Let me handle this case and you'll never hear me complain again.'

Brown Owl scratched his golden chin, producing a metallic scraping sound which knotted Peace's insides. 'You could be killed.'

'Let me worry about that,' Peace said, feeling a pang of joyous relief as he realized Brown Owl was weakening. 'I'm ready to face any danger in the galaxy.'

Chapter 3

'Alien porn,' Superintendent Glauber said, apparently deriving so much gloomy relish from the phrase that he felt compelled to repeat it. 'Alien porn. Who would have thought it could cause so much trouble?'

'What exactly *is* the problem?' Peace said, glancing about him with some curiosity. The Cosmic Pharmaceuticals office was octagonal in shape and on the highest point – about ten metres above sea level – of one of the few islands on the planet Golborne. Transparent walls revealed that the island was less than a kilometre across and surrounded by an ocean of yellowish muddy water or perhaps watery mud. The surface was speckled with a pattern of broad-leaved blue-green plants, like small rafts, which began at the constricted shore and stretched out to the limits of vision. Above the somewhat uninspiring vistas, the sun was represented by a circular patch of brightness in the continuous cover of leaden cloud.

'I thought you would have been fully briefed before you came here,' Glauber said, a look of suspicion appearing on his peppery red countenance. 'You don't look like an Oscar to me.'

'Glad to hear it,' Peace replied. 'Any human being who looked like an Oscar would be in need of urgent medical care.'

'But you look so . . . ordinary. Have you any credentials?'

'Here's my badge.' Peace groped in a pocket of his vastly expensive and conservative denim suit and brought out the badge the Oscars had prepared for him. It was of solid platinum nearly a centimetre thick, inlaid with gold and heavily encrusted with the finest diamonds. The fortune it must have cost was evidence of the high regard in which he was held by the Oscars but, because of the impractical streak in their nature, it had not been provided with any means of attaching it to his lapel. He had tried using a piece of surgical tape and

36

a safety pin, but the badge kept falling off and he had decided
to keep it in his pocket for safety. He handed the glittering
emblem across the superintendent's desk.

'That will do nicely,' Glauber said in reverential tones as he
fondled the badge. 'Are you a very senior officer with the
Oscars?'

'Let's just say I'm a special agent. Now, what's the problem
here?'

'Well, as you know, this planet is the only source of the drug
melancholin, commonly known as glum.' In contrast to his
previous attitude, Glauber was becoming effusive. 'It is
extracted from the petals of *Nuphar melancholium*, or the
suicide lily. There is only one tiny flower to about ten square
metres of floating pads, and it has to be gathered just before it
sheds its petals. That is an incredibly difficult operation,
because at that stage the flowers are so sensitive that the
slightest vibration of the plant causes the petals to drop off
and immediately lose their potency.'

'I can see why powerboats and helicopters are no use,' Peace
said. 'How *do* you harvest the drug?'

'Golborne was uninhabited when we found it, so we bring in
workers from other watery and swampy worlds. Have you ever
seen a squelcher?'

Peace thought back over the myriad alien beings he had
seen while in service with the Space Legion. 'I don't think I've
had that pleasure.'

'It's no pleasure,' Glauber said as he touched a control panel
on his desk. One of the office walls became opaque and there
appeared on it the image of one of the most unprepossessing
creatures Peace had ever seen. It was orange-brown in colour
and resembled an inflatable gorilla that had developed a slow
puncture, making it a mass of sags, bags and wrinkles. It had
at least three yellowish, rheumy eyes, but others could have
been concealed in the hairy flaps and folds which encircled the
domed head. Two red hemispheres like halved tomatoes, which
appeared to be nipples, adorned the torso, one above the other.
The squelcher had feet which were enormous in proportion to

its body – great, flat, spreading things, the size and shape of well-used pillows.

'Jehovah's jockstrap,' Peace breathed, reflexively shrinking back into his chair. 'Can you train a thing like that?'

'They don't need any training. They're intelligent, and they're also very light for their size. Evolution has given them bodies packed with hundreds of air sacs. They can move around on the lily pads without disturbing the glum flowers.'

'And you say they're intelligent?'

Glauber nodded. 'Many of them can speak quite good English when they feel like it, which isn't very often, because they're a surly lot. They are supposed to have quite well-developed cultures on a dozen or so worlds. We don't know *too* much about them, because the only landing rights they grant on their home worlds are solely for trade purposes. They're good customers for quite a few Earth products – canned fruit and vegetables, musical instruments, non-ferrous metal extrusions, bug sprays, and printing machinery . . .'

Glauber's flow of words slackened off and a haunted look appeared in his eyes. 'Printing machinery! That's the cause of all the trouble. The one aspect of human culture that the squelchers seized on . . . took to it like a duck to water, they did . . . was magazines. Not books so much, but for some reason they absolutely *love* glossy magazines. They just can't get enough of them – and you know what that has led to.'

Peace frowned. 'Big sales of Swiss watches and Victorian conservatories?'

'No!' Glauber, a hefty fifty-year-old whose sleeveless shirt displayed impressively knotted musculature, leaned forward across his desk and his already florid complexion deepened in colour. 'Warren, is there something wrong with your memory?'

Peace grinned, deciding to ease the tension in the atmosphere with a little humour. 'I don't know. I can't remember having forgotten anything.'

The sally evidently failed to achieve its objective, for Glauber's crimson countenance slowly developed purple patches, and Peace's startled gaze even detected traces of magenta here and

38

there. He gaped at Glauber, fearful that the superintendent's head might be about to explode.

'I'm sorry about that,' he said quickly. 'My memory *is* a bit dodgy. I had total amnesia for a while, due to no fault of my own, and I'm not sure if I'll ever fully recover.'

Glauber took an audibly deep breath. 'All right, Warren. We were talking about alien porn. When the squelchers are returning from leave they bring loads of magazines back with them. Magazines with dirty pictures! The magazines get circulated around the workforce, and they have a terrible effect on production.' A look of distaste appeared on Glauber's choleric features. 'They're a randy, sex-crazed lot, these bloody squelchers.'

Peace smiled tolerantly. 'But if they're away from their wives or mates or whatever for a long time it's only to be expected that they'll take an interest in sexy magazines.'

'They don't just take an interest, as you put it,' Glauber snapped, his expression changing to one of outright disgust. 'Just staring at the pictures gives them . . .' He paused and glanced around his office as though fearful of being overheard '. . . *orgasms!*'

Peace resisted an urge to laugh aloud. 'What harm does that do?'

'What *harm*?' Glauber bellowed. 'Would you like to see a squelcher having a climax?'

Peace thought the matter over. 'No.'

'Well, you're going to,' Glauber said grimly. He again touched the control panel on his desk and the frozen image of the squelcher on the wall changed to a moving sequence which depicted one of the gorilla-like beings standing on a green raft of lily pads. The squelcher was holding an open magazine in both hands. Peace could not see the illustration which was under scrutiny, but he could tell that it was having a powerful effect. The squelcher began by emitting loud sniffing and snuffling noises. Soon its eyes were bulging and its tongue, which resembled a very old blue-and-green sock, was hanging out. Mesmerized against his will, Peace saw that the alien's vertically arranged nipples were swelling like red balloons.

'The squelchers really hate anybody spying on them. They have an incredible sense of smell – usually they can scent you before they see you – but I managed to tape this with a hidden camera,' Glauber whispered. 'Just watch what happens next.'

Unable to avert his eyes, Peace watched as the squelcher gave a convulsive shudder, dropped the magazine and sprang into the air. The floppy orange body rotated while it was aloft, making the creature land on its back with an impact which rocked everything in sight. The alien's stubby arms and legs were rigidly sticking upwards, and its whole ungainly form was quivering violently in what Peace deduced to be paroxysms of ecstasy. The vibrations quickly spread into the underlying quagmire, causing ripples to spread outwards, and the image began to bounce as the camera was affected.

'That goes on for about twenty minutes,' Glauber said, breathing heavily as he switched off the picture and returned the wall to its former transparent state. 'And by the time it's over every bloody glum blossom within two hundred metres will have been shaken off its stem and destroyed. Now do you see why we have to stamp out this filthy porn trade?'

'Yes, but it doesn't seem much of a problem,' Peace said. 'All you have to do is ban the importation of all magazines.'

'Do you think we didn't try that?' Glauber looked indignant. 'Nooglenorker – that's the barstool lawyer representing the squelchers' union – soon put a stop to it. Under galactic law it's illegal to interfere with the free flow of goods and information.'

Peace thought for a moment. 'But that doesn't cover zee feelthy peectures, does it? Why not just prohibit pornography?'

'Hah!' Glauber exclaimed, so forcibly that Peace's eyes widened in shock. 'There's the rub! How do you tell what is alien porn and what isn't?'

'Once you've seen one member of a species, it should be easy enough to decide what gets their old gonads in a tizzy.'

'You think so?' Glauber pointed at a table on which, previously unnoticed by Peace, were dozens of magazines, all of them open at the centrefold. 'Take a look at those and find me the squelcher equivalent of Lola Grabdick.'

'Who's Lola Grabdick?' Peace said as he stood up.

The superintendent looked embarrassed. 'Oh. I *think* that's what one of the current porno queens back on Earth is called. I'm not sure, of course. I don't know why that name came into my – ' He broke off and gave Peace a ferocious glare. 'Why are you interrogating *me*? Take a look at the magazines, man! If you're such a goddamn expert on ET erotica you shouldn't have any trouble spotting the porn.'

Peace went to the table and examined the magazines, all of which were in remarkably grubby condition and were giving off a choking papery smell. He had fully expected to see pictures of some creature that was recognizably a squelcher, or close-ups of some parts of the nauseating squelcher anatomy, but the centrefold illustrations seemed to have no coherence or relevance to anything. One portrayed the most revolting ten-legged crustacean Peace had ever seen; another had a kind of warty caterpillar with sets of carnivorous jaws at each end; another looked like a robot which had been designed by an insane marmoset; another resembled nothing so much as a hippo which had been run over by a tank. Most of the pictures were of unprepossessing life forms, some adorned with bizarre clothing, but not one of the subjects looked anything like a squelcher. Other pictures seemed to be straightforward representations of flowers, rock formations, oddly shaped beds, clouds, heaps of varicoloured berries and beans.

'Well?' Glauber said maliciously.

'I have to admit,' Peace replied slowly, 'that I don't see any likely candidates for the female of the species.'

'We don't even know if there *is* a female of the species. The bolshie buggers will tell us nothing.' Glauber clenched his fists in impotent anger. 'If they weren't the only ones who can harvest glum I'd fire the whole bloody lot.'

'Are you sure these *are* pornographic pictures? Has the text ever been deciphered? For all we know, what you have here are cookery and fashion zines.'

'The text is indecipherable,' Glauber said. 'These *might* be general magazines, but it's obvious that the publishers always include a dirty picture just to pander to the depraved tastes of my so-called workers. It's a filthy racket! They're making money at my expense!'

'Isn't that mostly conjecture?' Peace said, hoping to introduce a note of reason to the conversation.

'Conjecture my ass,' Glauber shouted. 'I *know* these are dirty books. I personally gathered up every one of them while their owners were busy going through their disgusting orgasms, generating tidal bloody waves, destroying thousands of monits' worth of good flowers. I tell you, there is something obscene and immoral and perverted in every one of those pictures. If I could figure out what it is I could ban them. The damned squelchers are laughing at me ... and wanking me into the poorhouse ... and I want to know what you're going to do about it.'

'Me!' Peace was about to protest at the unfairness of the superintendent's demand when he recalled that he had begged Brown Owl to give him this assignment, and that it was vital for him to make a success of it. Unless he proved himself capable of dealing with the case the Oscars were likely to fret about his welfare and put him under closer guard than before. He studied the strewn magazines again, with what he hoped was an air of professionalism, and an idea began to flicker in the deeper recesses of his mind.

'These magazines are all open at the centrefold,' he pointed out.

Glauber nodded without showing much interest. 'What of it? That's the best place for a sexy picture.' He paused and again looked embarrassed. 'At least, I *suppose* that would be the best place ...'

'I've decided what I'm going to do,' Peace said triumphantly. 'I'm going to set up a checkpoint at the spacefield, and I'm going to inspect the incoming squelchers' baggage, and when I find any magazines I'm going to rip out the centrefolds and incinerate them.'

Glauber's expression brightened, but only momentarily. 'They won't like it, you know. They're sure to cause trouble. I know the squelchers are a pretty scrawny lot, but there are hundreds of them – and only a dozen or so humans on the whole island, including you.'

'Don't worry about that.' Peace gave a nonchalant wave of his hand. 'I have my methods.'

'I wish you luck.'

Peace made for the door then realized that a familiar comforting weight was missing from his side. He turned and said, 'I'd like to have my badge back, please.'

'Badge?' Glauber looked puzzled. 'What badge?'

Peace sighed. 'The one made of platinum and gold and diamonds. The one that's dragging your right-hand pants pocket down to the floor.'

Glauber reached far into his pocket and brought out the gleaming disk. 'This bauble? Anybody can make a mistake.'

'You've said it,' Peace replied sternly, removing the badge from the clasp of fingers which, while offering no real resistance, showed a strange reluctance to be separated from the massy object. It was as though the very molecules of Glauber's hands had an affinity for precious metals.

As Peace walked away from the office it occurred to him that he had little sympathy for Glauber, and that he could have been pressed on to the wrong side in what was scarcely more than a domestic squabble. He had to ignore all qualms of conscience, however, for if he failed in his mission he was likely to find himself back on Mildor IV, trapped in an iron box and restricted to a diet of lettuce leaves and carrot juice.

The spaceport on Golborne consisted of little more than a long, narrow prefabricated shed. It had a low barrier and gate near the 'inner' end. Peace had set up his checkpoint close to the gate, and he was facing a crowd of perhaps two hundred squelchers who had just returned from home leave on the weekly local flight. The ungainly, simian-looking aliens were a colourful lot, with their holiday hats and bandanas and bright-hued shoulder bags.

Peace, having noted that glossy magazines were projecting from many of the bags, turned to Ozzy Drabble and Hec Magill, who were standing just behind him. The two Oscars, his own personal bodyguard, had been waiting in reserve in an orbiting ship since his arrival on Golborne.

'Here we go,' Peace said to them. 'Are you ready to do your stuff?'

Drabble and Magill nodded, highlights flowing on their golden features. Each took a thick steel reinforcing bar from a heap on the floor and began destroying it by pinching bits off the end with his fingers. The process created hard snapping sounds which were painful to the ear. Peace nodded his approval, and turned to address the crowd of squelchers.

'My name is Warren Peace,' he called out, 'and I have been empowered by the Company to take whatever steps I deem necessary to prevent the importation of printed matter of a distasteful nature.' *That was too wordy*, he thought, as the squelchers gazed at him in silence. *Better keep it direct and simple* . . .

'Accordingly, every worker who is carrying printed matter will bring it to this table for inspection. Anything I even *suspect* of being offensive will be confiscated. You may now approach the checkpoint in single file.'

There was little doubt that Peace's message had been well understood because the squelchers began shuffling their huge feet and muttering to each other in angry tones. Even though they were speaking in perhaps a dozen alien tongues, there was a note of resentment in the composite sound which transcended all language barriers. Peace sat bolt upright in his chair and tried to assume the kind of stern and fearless expression that a Lawrence of Arabia or a Sanders of the River might have used to quell a rebellious mob. His principal worry was that the squelchers would have as much trouble interpreting these subtleties of countenance as he had in trying to read the flabby horizontal folds which fate had obliged the aliens to accept as faces.

The first alien to reach the desk was clutching a glossy magazine close to his chest and was obviously displeased about the new immigration controls. 'I don't think it's legal for you to confiscate our magazines,' he said in a surprisingly thin, high voice. 'What if I refuse to hand mine over for inspection?'

Other squelchers pressing forwards behind him whinnied their approval of the question.

'Then you'll have to deal with my two friends,' Peace replied, indicating Drabble and Magill with his thumb. Aware of having become the focus of interest, the two Oscars stepped up their act. Drabble struck himself on the forearm with a steel rod so forcibly that the metal coiled itself like a snake, while Magill began tying another rod in dainty bows. The uncooperative alien watched the performance for a moment, seeming to deflate a little with each passing second, then slapped his magazine down on the desk.

Peace was pleased that a good precedent had been created. He too had doubts about the legality of what he was doing, and he was glad that the Oscars had been able to intimidate the alien without any actual threats being uttered. He opened the magazine at the centrefold and was slightly taken aback on seeing a picture of a large woolly marsupial with a head like that of a walrus. The creature was leaning against a counter and eating from what looked like a pile of living eels. Peace, whose spell in the Space Legion had accustomed him to aesthetically-challenged life forms, gave a shudder of distaste as he took in the extent of the being's ugliness. He was beginning to suspect that the squelchers were members of one of those complex multi-sexual species in which reproduction was achieved by many kinds of unlikely pairings. If that were the case, he felt sorry for the squelchers. Fate had dealt them a lousy hand when it came to looks and then compounded the joke by forcing them to couple with some of the most revolting biological specimens the worst planets of the galaxy had ever spawned.

Feeling guilty but yet determined to do his duty, Peace brandished the open magazine in front of the squelcher's face. 'What do you think of that?'

The alien rearranged the folds of its face to uncover two extra eyes and focus them on the centrefold. At once it began to emit loud sniffing sounds and its whole sagging body began to ripple. Its striped tongue began to quiver, puffs of vapour

45

came out of its ears, and the half-tomatoes of its vertically arranged nipples started to swell alarmingly.

'Well?' Peace demanded.

'Doesn't mean a thing to me,' the squelcher said, speaking with some difficulty because its tongue had begun to coil and uncoil rapidly, hurling drops of saliva in all directions.

'I've got a word of advice for you,' Peace said sternly. 'Never try to play poker.'

He grasped the centre pages of the magazine, ripped them out and dropped them into the molecular disintegrator he had positioned beside his desk. The box-like machine emitted a greenish flare, showing that the offending pages had been converted to microdust. He checked the new set of middle pages and saw that they contained nothing but advertisements for refrigerators and washing machines, all of Terran design. Even the most cunning purveyor of alien porn would have been unable to conceal objectionable material in these.

'Let that be a lesson to you,' Peace said, closing the magazine and handing it back to its owner. He had expected a fresh outburst of complaints, but the squelcher, after taking a few seconds to recover from its state of sexual agitation, quickly returned to normal, with no apparent signs of resentment.

'Will that be all?' the squelcher said in polite tones, thrusting its orange-haired abdomen forward invitingly. 'Or would you like to conduct a body search?'

The thought was enough to make Peace feel queasy. 'Pass on through,' he said, repressing the idea that the alien was making fun of him in some way. 'Let that be a lesson to you,' he repeated, unable to think of any original comment. 'Think yourself lucky! You've got off lightly this time.'

He kept muttering the same forms of words, with only slight variations, as the rest of the incoming alien workers began filing past his desk. To his relief the entire batch submitted without complaint to having their magazines stripped of the centre pages. His concern had been less with his own safety than with the prospect of what would have happened had Drabble and Magill had to exert force against the squelchers. It was central to the Oscars' creed that they should always try to act as *gentle* giants, but he had seen the golden supermen – momentarily forgetful of their physical power – run straight through masonry walls in their eagerness to catch up with offenders. He had a feeling that the squelchers' low-density, squishy bodies would have been reduced to something spectacularly unpleasant had the Oscars tried even to twist their arms or slap their wrists.

In less than an hour, having destroyed perhaps a hundred centrefolds, he had cleared all the arrivals and the hall was standing empty.

'Thanks for your help, fellows,' he said to Drabble and Magill. 'You can take your ship back up into orbit now. In fact, if you want to take some time off at HQ you could shoot back to Mildor IV and tell Brown Owl how well I've done.'

'If you've got the problem licked you could come back with us and report in person,' Magill said.

'Mustn't be too hasty,' Peace stalled. 'It would only be fair to the superintendent if I stayed on for a couple of days just to make sure my plan is working all right. Why don't you fellas go off on your own for a while? Take a little break? You could play a few rounds of hide-the-asteroid. You'd enjoy that, wouldn't you?'

Magill shook his head. 'We couldn't leave you on your own here, Warren. This place is pretty exposed if Jeeves decides to mount an attack.'

'You worry too much about Jeeves,' Peace replied, concealing his annoyance that the Oscars were such persistent guardians. So anxious was he for a taste of true freedom that he had convinced himself that the arch-enemy of the Oscars posed no real threat to his well-being. Peace had been escorted straight to Golborne, without being able to visit any recreational hotspots on the way, and he could see that he was in danger of making a similarly uneventful return trip. His only hope of a medicinal taste of the high life lay in shaking the Oscars off his heels, and obviously that was going to be no easy matter.

'It's *impossible* to worry too much about Jeeves,' Magill said portentously. 'We'll be up there, Warren, keeping a close eye on you.'

That's what I was afraid of, Peace thought as he watched the two gleaming giants stride away in the direction of their ship. He turned and went into the octagonal administrative building.

'That's it,' he said as he walked into Superintendent Glauber's office. 'The first stage of Operation Centrefold has been completed. I think I can safely say that you won't have any more production problems with glum.'

Glauber's face brightened. 'So you'll be leaving right away!'

'No, no,' Peace said hastily. 'I've got to hang around for a while. Just to make sure everything is OK.'

Glauber's face darkened. 'I see.'

'Don't look so . . . if you'll pardon the pun . . . glum,' Peace said with forced cheerfulness.

Glauber gave him a baleful stare. 'That wasn't a pun. You used the word in its correct sense in both cases. A pun is when you give two different meanings to one word, or when you attach two different homonyms to one meaning.'

'Thank you, *professor*,' Peace said as he turned on his heel and left the office. *What's the forking universe coming to,* he thought, *if you can't make a little joke without getting a forking lecture in English grammar? I've got to get out of this place as soon as possible – but without my two brass buddies tagging along.*

Chapter 4

The only thing Peace liked about his quarters was that the bathroom, instead of being equipped with a sonic shower cubicle, featured an old-fashioned tub. He had never approved of sonics, partly because they lacked the sybaritic luxury of a good soak in hot water, partly because they were too complicated – and he knew himself to be prone to accidents.

After the nervous tension of facing two hundred squelchers at the spaceport, he had decided to have a relaxing bath. He had drawn a goodly quantity of water at exactly the right temperature and now he was lying in it, gently poaching his cares away. Only his face projected above the water at one end of the tub, while at the other his large toes peeked up like two tiny pink islands in a vapouring sea.

This will do me a lot of good, he thought. *A period of meditation and pure relaxation. Just what the doctor would have ordered! Even I can't get into trouble here. Tranquillity, blessed tranquillity . . .*

He lay without moving for a couple of minutes. Then came the realization that he was getting a surfeit of peace and tranquillity. In fact he was becoming pretty bored. After almost a year as an Oscar, had he been restored to the human condition only to soak in warm water like a sponge? His immediate answer was in the negative, but it seemed a shame to quit the bath so soon after taking all the trouble to prepare it. He tried to do some constructive meditation, but his mind was annoyingly blank.

Another minute dragged by, and Peace was beginning to wonder if ennui could be terminal when his gaze fastened on the two faucets at the other end of the tub. They were two very ordinary plumbing fitments, and until now he had paid them no attention, but all at once they had become the only items of potential interest in the uneventful microcosm of the tub. They loomed on the horizon like strange silvery towers on a mist-shrouded shore.

I know what I'll do! he thought, suddenly inspired. *I know how to generate a bit of excitement – I'll stick my big toe into one of the faucets! That'll be good for a giggle!*

Raising his right leg very gently, because the slightest movement caused water to slop into his near-submerged mouth and nostrils, he brought his big toe up to the nearest faucet and then slid it into the metal orifice. There was a moment of vaguely Freudian pleasure as he felt the coldness of the metal encircle his toe. A second later the same chill penetrated to the muscles of his foot and, taken by surprise, the muscles went into spasm.

The pain was enough to make Peace howl with anguish, but the sound failed to escape his lips because the powerful cramp in his instep caused a reflexive arching of his body and his face was abruptly plunged below the water. In one instant he was a lordly Neptune placidly surveying his private little sea kingdom; in the next he was back to being plain old Warren Peace, half-drowning at the bottom of a bathtub. He heaved his head and shoulders up into the air, his mouth horribly contorted as it spewed soapy water, and dragged his toe out of the faucet.

Emitting raucous choking sounds, he forced himself to an upright position and struggled out of the bath. On coming into contact with the cool plastic of the floor, his right foot, not content with the havoc it had already created, went into a new set of violent spasms, a paroxysm of cramps which made all five toes snap up and down like the flippers on an antique pinball machine. Appalled at the sheer treacherousness of his foot, Peace hopped towards the warmly carpeted sanctuary of the apartment's main room. He reached it just as the burly figure of Superintendent Glauber came in through the other door.

'What are you up to?' Glauber demanded suspiciously. 'Who have you got in the bathroom?'

'Nobody.' Peace summoned up as much dignity as he could

considering that he was naked, dripping wet and standing on one foot. 'I got stuck in the faucet, that's all.'

'You got stuck in the – !' A look of utter revulsion appeared on Glauber's florid countenance. 'Listen here, Peace. Other people have to use that tub after you, you know.'

'What are you implying?' Peace grabbed a cushion from the nearest chair and clasped it to his groin. 'And what makes you think you can just barge into my rooms, anyway?'

'I'll tell you what,' Glauber bellowed. 'Your smart-ass idea about ripping out the centrefolds isn't working.'

'You're joking!'

'Joking! *Joking*! The new magazines have spread through the plantation like wildfire. Things are worse than ever! Half of my workforce have orgasmed themselves into a coma. The filthy, oversexed perverts . . . setting up tidal waves . . . wiping out my bonus . . .' Temporarily lapsing into incoherence, Glauber resorted to shaking his massive fist under Peace's nose.

Peace gaped at him in consternation. 'But I checked the pictures underneath the original centre spreads. There was nothing but fridges and sun loungers and the like.'

'You must have missed something!'

'I *can't* have done,' Peace said firmly. 'This calls for a bit of first-hand investigation. I'm going to go out there and see things for myself!'

The sea-boots resembled two pneumatic bolsters with centrally located straps which looped around the operator's feet. Peace had noticed a couple of men scooting about the inshore waters on them with nonchalant ease, and he anticipated no difficulty in learning to do the same. Water sloshing about his ankles, he stepped gingerly on to the boots, which were being steadied for him by a Cosmic Pharmaceuticals employee, and squirmed his feet into the securing straps.

'There you go!' The CP man, a jovial and tubby little Asian named Cedric, handed Peace the propulsor control unit. 'This is going to be funny as hell. I'm going to get a kick out of this. Anybody who tries to run a pair of boots with no tuition is just

51

asking for trouble. I offered to show you the ropes for next to nothing, but . . .'

'Next to nothing!' Peace was scandalized. 'Do you call a hundred monits next to nothing? I've got better things to do with my money.' He refrained from mentioning that the better things he had in mind mainly consisted of the monumental blow-out planned to take place as soon as he could get to a reasonably civilized planet without his ruby-eyed chaperones in tow. 'Anyway, what's so hard about floating around on a pair of little airbeds?'

'Perhaps nothing,' Cedric said with a shrug, assuming a look of Oriental indifference. 'Perhaps it's all in the mind. Why don't you try it out?'

'Just watch me!' Peace had intended to depress the GO button very gently, but he had been stung by Cedric's attitude and as a result his thumb came down quite hard on the handset. The sea-boots surged forwards beneath him with silent force and on the instant he found himself wildly flailing his arms as he fought to remain upright.

He managed to retain his balance and was about to congratulate himself when he made the unhappy discovery that the boots had chosen slightly divergent courses through the yellow water. He exerted all the power of his thighs in an attempt to correct the situation, but the boots stubbornly continued on their separate ways. In a matter of seconds his legs were almost at full stretch, and he was in a panic in case the canoes had enough power in their paramagnetic propulsion units to tear him apart. He made a lightning assessment of his plight and decided that given the choice of disengaging one foot and toppling ignominiously into the sea, or being snapped in half like a wishbone, the former was infinitely preferable. He tried to withdraw his left foot from its strap and was appalled to find that lateral forces had bound the two inextricably. By now he was practically doing the splits, with urgent torture signals coming from his hip joints, and in an extremity of fear he suddenly remembered the hand-held controls.

He pressed the STOP button and emitted a groan of relief as the sea-boots promptly began losing way and became more tractable. Dragging them together with trembling legs, he coasted to a halt then looked back and gave Cedric a reassuring wave. Cedric, who was doubled over with laughter, waved back. Peace studied the control unit for a moment, deduced the meaning of some curved arrows, and with a great deal of hesitancy persuaded the boots to do a U-turn. Encouraged, he set off at slow speed back towards the shore, but again the boots showed an infuriating tendency to part company.

His abused muscles and joints were protesting so much at the renewed ordeal that he was forced to consider an undignified plea for help. Suddenly inspiration struck. It came to him that it was the length of his legs which was giving the boots too much scope for their wayward antics. He sank down on to his hunkers and immediately found he had a much greater degree of control. Smirking with pleasure and triumph, he motored back towards land at a respectable speed, and even managed to stop a few metres out from the shore with a rather showy broadside turn.

'What have you got to say about that?' he called out to Cedric.

'Nuts,' Cedric replied.

'If there's one thing I can't stand it's a sore loser,' Peace said reprovingly.

Cedric shook his head. 'I'm not a sore loser. I'm just explaining why you can't go around on sea-boots hunkered down like that.'

'Pray tell why not?' Peace said in his snootiest voice. He had barely uttered the words when he noticed a commotion just ahead of his knees in the narrow strip of water between the boots. An instant later a hideous, bright red creature resembling a miniature crocodile lunged up out of the water, snapping with ferocious jaws. Peace gave a bleat of panic and straightened up, just in time to save himself from an unthinkable injury. Disappointed, the ugly reptile swam away, sinking out of sight as it went.

'Does that answer your question?' Cedric said, chortling.

Peace's mouth opened and closed several times before he

was able to speak. 'You . . . you should have warned me about the . . . the . . .'

'Gondoliers. That's their official name, but we usually call them gonadiers – for reasons I don't need to explain.'

'You should have warned me.'

Cedric shrugged. 'You should have paid for some essential tuition.'

'And be ripped off for a hundred!'

'There's worse rip-offs than that around here,' Cedric said with an obscene grin. 'As you nearly found out.'

Still quaking over the narrowness of his escape from mutilation, Peace shook his fist. 'I'm going to report you to Superintendent Glauber for this.'

'Go ahead,' Cedric said, looking unconcerned. 'He was looking forward to his cut out of the hundred.'

Dismayed by the whiff of corruption, and no longer convinced that his was a just cause, Peace activated the sea-boots and carefully turned their prows towards the open sea. This time, knowing what to expect, he suppressed the boots' every deviation before it got properly started, and in a short time he was – with reasonable confidence – making silent, stately and upright progress through the calm waters.

Ahead of him, under a canopy of diluted sunlight, lay an expanse of custard-coloured sea liberally sprinkled with what appeared to be very small islands. The islands were conglomerations of lily pads, and widespread upon them, their shapes rendered two-dimensional by low-lying mists, could be seen squelchers going about the delicate task of harvesting glum blossoms. When he passed near workers they ceased their activities and glowered at him until he had drifted away – a reminder that they disliked being under surveillance.

The scene was charming in its own way, a worthy subject for a latter-day Turner, but had a keen-eyed Cosmic Pharmaceuticals shareholder been present he would have been upset by evidence that productivity was not at the optimum level. As Peace scanned his surroundings he was able to discern, here and there, the unmistakable silhouettes of squelchers

54

who had abandoned themselves to the pleasures of vicarious sex.

The creatures were either holding magazines widespread in front of their faces, or had already fallen over on their backs and – stubby limbs thrust in the air – were quivering and bouncing, sending tremors through all the lily pads in the vicinity. One part of Peace's mind began to feel mildly envious: it was obvious that a squelcher orgasm was like a full-scale orchestration of pleasurable sensations compared to a human male's brief solo on the piccolo.

Feeling uncomfortably voyeuristic, he kept sailing out from the island until he reached an area where the mist was thicker than usual and only one squelcher was dimly in view. Peace backed off a little to ensure that he could not be spotted by the alien, then took a pair of electronic binoculars out of a pocket. The view through the little instrument, with mist eliminated, clearly showed the squelcher carefully shuffling around a patch of lily pads, gathering tiny blossoms and putting them into a bag.

The alien worked steadily for about twenty minutes, and Peace was starting to become bored and fidgety when another squelcher appeared on the scene. This one was actually walking on the surface of the water in a kind of aquatic shuffle, buoyed up by its enormous feet, and it was carrying several magazines. It approached the worker, handed over a magazine, received money in exchange and slopped off into the murky distance with the energetic gait, common throughout the galaxy, of a petty crook going about his chosen profession.

'Aha!' Peace murmured, adding, with no attempt at originality, 'Now we shall see what we shall see.'

He watched intently as the squelcher opened the magazine directly to the centre pages. The angles were such that Peace could not see what was on the pages, but there was no doubt that the content was a very good example of alien porn. The squelcher began its gratification routine with the usual preliminary sniffing and snorting noises, so loud that they reached Peace's ears over the considerable intervening distance; then followed the bulging of the eyes and the protrusion of the revolting, blue and green tongue.

The magnified binocular image showed the squelcher's vertically arranged nipples swelling like little pulsating crimson balloons. A few seconds later the alien sprang into the air and fell on its back with an impact which sent wavelets racing through the surrounding lily pads. All four of its limbs were sticking straight up and quivering with the rest of its flabby body.

Peace had been told by Glauber that the alien's ecstatic coma would last for about twenty minutes, giving him plenty of time to inspect the magazine which had fallen from its nerveless grasp. He activated the sea-boots and, with a growing sense of scientific excitement, scudded forwards through the tendrils of mist. As soon as the raft of vegetation was visible to the naked eye, he slowed down and approached it gently in silence, even though it appeared that stealth was quite unnecessary. The orange-haired alien, looking more than ever like a partially deflated rubber gorilla, was oblivious to all that was going on around it. Quivering, snuffling and drooling profusely, it was lost in an internal world of alien biological delights.

Luckily, it had swooned right at the water's edge, so Peace did not have to risk crawling on to the lily pads to retrieve the magazine, which was lying open at the centrefold. Taking care not to lose his balance, he leaned over sideways, picked up the magazine and scanned the illustration on the double page.

It showed two large sets of hexagonal wrenches – open-ended and ring-type – tastefully arranged in order of size.

With a cry of mingled surprise and bafflement, Peace leafed through the rest of the publication. All the pictures were of wide-wheeled swamp bikes, engine blocks, performance analysers and varieties of hand tools, most of them of Terran origin. In spite of the indecipherable text, Peace was left with no doubt that he was holding some kind of bike freaks' journal. Nothing could have been less erotic than the solemn arrays of screwdrivers and comfy-sprung saddles, and yet he had seen for himself the effect they had had on the zapped-out squelcher.

A disturbing new thought entered Peace's mind. He had toyed with the notion that the squelchers could have a multiplicity of sexual attractors – but was it possible that they could be turned on by *anything*? Come to think of it, was *he* safe? Could it be that the ugly brutes went into a kind of super-heat now and again, and in a berserk frenzy of desire launched themselves upon anything that had a suitable orifice?

Peace was still plumbing the grim possibilities of this new idea when it gradually came to him that, for several seconds, he had been absent-mindedly listening to a strange tearing and munching sound. He glanced around and to his dismay saw that a gondolier, possibly the selfsame bright crimson horror which had lunged at him earlier, had inched its way on to the raft of lily pads and was busily eating the recumbent squelcher.

It had created a sizeable rent in the flabby tissues of the squelcher's side, from which something like a yellowish frog-spawn or tapioca was dribbling. The victim of the attack seemed totally unaware of what was happening. It lay placidly on its back, still sniffing, still quivering with unknowable ecstasies. Given the sheer lethality of the gondolier's jaws, Peace was surprised that much more damage had not been done to the squelcher, but its skin and connective tissues appeared to be as tough as the plastic used to bind packs of beer cans. It was clear, however, that the squelcher was in mortal danger.

'Hey!' Peace shouted. 'Get off!'

The gondolier turned one malign eye in his direction, but continued with its repast.

Peace swore and, unable to think of any other course of action, pressed hard on his GO button. His intention was to run over the gondolier with his puffy canoes and perhaps frighten it away. The sea-boots surged forward under full engine power. The prow of the right one slid up over the gondolier's scaly back, but the villainous little beast was not in the least intimidated. It rounded savagely on the boot and bit into it. The boot promptly lost most of its buoyancy, causing Peace to develop a severe list to starboard.

Feeling the water rise up around his leg he gave a wail of consternation, knowing that if he splashed in beside the crimson nightmare he could easily become the next item on the menu. The gondolier appeared to have reached the same conclusion, because *both* of its eyes were now greedily fixed on Peace as he fell sideways. He threw himself on to the lily pads, frantically wriggling his feet out of the boots' securing loops, and tried to scramble to safety.

Panic and the instability of the leafy platform kept him floundering in the one spot, the lower half of his body in the water and vulnerable to unspeakable savagery. He glanced back, wondering why he had not already been emasculated, and saw that the gondolier was making unexpectedly hard work of shredding up the boot it had attacked. It appeared to have something indigestible in its throat and was twisting its head this way and that as it gagged up the unacceptable object, along with tatters of sea-boot skin. In a second it would be free to resume its pursuit of something more to its taste.

The little git is choking on an engine! The realization that the gondolier had tried to swallow the sea-boot's paramagnetic motor sent a flash of inspiration through Peace's mind. Grateful that the boots' remote controller was still at the end of its wrist cord, he jabbed hard with his thumb on the GO stud.

The effect was immediate, and immensely gratifying.

The superb little engine instantly developed full thrust and torpedoed its way down the gondolier's throat and into its stomach. Unable to make any more headway within the reptile's digestive tract, the engine promptly bore its new host out towards the open sea. The last Peace saw of the gondolier was its eyes glaring at him in a complex blend of astonishment, accusation, fury, disillusionment, cynicism, bitterness, feral hatred and reproach as it was swept away – backwards – at high speed, gradually sinking beneath the ochreous water.

The other boot, having escaped any damage, went skimming off in a different direction and was soon lost to sight in the mists.

'Wha . . . What's going on here?' The weak voice came from the squelcher. It had emerged early from its ecstatic coma –

58

not surprisingly in view of the hideously oozing wound in its side – and was gazing up at Peace in bewilderment.

'I was just passing this way, and I couldn't help noticing that one of those gondolier things had started to eat you while you were . . . er . . . indisposed,' Peace said. 'I drove it off.'

Folds of flesh rearranged themselves on the squelcher's face, uncovering an extra green eye which regarded Peace with a luminous intensity. 'You saved my life!'

Peace shrugged. 'Anybody would have done the same thing.'

'Not true! Glauber would have let me be devoured a dozen times over rather than risk his despicable hide. This is the first time in my experience that any human . . .' The injured squelcher paused and studied Peace's face for a few seconds. 'Say, aren't you Warren Peace? Aren't you the one who ripped the middle pages out of all the magazines this morning?'

'I was only trying to do my job.'

'That's all right,' the squelcher said graciously. 'I'm sorry I didn't recognize you at once, but you humans . . . I hate to say this, Warren, but you humans are so *ugly* that you all look the same to us. Not only that, but you *smell*.'

Peace produced an unnatural smile. 'Quid pro quo.'

'What does that mean?'

Peace's smile became even more strained as he realized he had only the vaguest understanding of the Latin term. 'I'm not quite sure.'

'Great! My name is Nooglenorker. I'm training myself to be a properly qualified lawyer and I recognize high-class double-talk when I hear it. You and I can help each other, Warren. If you teach me a bit more of that . . .' The alien raised itself up, apparently intending to shake hands or paws with Peace, then glanced down and for the first time became aware of the full extent of the injury to its side. It gave a quivering bleat of anguish and sank back down, fixing Peace with an imploring look.

'Don't worry,' Peace said. 'I'll get you back to base.'

'How?'

'Like this.' Peace cupped his hands around his mouth and

began to yell for help, praying there were a few alien workers within earshot who were not erotically delirious.

'Two days that character has been in there,' Superintendent Glauber said in a doleful voice. 'That's one of my best suites, you know. It's there for the benefit of visiting CP executives. It was never meant as a hidyhole for work-shy bogtrotters.'

'Work-shy!' Not for the first time, Peace was stung into an angry response. 'Do you realize Nooglenorker could easily have died? It was lucky there was a surgeon-errant from the White Foundation passing through this sector. Apart from the humanitarian aspects, if we hadn't been able to get a medic here in time to do the operation, Nooglenorker's relatives would have put in one hell of a compensation claim.'

Glauber sneered. 'Some chance! Nooglenorker brought it all on himself. Nobody could claim he was attending to his duties when the gondolier chewed him up.'

'No, but—'

'But me no buts,' Glauber cut in. 'I'll tell you something for nothing, Warren. I've only been here a couple of years, but that was plenty of time for me to start *hating* the damned squelchers. Sniffing around here, sniffing around there! Even when they're not indulging in their disgusting self-pollution antics, they keep sniffing at me like I was something the cat had dragged in. If you ask me—'

'Sniffing!' Peace exclaimed, as a startling thought began to form in the deep recesses of his mind. He started tapping his pockets in search of the notebook he had obtained from the CP stores two days earlier in order to jot down observations and theories about squelcher behaviour.

'You got fleas or something?' Glauber said, scowling.

'No fleas, but I think I might have the solution to your alien porn problem.'

'You're kidding!'

'No kidding.' Peace put on an enigmatic smile. 'And you were the one who put me on the right *scent*, if you will excuse a small pun.'

'Pun?' Glauber glowered at him, his complexion deepening.

'Listen, Peace, we've already established that you don't know the first thing about puns. Are you going to tell me what you have found out?'

'Who knows?' Peace did another inscrutable smirk as he tapped the side of his nose. 'Knows . . . nose . . . ?'

Glauber jumped up from behind his desk, with an inarticulate cry of rage, and had taken a couple of menacing steps towards Peace when an unmistakable sound filled the office. From the audio monitor linked to Nooglenorker's room came the distinctive sniffing and snuffling that squelchers always emitted before going into sexual delirium.

'Nooglenorker must have come out of the anaesthetic and started to . . .' Glauber's crimson features twisted in a look of disgust. 'The filthy sex maniac! How did he get hold of pornographic material so soon? That's what I'd like to know. Couldn't even wait for his stitches to come out! I'll soon put a stop to that game!'

He strode to his office door and set off at high speed along the short corridor which led to the hospitality suites. Peace followed in his wake, gratified at having the chance to test his new theory so soon after its formulation. On reaching Nooglenorker's quarters, Glauber threw the door open and hurtled straight into the bedroom, with Peace close on his heels.

Even Peace, whose sympathies had swung towards the aliens, had to admit to himself that Nooglenorker in heat was not a pretty sight. The squelcher was standing by the bed, his floppy form made even uglier by having been shaved on one side to accommodate a large surgical dressing. Nooglenorker's whole body was quivering, the nipples were pulsing alarmingly, he was sniffing like a bloodhound, and at least three of his eyes were intent on the small book he was holding in both hands.

'That's not a porno zine,' Glauber said. 'What is it?'

Peace gulped. 'It looks like my notebook. I must have left it here.'

'Your notebook!' Glauber's red-tinged eyes regarded Peace with outrage and revulsion. 'What did you draw in it?'

'Nothing,' Peace said indignantly. 'Nothing at all.'

'*Nothing*?'

'Yes, and this goes to prove my new theory that—'

'Do you take me for a complete fool?' Glauber snarled. He darted forward, with surprising speed for one of his bulk, and snatched the book from Nooglenorker's unresisting hands. Nooglenorker, who until that moment had been quite unaware of their presence, gave a whimper of dismay and sagged down on to the bed. Ignoring the squelcher, Glauber scanned the open centre pages of the notebook and his jaw sagged as he saw that they were totally devoid of script or drawings.

'I can't take any more of this,' he bellowed in a voice thick with rage and frustration. He threw the notebook down, grabbed Nooglenorker by the loose skin of the upper chest and dragged the alien to its feet. 'This is the end of the road for you, Nooglenorker. If you don't tell me what it is that turns you on I'll rip your disgusting body apart. What have you to say to that? Eh? Eh? Eh?'

Nooglenorker's response was, to say the least of it, quite unexpected.

'Do it to me, darling,' the squelcher said in a dreamy, not-with-it voice, then thrust his blue and green tongue – the tongue which so much resembled a putrid sock – right into Glauber's open mouth.

'Ger-*awllcchh*!' Glauber cried in a terrible voice, pushing Nooglenorker away from him and clasping both hands to his throat. 'Oh, God! I've been violated by a filthy ... I've been poisoned! Get me to a medic!' He lurched to the door and clung to the frame for a moment to cast a distraught and venomous look back at Nooglenorker and Peace. 'I'll get you for this as soon as I get my mouth douched and disinfected and irradiated and sterilized. I'll get *both* of you. You'll see! I've got a gun, and I'm not afraid to use it on ...' His voice faded as he stumbled out of the suite and into the corridor.

Somewhat taken aback, Peace turned to look at Nooglenorker. The alien, who had dropped on to the bed, was sitting up and looking around the room with a bemused expression.

'Wha— what's been going on here?' he said weakly.

'Glauber and I came in while you were ... mmm ... starting

to enjoy yourself. As you know, he's been trying to find out exactly what it is in the magazines that gets you guys going, and when he saw the notebook pages were blank he lost his head a little and he grabbed you and said he was going to tear you apart – but you managed to drive him off.'

'Really?' The squelcher sounded quite proud. 'What did I do?'

'You rammed your tongue into his mouth.'

'Yug-*aarrgghh*!' Nooglenorker cried in a terrible voice, clasping both hands to his throat. 'Oh, God! Maybe I have poisoned myself! Maybe I'll die a horrible death of some loathsome disease, Warren. A ghastly and lingering death!'

'You needn't worry about the lingering side of it too much,' Peace said. 'Glauber has gone to fetch his gun.'

'That settles it. I'm getting out of this cursed dump.' Nooglenorker jumped up, clutched his side, swayed briefly on his vast feet and started an ungainly but energetic shuffle towards the door. 'It was nice knowing you, Warren.'

'You too,' Peace said, giving the alien's pneumatic upper arm an affectionate squeeze. 'Just one thing before you go . . .'

Nooglenorker paused in the doorway. 'Yes?'

Peace gave him a broad wink. 'The secret is safe with me. This is against the Oscar rules of conduct, but I promise not to reveal anything to Glauber – even though he was the one who called us in on the case.' Peace winked again. 'You can trust me to keep a secret.'

'Secret?' Nooglenorker glanced apprehensively along the corridor, obviously concerned in case Glauber should come into view brandishing a gun. 'What are you talking about, Warren?'

'Alien porn!' Peace tried winking with each eye in turn in order to get his message of camaraderie across, but the strain on his cheek muscles was too great. 'It's the smell, isn't it?'

'The smell?'

'Yes, the smell of paper,' Peace said triumphantly. 'The first inkling came to me when I heard that squelchers relied as much on smell as on eyesight for getting about. Then there was all the sniffing you do just before . . .'

'Let me get this straight,' Nooglenorker interrupted. 'Are

you seriously suggesting that we can get off . . . on the smell of paper?'

'Odours are evocative, and the smell of paper can be one of the most evocative of the lot.'

'Warren, have you any idea of how *kinky* that sounds?' Nooglenorker eyed Peace from head to foot with what seemed to be the utmost distaste.

Peace was dismayed. 'But I was so sure! You mean it *isn't* the lovely, creamy, musky, papery smell?'

'You should seek some kind of professional help, Warren – and the sooner the better.' With a final scandalized shake of the wattles, the squelcher moved out into the corridor.

'Please!' Peace ran after Nooglenorker. 'You can't leave me in suspense like this. I've got to know what it is that gets you going. You can trust me not to talk.'

'Sorry.' The alien kept on walking.

'I saved your life.'

The alien stopped walking, stood for a moment with drooping shoulders, then turned to face Peace. 'That isn't fair.'

'Sorry, but I've got to know.'

Nooglenorker hesitated. 'You promise not to say anything to Glauber?'

'Cross my heart.'

'All right then.' Nooglenorker glanced up and down the corridor, making sure of not being overheard. 'If you really must know – it's the staples.'

'The *staples*!' Peace took a step backwards. 'Is this some kind of a sick joke?'

'I'm serious,' Nooglenorker assured him. 'You see, our reproductive cycle is much more complicated than yours. We have six different sexes . . . in six different forms . . . all of whom have to fertilize each other in turn. I'm a member of the fourth sex, which is mainly distinguished by the presence of these.' With a strangely coy and delicate gesture, the squelcher indicated the red hemispheres on its torso.

Peace frowned. 'What's so unusual about a pair of nipples, even if they're one above the other?'

'They aren't nipples,' Nooglenorker said in demure tones

which sounded grotesque coming from an orange-haired gorilla. 'They're my gamete sacs, and an extremely well-developed pair they are, even if I say it myself. I often get complimented on them, and several times I've been asked to pose for glamour magazines, but of course I wouldn't agree to that sort of thing unless it was artistically—'

'The staples,' Peace cut in impatiently. 'What about the staples?'

'Well, you see, a member of our *fifth* sex has two sets of twin-pronged ovipositors on his trunk. When my mingle-time finally comes . . . and I see my ideal partner . . . we will cling together and his prongs will penetrate my gamete sacs and . . . and . . .' Nooglenorker's voice degenerated into a series of sniffles, his half-tomatoes began to swell and the hulking, loose-packed body gave a preliminary tremor.

'Get a grip on yourself!' Peace cried in consternation. 'Have you no shame?'

'I guess I got carried away,' Nooglenorker said apologetically, obviously striving to bring the symptoms of arousal under control. 'My mingle-time must be nearer than I thought. I'd better get back to Billinge – that's my home world – as soon as possible.'

'I'm getting out as well, before Glauber shows up again,' Peace said, falling into place beside the alien as he headed for the building's main exit. 'Have I got it right about the magazine staples? They look so much like fifth-sex ovipositors that the sight of them just flips a squelcher over?'

'Correct. When you pulled out the centrefolds, all you did was erect the prongs a little and make the magazines even sexier. We're fairly liberal about pornography back on Billinge – ordinary photographs are OK – but no publisher is allowed to use staples.'

'I see.' Peace fell silent for a moment as vast new tracts of understanding were opened to his mind. Truly there were more things on Earth and in the galaxy in general than were dreamed of in somebody-or-other's philosophy. He and Nooglenorker reached the lobby, drawing some attention from a few CP personnel, and hurried outside. The little landing field, beyond which a sea of green-stippled yellow stretched to the horizon, was completely empty.

'I was hoping a ship would be in,' Nooglenorker said in a despairing voice. 'How will I get away from Glauber?'

'Leave it to me.' Peace slid a hand inside his shirt and brought out the subetheric whistle which Brown Owl had insisted he should wear at all times. He raised it to his lips and blew a long blast. There was no sound, but he knew that Ozzy Drabble and Hec Magill would hear the signal clearly in their orbiting patrol vessel.

'My friends will have a ship here before you know it,' he said. 'Let's get out on the field and be ready for them.'

'Thanks, Warren.' Nooglenorker set off immediately, his elbows pumping as he tried to gain speed on feet which had been designed for slithering through quagmire. 'I won't forget you for this.'

'Think nothing of it.' Peace began to feel magnanimous as it came to him that his spell on the depressing mudball of Golborne was nearly over. 'Just tell me one thing before we part. *Are* there any pictures of fifth-sex mates in the magazines the workers keep bringing in?'

'Dozens. But they're not as sexy as the staples.'

'Had I any chance of identifying one of them?'

'I doubt it. All *you* would have observed is something resembling a perfectly ordinary tree.'

'A tree!' Peace was astounded. 'You're going to do it with a tree!'

'Not just any old tree, Warren. *My* tree will be sentient, sensitive, caring, concerned for me without being too possessive, capable of adjusting its own needs so as not to intrude on my own essential living space . . . and . . . and . . . it will also have those gorgeous ovipositors growing out of its trunk at exactly the right height to spear my gamete sacs . . . and when we get together . . .' Nooglenorker's voice began to quaver and he gave a couple of tentative sniffles.

'And you had the nerve to accuse *me* of being kinky,' Peace said accusingly.

'Quid pro quo!'

'You don't even know what that means.'

'Neither do you.'

'Maybe, but I'm more entitled to . . .' Peace broke off as a loud report blasted out behind him, followed by the sound of a bullet richocheting off the spacefield ferrocrete. 'Fork me pink! Glauber has gone mad! He really means to kill us!'

He increased his speed, then slowed down again in an agony of trepidation as he saw that his ungainly companion, hampered by the enormous squelcher feet, could go no faster. Glancing back, Peace saw that Glauber, brandishing what seemed to be an old-fashioned revolver, was skimming over the ground like a champion sprinter. In a matter of seconds he would be so close that it would be impossible for him to miss, even with an antique weapon.

'Ozzy and Hec,' Peace mumbled to himself in a panic, 'where are you?'

As if in answer to his question, a spaceship solidified in the air twenty metres above him. It immediately swooped to ground level and landed, shutting Glauber off from view. Peace heard his pursuer give a howl of frustration as the 200-metre-long metal barrier clumped into place in front of him. Doors swung open in the ship's midsection and two ruby-eyed golden giants emerged. Peace, who had believed he had his fill of Oscars for life, gave a sob of relief.

'Come on, Noogle,' he panted. 'Into the ship! We'll be safe in there.'

'Noogle?' The squelcher slid to a halt. 'How dare you address me by my part-name! That privilege is reserved for members of the first and third sexes in the quarter after the fourth paramingle, and if you think I'm going to allow . . .'

'Get into the ship!' Peace shouted, dancing with urgency. 'Get in before that madman . . .'

'What's the trouble here, Warren?' Drabble said, bounding towards Peace. His voice, even though it came from the speech converter he wore at his waist, showed deep concern. 'Has Jeeves made a move against you?'

'Jeeves?' Peace had all but forgotten the galactic villain's existence. 'No! It's the superintendent, Glauber! He's gone crazy! He's trying to shoot me and my friend!'

'*What?*' Drabble and Magill exchanged glances and the lenses of their eyes flared in righteous anger. 'Just leave him to us, Warren.'

They nodded at each other then parted company, running towards opposite ends of the ship so as to be sure of intercepting Glauber regardless of where he appeared. They had barely got into their stride when the superintendent came barrelling around the corner of the ship's forward tower. He skidded to a halt, his expression changing as he saw the huge golden Nemesis bearing down on him at speed. Apparently realizing that his revolver would be useless against such an adversary, he threw the weapon down and ran back the way he had come, emitting high-pitched bleats of terror. The Oscars, feet throwing out sparks while cornering, followed him out of sight in hot pursuit.

'I think that takes care of our Mr Glauber,' Peace said complacently. 'I just hope Ozzy and Hec don't accidentally break bits off him while performing the arrest. Those boys don't know their own strength.'

Nooglenorker rearranged the folds of his face to regard Peace with an extra disapproving eye. 'You certainly have some very peculiar friends.'

'Listen to who's talking!' Peace snapped. 'There aren't any Douglas firs or horse chestnuts among *my* buddies. Buds! Do you get it! *Buddies!* I'm sorry, puns are a weakness of mine. But have you no gratitude?'

'I apologize,' Nooglenorker said. 'I think I must be suffering from PMT – pre-mingle-time tension. I want to thank you for saving my life, Warren, and I'll wait right here until your friends come back and I'll thank them as well.'

'I'm sure it won't take them very long to deal with . . .' Peace's gaze wandered idly in the direction of the ship and his voice trailed off as he realized it was sitting there . . . unattended . . . with the doors wide open . . .

His heart began to pound as it came to him that *this* was his big chance to head for the fun capitals of the galaxy with no puritanical supermen in tow.

'I can't wait with you,' he said quickly to Nooglenorker. 'I've got to go now. Look after yourself . . . and don't take any wooden nipples. I mean nickels. I mean . . .'

'What's the matter with you?' Nooglenorker demanded.

'Nothing. Just tell Ozzy and Hec not to worry about me. I'll be OK – Jeeves or no Jeeves.'

Before the squelcher could reply, Peace had darted across the intervening distance and into the ship. He slammed the doors shut and sprinted into the forward control centre. His familiarity with every panel in the room enabled him to activate all the systems at lightning speed, and within ten seconds the massive vessel was rising into the sky.

A large screen showed the landing field swiftly falling away beneath. One of the Oscars was visible, with the inert form of Glauber slung over his shoulder; the other was looking upwards and making pathetic beckoning gestures.

'Sorry, fellas,' Peace murmured with a grin. 'I've got some therapeutic high living ahead of me. Perhaps we'll bump into each other again some time.'

He lowered himself into the main command seat and gently increased the ship's speed to a modest fifty light years an hour. It would be advisable to get out of the general region before Drabble and Magill could commandeer another ship and come after him, but he also needed a little breathing space in which to calm down and plan his immediate future. He relaxed into the comfortable curvatures of the seat and watched the local sun shrink and dim until it was lost in the background of stars.

Where shall I go first? he wondered. *Should I head for familiar territory, such as Parador, or should I take a look at one of the newer casino worlds?*

The problem, unlike those which had been plaguing him in the last few days, offered pleasurable mental exercise. He was leaning forward to call up a gazetteer of recreational planets when something strange happened.

The forward viewer, which had been showing dense star

fields, suddenly emitted a brilliant wash of blue light. It blinked on and off several times, making Peace feel giddy, then the image of a plump, white-haired man appeared on the screen. He had smooth pink skin, humorous grey eyes, a nose which was very slightly bulbous, and quirky lips which hinted at a sensitive and generous nature. One silver kiss-curl adorned the centre of his forehead. Altogether he was just about the cheeriest and most avuncular person Peace had ever seen – which made his electronic invasion of the control room all the more difficult to explain.

'What's going on here?' Peace said in a voice which was as reasonable as he could make it. 'Who are you?'

'My name is Jeeves,' the image replied. 'I don't like you, Warren Peace. And if you have listened to me this far you are now caught in the most sophisticated trap ever devised for one individual.'

Don't make me laugh, Peace thought.

He had intended to say the words aloud, but had to be content with running them through his mind because – much to his dismay – he found himself in the grip of a paralysis so profound that he could not even move his lips.

Chapter 5

'Would you like to hear what's going to happen to you next?' Jeeves said. He smiled as he spoke, making his face more cherubic than ever.

'There's no need for me tell you anything,' Jeeves went on cheerfully, 'but I always think it adds to the fun. Would it surprise you to learn that you're going to die, Peace? You will meet your death in only a few scant minutes from now – a *splendid* death – so would you like to know all the details? Would you like me to tell you the precise method of your execution? Peace? Peace?' Jeeves's image on the screen leaned forward, looking puzzled. 'Peace, why don't you answer my questions?'

Because I'm paralysed, you berk, Peace fumed in silence, annoyance momentarily displacing mortal fear.

'Is it because you're paralysed?'

Brilliant!

'It's because he's paralysed, boss.' The voice, coming from somewhere off-screen, sounded vaguely familiar to Peace. He tentatively placed it as belonging to one of the pair who had been involved in launching the pryktonite boulder against the assemblage of Oscars at the Galactic Jamboree. Wimpole! That was almost certainly the name.

'I realized he was paralysed all along,' Jeeves said petulantly. 'Kindly reduce the intensity of the Vogt ray so that the pathetic wretch can utter his last words. I rather like listening to last words.'

'Okay, boss.'

A few seconds later Peace felt a faint tingling sensation sweep through his body. He immediately tried to reach for the controls of his ship, but there was no muscular response apart from a slight twitching of his fingers.

71

'It's no use, Peace,' Jeeves said, his benevolent smile returning. 'You are in my power, and nothing can save you. At this very moment two small black holes are converging on your ship from opposite directions. When they collide you will be squarely in between, and you will be converted to molecules, to atoms, to particles, to quarks, to *bits* of quarks.'

Wishing he had been sensible enough to remain with his Oscar bodyguards, Peace swivelled his eyes to take in the side view screens. He gave an involuntary whimper of panic as he discerned two expanding purplish disks, each fringed with tangential flickers of blue radiance.

'Don't strain your shifty little eyes,' Jeeves advised happily. 'Yours will be the most comprehensive death ever inflicted on a human being, and the beauty of it is that you won't be able to tell when the black holes are about to hit you. They are, by definition, invisible. You won't be able to see a damned thing. What have you to say to that?'

Peace was in no mood for astronomical trivia, especially under threat of death, so he seized the chance for a futile gesture of defiance. 'You're wrong about my not being able to see anything. I can see two purply-brown disks.'

'*What*?' A vertical wrinkle appeared under Jeeves's kiss-curl as he turned to address his off-screen companion. 'What's the meaning of this, Wimpole?'

'There wasn't no time to find three proper black holes in a cluster, boss,' Wimpole said defensively.

'Three? *Three*? I told you to bring *two* black holes.'

'And howja think I was gonna transport them? I had to find a big black hole and steer the two small ones into it at the right speed and angle to make them come outa the worm hole near Golborne.'

Jeeves gave a faint sniff. 'It sounds a simple enough job to me.'

'Yeah? Well, you should try it some time.'

Wimpole was now sounding quite aggrieved, but Peace was unable to take pleasure in listening to his enemies falling out. The disks in his lateral screens were visibly swelling at an accelerating rate and he guessed they would meet – with him in between – in only a minute or so.

'Don't be impertinent, Wimpole,' Jeeves said. 'I supply you with expensive mass-moving equipment and you can't even round up two little black holes!'

'Puce holes is nearly as good.'

'Puce? You fool, Wimpole!' Jeeves's doll-pink features again attempted to register fury, but the best they could do was to pucker slightly, like those of a baby with mild colic. 'Don't you know that when puce holes collide they have a tendency to . . .?'

Peace strained his eyes, anxious to hear any astrophysical tidings which could relate to his chances of survival, but events had begun to move too swiftly. There was a clamour of alarm bells and klaxons. His lateral screens emitted bursts of violet brilliance. Peace gave a loud despairing wail as he realized that the puce holes were meeting and combining all around him. He had entered the last microseconds of his life and was only able to complete his final thoughts because event horizons were clashing with each other, wrestling and entwining like eels in a basket, prolonging his annihilation. There followed a curious and startlingly inappropriate moment during which he seemed to be flying at high speed past arrays of neon signs, and over colour-reversed images of Finland . . .

Then the ship gave a sickening lurch – and calm silence descended upon everything.

Peace had been gazing at the star fields portrayed in his view screens for quite a long time before he was able to accept the fact that he was still alive.

He gave a quavering sigh of relief, scarcely able to credit his good fortune. It seemed that Jeeves had been fully justified in doubting the efficacy of puce holes as instruments of death. Apparently, as far as Peace was concerned, the only result of the astronomical collision had been to hurl him into another part of the galaxy. All he had to do now was to return surreptitiously to the Oscars' headquarters and place himself under their protection. The good old Oscars! Who could ask for better friends? With benefit of hindsight, he could see that he had not taken their warnings about Jeeves seriously enough. In future, once he was reunited with his golden-hued allies, he was going to play safe and stop all immature hankering after pleasures of the flesh.

As if in reward for his new virtuousness, Peace slowly became aware of an astonishing piece of good fortune. He had been paying little attention to the star patterns shown on his screens, assuming they would be totally alien to him, as was to be expected when a ship had been deposited at a random location in the galaxy. Finding the way back to the explored sector had promised to be a long and difficult task. Now, however, it was dawning on him that he could see some stellar groupings which looked quite familiar. Senses suddenly acute, scarcely able to believe his luck, he scanned the view panels and almost at once found the only classical constellation he knew really well.

Orion!

It had no distortions that he could detect, which meant that he had emerged from null-space perhaps only one light year from Earth!

Peace's jaw sagged as he weighed the odds against such a fortuitous coincidence. Then a possible explanation came to him via dim memories of an article he had once seen in the back pages of the *New Scientist*. It was to do with nostalgia – a recently discovered property of certain particles which gave them an affinity with the location in space-time in which they had first become part of stable atomic structures. His ship had been constructed on Earth, and the inanimate homesickness of its elemental constituents had caused it to materialize as close as it could to its point of manufacture.

Peace's lips quirked as he thought about what might have happened if the nostalgia effect had been stronger. His ship might have emerged from its null-space transit within the gates of the factory where it had been built. Pleased at having reached a rational and scientific explanation for his proximity to his home world, he turned his attention to an ultra-bright star which dominated the screen on his right.

With luck now running his way, he could reasonably expect to find that it was none other than Sol. That being the case, he could be on Earth in only a few minutes, and there were lots of high-class pleasure cities on Earth. Perhaps he had been too quick in deciding to go crawling back to the Oscars, cap in hand. He could see that it was advisable for him to go into a kind of monastic seclusion, to avoid being assassinated by Jeeves, but his spiritual forefathers had long recognized the need for a good blow-out before a period of abstinence. That was what Mardi Gras was all about, and who was *he* to cast doubts upon the teachings of history's greatest religious leaders?

'All right!' He flexed his fingers several times, like a concert pianist preparing to give a recital, and addressed himself to the control console. The first thing he did was to put a selective monitor on all astrogation beacons associated with the bright star. The result was complete silence.

That's odd, he thought, frowning. *Either they're not sending – which hardly seems likely – or I'm not receiving.*

He ran his gaze over various instrument zones, hoping to identify a simple malfunction somewhere, and it was only then that he noticed something very strange about his view screens. The images of the myriad stars, which should have been steady points of light, were changing in intensity. The fluctuations were rapid and irregular, causing some stars to dim almost to invisibility while others were increasing in brightness as though on the verge of going nova. Repeated many thousands of times over, the phenomenon made the perceived universe seem alive, like a vast swarm of fireflies.

Peace's first thought was that the ship's power supply had developed a serious irregularity. He searched the control console and found areas where many indicator LEDs were behaving erratically. Digital displays which should have been glowing with serene steadiness were shifting like numbers on a gambling machine, giving wildly nonsensical readings. The artificial gravity in the control room also began to vary, producing queasy surges in Peace's stomach. All of a sudden his newfound conviction that fortune was on his side seemed

75

naive in the extreme. It was becoming quite obvious that the ship, as a result of running the hyper-geometrical gamut, had suffered distortions in its nano-engineered control matrices. As a result, it was now being overtaken by catastrophes which could easily result in his death.

There's no need to panic, he told himself. *AESOP can handle this. After all, that's why they install Automatic Electronic Spaceship Operators and Pilots in the first place. Computers like that are designed to deal with every possible emergency. No matter what goes wrong with a ship, no matter how great the potential disaster, AESOP, with his awesome artificial intelligence, can take care of it.*

Peace directed his gaze towards AESOP, a medium-sized but authoritative-looking black box mounted on the wall above the control console, and said, 'Over to you, pal. What are you going to do?'

AESOP responded by emitting a few curls of smoke, followed by an explosion of violently fizzing magenta sparks. A second later most of the control panels in front of Peace went dark.

'Thanks a lot, pal,' Peace said bitterly, as he looked over the console and began to assess the damage. The lights and air generators were still working, but as far as he could tell at first glance, all other auxiliary systems, including artificial gravity and communications, had ceased to function. Even the lighting in the control room was unsteady. In his experience such failures were always progressive, so he made an immediate decision to head for Earth while the ship's propulsion transceivers were still working. The relevant flight control computers seemed to be dead, so he went over to manual.

He activated the drive circuits, identified the target star and called for the modest speed of one light year per hour. Accustomed though he was to unpleasant surprises, what happened next caused him to freeze in his chair, the blood draining from his face. He had expected a gradual increase in the overall brightness of the designated star, but instead it flared up like an automobile headlight which had just been switched on – a phenomenon which told him he was travelling at thousands of light years an hour. With no computers to promote the idea of self-preservation, the ship was likely to dive into the heart of the sun in a matter of seconds.

Peace hit the STOP bezel with all his strength, and the terrifying plunge through space ceased on the instant. His eyes closed themselves from sheer relief. Now quivering with sheer nervous strain, he gripped the arms of his chair with clammy hands and tried to work out what had gone wrong with the ship. A treacherous instability seemed to have developed in all its electrics and electronics, as was indicated by the fluctuations in everything from the images in the view screens to the output of the lighting system.

This is awful, Peace thought. *I've got to get out of this forking junk heap before it kills me.*

He opened his eyes and gave a whimper of gratitude as he was greeted by the sight of the Earth–Moon system floating, albeit unsteadily, in the forward view panel. Nothing had ever seemed more beautiful. Praying that the ship would exercise some degree of self-restraint, he put the controls into the landing manoeuvre mode and slid his thumb on to the miniature joystick in the arm of his chair. Cautiously, with icy perspiration stinging his forehead, he advanced the stick the smallest possible distance.

The unequal globes of Earth and Moon gently and meekly increased in diameter. Greatly encouraged, Peace resisted the urge to demand greater speed. He guided the ship towards the daylight side of the planet, where he could see the whole of the north American continent conveniently laid out before him, right way up, exactly as it had always appeared in old science fiction illustrations. As the smooth approach continued, it became apparent that the ship was going to touch down somewhere in the region of South Dakota or Nebraska.

Peace had nothing against those states, but he had grown up on the west coast and, after the succession of harrowing experiences to which he had recently been subjected, felt a sentimental urge to make landfall in his beloved home state of Califanada. Almost of its own accord, his thumb exerted a faint lateral pressure on the joystick, just enough in normal circumstances to nudge his descent path a little to the west.

The ship's response was instantaneous and appalling.

The image in the forward screen ballooned and began to spin, evidence of a tremendous increase in speed accompanied by a total loss of stability. Peace tried to decelerate and cancel the rotation simultaneously, but his frantic thumbing of the joystick only goaded the ship into new displays of perversity. The sunlit landscape started whirling away to one side, and then Peace was hurled into a terrifying low-altitude dash across the continent. He barely had time to recognize the outlines of Cape Cod and the Gulf of Maine before he was out over the Atlantic and speeding towards Europe.

The ocean flashed by beneath him in a few petrifying seconds, darkness looming ahead as he drew close to the planet's terminator, the boundary between day and night. There, in twilight, was Ireland. He crossed the Emerald Isle in the blink of an eye and saw ahead of him the north-western part of England, its mountains and lakes already lost in sombre shades of grey and black.

Peace gave a moan of despair as the ship made an abrupt downward swerve and headed for a steep hillside which bordered a long, narrow stretch of water. Unable to think of a more constructive reaction, he again pounded his fist on the glowing crimson square of the STOP bezel, cutting off all power to the drive transceivers.

The ship obliged him by coming to a standstill – about ten metres above the surface of the lake. There followed a moment of weightlessness, during which the massive vessel was obeying the dictates of gravity; then came a cataclysmic *boom* which could have been the opening shots of Armageddon. Partially stunned by the incredible blast of sound, Peace was also driven deeply and painfully into his seat as a result of the impact with the water. In the same instant the control room was plunged into total blackness.

Driven by a choking claustrophobia and fear of drowning, he lunged out of the control seat, groped his way through the darkness to the nearest door and pulled it open. Water gushed in around his shins with unexpected force, almost carrying him off his feet. He dived forward, above the incoming flood, and found himself breasting the chill waters of a British lake at night. A few stars glimmered weakly in the murk overhead, and an equally feeble sprinkle of lights was all that marked the distant shore. Behind him, the ship emitted vast gurgling and belching noises as it took in water and entered on its slow descent to unknown depths.

There is one consolation in all this, Peace told himself as he began to swim towards dry land. *Things are bound to get better from now on.*

Chapter 6

For a brief period it seemed that the coldness of the water would not be much of a problem.

It was bad, he decided, but not *too* bad. Admittedly, the lights of the shore seemed far more distant than his aerial view of the lake had prepared him for, but he was young and strong, able to call upon vast reserves of physical power and endurance. No matter what Herculean test lay ahead he was bound to triumph because of his vast reserves of physical power and endurance.

And then, with quite astonishing alacrity, his vast reserves of physical power and endurance faded away.

The internal treachery began as a cramp in his right foot, possible a legacy from the encounter with the cold bath faucet on Golborne. Before Peace knew what was happening the seizure had progressed up his leg as far as the knee, bringing unspeakable agony, and causing him to do something which was diametrically opposed to the intentions and philosophies of any dedicated swimmer.

He sank.

On the way down he swallowed a stomachful of water, and while struggling back up to the surface drew a similar amount into his lungs. Finding himself once again in a milieu where, in theory, air was freely available he tried to take in the maximum amount, but a severe bout of coughing, gasping and retching effectively thwarted that ambition. He sank again. This time the descent was curtailed, thanks to the efforts of his three functional limbs, but by the time he got back to the surface he was in genuine fear of his life.

After a moment of snorting and puking water, he located the shore lights and set off in that direction, using a new kind of side-stroke – loosely based on that of the shrimp – in which his paralysed leg was dragged behind. It was not an efficient means of progression, and the more he persisted with it the farther the land seemed to be. He was beginning to wonder if he was actually swimming backwards, when, mercifully, the circulation was restored to his leg and it started to move again.

In spite of his improved performance, the swim proved to be a drawn-out and gruelling affair, a watery nightmare, and by the time he reached the shallows his body was suffused by a painful numbness. *This isn't fair*, he thought. *Numbness implies an absence of sensation, but I'm numb – and it HURTS!* He forced himself upright, shivering violently, and waded a final few paces on to dry land.

His first reaction, after he had knuckled his eyes and looked around, was a dull surprise at how dark his surroundings were. All right, he was in a rural part of England, but this was the twenty-fourth century and no citizen on Earth was required to stumble blindly around at night, stepping in doggy poos and tripping over unseen obstacles. The absence of illumination was somewhat strange and disturbing.

He moved forward a few paces across a margin of pebbles and high grass and found himself on a narrow but well-paved road. The darkness seemed less intense to his right, so he set off in that direction. His shivering, which had been bad enough when he first emerged from the water, became so fierce that he seemed to be doing a kind of tribal dance. As he progressed laboriously and unsteadily along the road he could not help being aware of his total lack of dignity, and he began thinking wistfully about how different things would have been were he still an Oscar. Untroubled by lack of air or buoyancy, he would simply have strolled along the bed of the lake, all the while sending out a subetheric call for assistance. It was quite possible that a spaceship crewed by his jolly golden friends would have been there, waiting for him, by the time he had reached the shore. Yes, there was a lot to be said for being an Oscar and having such reliable allies close by at all times.

Peace sighed through chattering teeth and concentrated his gaze on the glimmers of yellowish light which were beginning to appear in the murk ahead. Gradually he discerned the outlines of an ancient-looking stone building. It had a steep roof and small windows adorned by flower boxes. As Peace drew even nearer he saw a square signboard hanging above the building's front entrance, and a tremulous flicker of hope began to gleam through his misery. *Could it be . . .? Could it really be that . . .?* Pure joy geysered within him as he made out the words 'Duck and Fiddler' on the sign, and realized he was approaching a country pub.

Moaning aloud with anticipation, he speeded up his witch doctor's dance. As he reached the stone steps of the entrance he noticed that the wall-lamps which flanked it were powered by antique gas mantles, or very good reproductions. *Somebody has gone to a lot of trouble to preserve the Olde Worlde atmosphere of this place*, he thought. *That probably means they take very good care of the beer.*

The heavy oak door had authentic stained-glass panels and an old-fashioned thumb latch, further boosting Peace's expectations. He opened the door and almost swooned with pleasure as he was surrounded by warmth from a log fire, plus the rich aromas of good ale and tobacco. The stone-flagged room he had entered was empty except for a large ruddy-cheeked man standing behind a bar which glistered with copper and glass.

'Hi!' Peace quavered. 'I need . . . I need a . . .'

'Good Lord, sir!' the barman said, starting out from behind his counter. 'What has happened to you?'

Peace tried to control the vibration of his jaw. 'Ship . . . lake . . . sank . . . swam . . .'

'Good Lord, sir! Were there other passengers? Shall I fetch help?'

'No need . . . alone . . .'

'You're lucky you didn't catch your death.' The barman gripped Peace with massive hands and guided him to a leather armchair close to the crackling fire. Peace sank into it with gratitude, feeling colder than ever as the heat of the flames reached his skin.

'We'd better get you out of those wet clothes, sir,' the barman said, 'otherwise you'll catch pneumonia.'

'There's no need for that,' Peace replied. His hitex shirt and trousers had already repelled most of the water picked up in the lake and would soon be dry. 'What I really need is a glass of beer.'

'You'll get no ale from me,' the barman announced sternly, shaking his head.

'But ...' Peace's voice failed as a terrible new thought occurred to him. Was it possible that this place, so inviting in all its aspects, was one of those temperance establishments where cranks gathered and *pretended* to have a good time? He stared up at the barman in abject pleading.

'Rum is what a man in your condition needs, sir,' the barman said. 'Hot buttered Navy rum – and plenty of it.'

'You're absolutely right.' Peace blinked to ease the thankful prickling in his eyes. 'Why didn't I think of that?' He winced as a trickle of water slid from his scalp and down his back. 'And could I have a towel to dry my hair?'

'Leave it to me, sir. By the way, my name is Fred. Fred Cherry. I'm the landlord here, and always at your service.'

'My friends call me Warren.'

'It's a pleasure to meet you, Warren. We don't get many American gentlemen in these parts.' The large, waistcoated and aproned figure of Cherry hurried away on the errand of mercy.

How pleasant, how civilized! Peace thought as, shivers beginning to abate, he slipped off his shoes and allowed the warmth of the fire to penetrate his feet. *I had no idea that places like this still existed – even in England. I think I'll come back here for holidays.*

He rubbed his hair dry with the rough towel which arrived within seconds, and accepted with trembling hands the pewter mug which Cherry brought a couple of minutes later. The landlord stood back, smiling benevolently, as Peace raised the mug to his lips. The aroma from the blend of hot dark rum and butter – his first encounter with alcohol in a year – was so exquisite that he was almost unable to take a drink, fearful of being disappointed.

'It's not meant for sniffing,' Cherry boomed. 'Get it down your neck, Warren.'

Peace took a small sip and a beatific smile spread over his face as sensations of purest pleasure, starting from his taste-buds, coursed downwards into his stomach and upwards into his brain. He took another sip and another, adding to the ambrosian warmth that was beginning to suffuse his system. He could not remember ever having been so happy. *This is more like it*, he thought. *I'm glad I'm not an Oscar any more. The poor chumps don't know what they're missing!*

'D'you know something, Warren?' Cherry said, sounding surprised. 'Your clothes look as if they're dry.'

Peace glanced down at himself. 'They *are* dry.'

'That's amazing! Truly amazing! Some new wonder material, is it?'

'No. Just ordinary water and dirt repellent.'

'Ordinary! That's a good'un, Warren.' Cherry laughed admiringly. 'More of that good old Yankee know-how, eh? The United States has a thing or two to teach us here in the Old Country.'

At that moment a brass bell tinkled above the entrance and two men came into the pub. Cherry hurried away to serve them, leaving Peace to ponder on what seemed a rather odd conversation. Hitex garments had been universally available for hundreds of years – so what had the landlord been talking about? Peace became aware that he was under discussion by the men at the bar. He gave a friendly wave in their direction and as they returned the gesture he noticed they were dressed like farmers, but not farmers of the twenty-fourth century. In place of the standard anti-gravity sled suits they wore what seemed to be tweeds, corduroys and clumpy leather boots. Peace linked the observation to several others he had made since plunging into the Earth's atmosphere, and an uncomfortable idea began to form in the back of his mind.

Had his encounter with the puce holes, which took place in 2387, thrown him backwards in time? Was this the England of, say, Queen Victoria?

Once the suspicion had established itself he was unable to make himself at ease. Time machines existed in his own age, but it was illegal to use them for forays into the past, so if he really was in Victorian England he was almost certainly stranded. In an era where one could die of measles or scarlet fever or stomach ulcers! And what about palsy and the ague, whatever they were? There was even a threatening entity, lurking in his meagre store of historical semi-facts, called HIV, which he was pretty certain was not a reference to Henry IV.

Even I couldn't be so unlucky, he thought in panic. *Surely this* has *to be the ultimate theme pub – one where even the customers like to dress up. I've got to check on what year this is!*

He scanned the large room, hoping to see a calendar, but nothing of the sort was in view. That left him with the considerable problem of locating himself in time through the men at the bar without appearing to be an idiot. It was all right to ask somebody what day it was, but not to know the *year*! He took a sustaining gulp of rum, stood up and sauntered across the stone floor to the bar.

'Back on your feet already, Warren,' Cherry said. 'Good man! I've been telling Alf and Josh here about your bit of bad luck. Losing your boat, and all that.'

Alf and Josh, squarely constructed men with weather-hewn features, shook hands with Peace. Their fingers were hard with calluses, reinforcing his alarm.

'What sort of craft was she?' Alf said.

'Standard star cruiser,' Peace replied, caught off guard. 'Usual sort of thing.'

'*Star* cruiser, eh?' Cherry looked oddly gratified. 'Top of the range, eh? It must have cost you a fortune, Warren. Do you want to get in touch with your insurance agents? I've been told the telephone in the village is working quite well this week.'

'I never bother about insurance,' Peace said, this time choosing a form of words he hoped would be neutral, regardless of which century he was in. 'I'll just pick up another ship when I need one.' He immediately wondered if he had said the right thing, because Cherry's ruddy countenance, already benign, became positively radiant.

'That's the way, Warren,' he said gleefully. 'No use having brass if you don't splash it around a bit and enjoy it! That's what I always say.' Alf and Josh gave a low rumble of assent.

Peace nodded. 'That's what I always say too.'

'We're all in agreement in that case.' Cherry beamed in pleasure at the happy coincidence, then a look of concern appeared on his well-padded features. 'Warren! What am I thinking of? Your pot is empty! Give it over and I'll top you up with the necessary. By the way, I trust you'll do me the honour of staying here tonight, or for as long as you need to get yourself settled and fettled?'

'Glad to,' Peace said as he handed over his mug. Cherry's concern for his welfare was quite touching, and it occurred to him that he could meet a worse fate than being stranded in a world of old-fashioned courtesy and kindliness. All the same, he *had* to find out what period of history he was in.

'Do you fellows like puzzles?' he said to Alf and Josh, taking a pen from his shirt pocket. 'Mathematical puzzles?'

Josh looked eager. 'Nothing I like better!'

'Good! You're going to love this one.' Peace handed Josh the pen and slid a beermat into place in front of him. 'Start by writing down the year.'

Josh nodded and wrote four digits: 2387.

Peace gaped at the number, as new questions crowded into his mind. The year was correct; he had *not* been hurled back into the past – but why did it seem that way? There was a mystery here, one that he had to solve . . .

'What next?' Josh said, pen poised.

'Huh?' Peace, who had forgotten about the puzzle, stared at the digits on the beermat and tried in vain to find some kind of a pattern in them. 'Divide by the number of days in the week,' he improvised.

'What are you lads up to?' Cherry said, rejoining the group with a vapouring mug of rum in his hand.

'Warren is showing us a great puzzle,' Alf said.

Peace snatched the mug and drank deeply, almost scalding his tongue in the process. Perhaps the best plan would be to

86

own up and admit his bafflement. But then he would become a laughing stock, and his pride would not permit that.

'What next, Warren?' Josh said, pen at the ready.

'Add on your shoe or boot size.' It suddenly occurred to Peace that a good way out of his predicament, instead of discreetly quizzing the locals, would be to catch some news broadcasts. 'Where can I watch some television?' he said to Cherry.

The landlord frowned. 'What's television?'

'You know . . . moving pictures,' Peace said with an indistinctness for which his parboiled tongue was only partly to blame. If these people, of the year 2387, had never heard of television something was definitely and terribly wrong.

'There was a bioscope down in Ulverston, but it closed a couple of years ago,' Cherry said. 'Nobody could put up with that shifty electric light going bright and dim all the time. Television, you called it. That's another Yankee word I've learned.'

Josh brandished the pen. 'What'll I do next, Warren?'

'Take away the number of . . . ah . . . degrees in a triangle.'

'You're looking a bit mithered, Warren.' Cherry leaned over the bar to inspect Peace's face. 'Would you like a bite to eat? The kitchen is closed, but I can do you a nice ham sandwich, home-cured. Or would you like to have a lie-down in your room?'

'No, thanks,' Peace said, again gratified by the attention. 'I'd like to stay right where I am for a while and perhaps try some of your beer after I finish this rum.'

'Just let me know when you're ready for it.' Cherry gave Peace a comradely pat on the shoulder, made as if to move away and then paused. 'By the way, Warren, do you want me to keep your bar account separate from your room account?'

'It doesn't matter either way,' Peace said cheerfully. 'I haven't got any money.'

He had often heard of blood draining from a person's face, but had never expected to see the phenomenon so graphically demonstrated. Cherry gazed at him with shocked eyes, while the ruddiness of his countenance sank downwards like red fluid escaping from a thermometer. He was completely immobile

87

for a second, petrified, then his mouth twisted into a weak semblance of a smile.

'You really got me that time, Warren,' he said in a faint voice. 'For a moment I thought you meant you really had *no* money. No money at all.'

'That's exactly what I did mean.' Peace found it difficult to understand why a kindly Olde Worlde innkeeper, dispenser of traditional hospitality, seemed concerned over such a trivial matter.

'But you must have a cheque book, letters of credit, traveller's cheques . . . somesuch like that.'

'None of those things,' Peace beamed. 'I will, of course, pay my bill in full – as soon as I have funds. Now, Fred, what is your normal procedure for dealing with somebody in my position?'

'My normal procedure . . .' Cherry reached under the bar and came up with a wicked-looking carving knife' . . . is to cut his frigging head off.'

'That's not very nice,' Peace said, shrinking back in dismay. Since breakfast he had been fired at with a handgun, sandwiched between two puce holes, trapped in a runaway spaceship, almost drowned – and now this! He had a feeling he was losing control of his life.

'Not very nice!' The colour was returning to Cherry's face in full force. 'What about you coming in here and pretending to be a Yankee millionaire?'

'I did *not*!'

'Who else has boats on Windermere?'

'I—'

'All you did was tip some water over your head. No wonder your clothes dried so fast! And to think I fell for it!' Cherry tightened his grip on the huge knife. 'You're going to pay what you owe me, or else . . .'

Peace raised his hands placatingly. 'Of course, I'm going to pay you. There can be no question about it.'

'How?'

'Well, maybe there can be *one* question about it.' Peace thought longingly of his platinum-and-diamonds Oscar badge, now lying in his jacket pocket at the bottom of the lake. It would have been an excellent article for barter. He sought inspiration and then remembered his wristwatch. In this curious rural backwater an advanced chronomod could be worth quite a lot of money.

'I'll give you this,' he said, undoing the watch's magnetic strap. 'I think you'll find it's worth at least five hundred ecus.'

'What's an ecu?'

Peace frowned as he ransacked his patchy knowledge of British history. 'Pounds? Yes, five hundred pounds.' He set the watch to local time, referring to a pendulum clock on the wall, and handed it over to Cherry.

The landlord fingered the sleek polychromatic casing and glittering strap, inspected the digital display and the numerous auxiliary controls. 'This is a fine-looking watch.'

'It certainly is.' Peace refrained from mentioning that it was also a powerful computer and an encyclopaedia, and could show in miniature just about every movie that had ever been made. He was developing a feel for the situation in which he had found himself, and reckoned he could judge when it was best to go softly.

'Look, Warren . . .' Cherry put his carving knife out of sight. 'I'm sorry if I got a bit edgy a moment ago. Things have been a bit tight recently, and . . .'

'Say no more about it,' Peace said grandly. 'I'm a man of wide experience and deep understanding; and now, if you don't mind, I think I'd like to sample some of your finest ale.'

'Certainly, Warren.' Cherry put the watch on his thick wrist and hurried away to the handpumps to fetch the beer. Peace smiled at Alf and Josh, who had been listening to the exchange with overt interest.

'What do I do next, Warren?' Josh said, pointing at his calculation on the beermat.

Peace groaned inwardly, wondering why life always had to be so complicated. Hoping that luck might be on his side for once, he said, 'Can't you see anything special about the number you've got?'

'No. Nothing at all.'

'Keep looking. It just needs a bit of thought.' Peace gave Josh an encouraging wink, seized the tankard of beer which had just been delivered to him and drank deeply from it. The bitter, malty, hoppy, complicated taste of a living beer was balm to his soul.

He relaxed again and, glad of the breathing space, was gazing quite contentedly around the room when the door opened to admit a new customer to the Duck and Fiddler. This was a tall, middle-aged man with a military bearing, wearing clothes which, although undoubtedly civilian and casual, nevertheless had a battle-ready look about them.

'Good evening, Hector,' the innkeeper called out as he turned to Peace. 'Warren, I'd like you to meet Colonel Hector Gooble, one of my best and most valued customers. He's here on holiday for a few days, but usually he spends his time with the Terran Interplanetary Defence Force.'

'Good to meet you, Hector.' As he shook hands with the newcomer Peace smiled to disguise the fact that he had never heard of any Terran Interplanetary Defence Force. Defence against what? Once again, there stole into his mind the conviction that something was terribly wrong – but how was he to determine what it was without giving away his own position? Humour? Could he put forward a few enquiries which were in the guise of jokes?

'I fully approve of the Interplanetary Defence Force,' he said jovially. 'You never know when those rotten Martians are going to launch an attack.'

Gooble took a sip of the beer which had just been served to him, then gave a solemn nod. 'Quite right, Warren. We have to watch the skies.'

Peace was still mentally reeling, wondering if Gooble had turned the joke back on him, when Alf, the quieter of the two farmers, made an unexpected contribution.

'You know, Hector,' he said, 'I saw an article in the *Tatler* last month, or the month before, which suggested that Mars could be uninhabited.'

'In that case,' Gooble said, smiling sagely into his tankard, 'who built the canals?'

Alf nodded. 'That's a good point.'

'It's a *very* good point.' Gooble gave the company a quizzical glance, looking every inch the soldier–statesman–philosopher. 'And don't forget – we have no idea of what kind of threat is posed to us by the Venusians.'

'Well said!' Cherry, Alf and Josh, obviously recognizing a clincher when they heard one, nodded vigorously.

Peace took another gulp of his beer, which was somehow beginning to lose its charm. *Fork me pink!* he muttered to himself. *I've either landed in some kind of retreat for well-off lunatics, or . . . or . . .* The thought fizzled out as his imagination failed to come up with a better explanation. He pummelled his brain for a moment then decided to try a new way of ferreting out information, one inspired by memory-shards of historic movies dealing with rivalry between Britain and the old USA when they were allies in some ancient war or another.

'I grew up on a farm in Kansas,' he lied, 'so I don't know much about space warfare and all that kind of thing, but I thought the Terran Interplanetary Defence Force was mainly run by the United States and Canada.'

'*What?*' Gooble slammed his tankard down on the counter.

'My ignorance is entirely to blame,' Peace said quickly, pleased with the promising reaction. 'I'm fully aware of that. I would love it if you could tell me something about the British component – so that I could spread the good word when I get back to Arkansas.'

'Kansas,' the landlord chipped in.

Peace nodded. 'That's what I meant to say. For instance, Hector, how many ships have you sent to Mars?'

'Son, you really *are* out of your depth in these matters,' Gooble said, barely suppressing a smirk. 'We haven't sent any ships into enemy territory – the journey would take too long. The policy is to sit tight and let them bring the war to us. Stretch their supply lines . . . that kind of thing . . .'

'But how fast can your ships go?'

'We get up to ten miles a second at the end of the launch burn.'

'Is that a fact?' Peace rubbed his chin while his overwhelmed brain tried to convert unfamiliar miles into familiar kilometres. A new and even more dismaying suspicion was beginning to form somewhere in his subconscious.

'You don't seem too impressed, Warren.'

'Oh, I'm *very* impressed, it's just that I'm not used to thinking terms of English miles. You know . . . coming from a remote place like Nebraska.'

'Kansas,' Cherry corrected.

'That's what I meant to say.'

Gooble winked, rather obviously, at the rest of the company, preparing them for a bit of amusement. 'So, Warren, with your New World upbringing and all that, how would you suggest we measure the speed of a spaceship?'

'In multiples of the speed of light.' Peace spoke without pausing to think, rising to the bait, then realized his blunder. 'I meant *fractions* of the speed of light.'

The hasty amendment had little or no effect of the listeners. They nudged each other and burst into derisive peals of laughter. Even Josh looked up from his laborious beermat studies to grin at his neighbours.

Gooble waited for the general mirth to subside, then dabbed his eyes as he spoke. 'My God, Warren, what do they teach at American schools apart from sports? Every school child in this country knows that light hasn't got a fixed speed: it varies from second to second.'

'It *varies*?' Peace was beginning to feel ill.

'Of course it does! Continuously! Over a range of about 40,000 miles a second. It's obvious you don't know very much physics, Warren.'

'Mathematics, neither,' Josh said, waving the pen accusingly at Peace. 'I've got 172 here, and I can't make heads nor tails of it.'

'Oh, I forgot,' Peace said distractedly. 'Divide by the number of fingers on one hand.'

He put Josh out of his mind as it came to him that his latest, and worst, suspicion had proved correct. His double impact with the puce holes had not thrown him back in time – it had hurled him into an alternative universe! This was still the

92

year 2387, but in a divergent time stream. His predicament was more dire than he had realized, because even though there was a faint hope of being rescued by a time machine from the wrong year, there would be no way of finding one's way home across all the trillions of probability universes that made up the infinite delta of time.

This is terrible, Peace thought as his beleaguered mind tried to weigh up some of the consequences of the situation. If the speed of light was always fluctuating, the propagation of electrical currents and fields would also be affected. It would be impossible to design an efficient electric motor or dynamo. Electrical engineering would have remained at a primitive level in this universe – he had already heard references to telephones and movie projectors being unsatisfactory – and, of course, the electronics industry would never have got off the ground. Why, science itself would have been hobbled!

Peace gave a quavering sigh as he grappled with more and more implications. He now understood why his spaceship and all its instruments had begun to behave so erratically as soon as they were transferred to this inconstant universe. He had been lucky to get out of the ship alive. Also, he now knew why the England in which he found himself had retained so many anomalous features of its Victorian past. Without the vast contribution of electronics, from radio to computers, technological progress would have been severely limited.

I'll have to be more careful than ever, Peace thought. *These people have no way of understanding how I got here, and if I give the game away I'll get locked up for sure. It's a good job I didn't say or do anything to get myself into trouble . . .*

'What sort of cursed watch is this?' Cherry shouted, pointing at the chronomod on his wrist. 'It doesn't even keep time!'

Peace's very bones went cold as he thought of all the electronic circuitry inside the gleaming case. 'It's quite *impossible* for that watch to go wrong,' he said, reassuringly, reaching out for it. 'Just a matter of some minor adjustment or another.'

'It had better be,' Cherry said. 'I'm getting a bit edgy again, Warren, and you know what happens when I get edgy.'

'It did come to my notice.' Peace took the watch and saw at

93

once that its analogue time display had gone haywire, the holographic hands twitching around the dial like insect legs in spasm. In desperation, he selected the encyclopaedia function as a test, held the watch near his throat and subvocalized: *How many teeth has an adult human being?*

'Asparagus,' the watch piped. 'Endearingly. Pelham. O. Interpretation. Bickerstaff. Indel – '

Peace managed to silence the fluting voice by pressing all the function buttons at once. He gave the awed onlookers what he hoped was a nonchalant grin.

'It's only some kind of newfangled child's toy! That's the *second* time I've been tricked by this Yankee carpetbagger – but it won't happen again!' Cherry, his face a caricature of outrage, was reaching beneath the counter, doubtlessly going for his knife, when the door of the pub was thrown open to admit about eight men. The noise they were creating made it evident they had serious thirsts.

'I'll deal with you later,' Cherry growled as he hurried away to great his new customers.

'You shouldn't provoke old Fred like that,' Gooble said quietly to Peace. 'It isn't safe.'

'He wouldn't really inflict bodily harm, would he?'

'Bodily harm! Fred would cut your throat for a shilling. He's totally obsessed with money, you see. He just can't help trying to short-change his customers. That's why the locals usually Spoonerize the name of this place: *they* don't call it the Duck 'n' Fiddler.' Gooble took a long swig from his tankard. 'I tell you, Warren, if you've even had a glass of water from Fred, and haven't got the wherewithal to pay for it, you're in danger of your life.'

'My God!' Gripped by fresh alarms, Peace glanced around at the fire-lit room, surroundings which no longer seemed so homely and welcoming. 'But what about the police? Surely, they wouldn't allow . . .'

'The Bow Street Runners? The Peelers? Don't make me laugh, Warren.' In spite of his request Gooble paused to give a cynical laugh. 'The fine specimens around here are all in Fred's pocket. *They* would cut your throat for sixpence.'

Peace gulped his own drink. 'What am I going to do? I don't even know which way to run!'

'And you don't know much about puzzles, either,' Josh cut in, pointing accusingly with the pen. 'I've now got 34.4, and for the life of me I can't see—'

'Let me look at that pen.' Gooble took the instrument from Josh's compliant fingers and studied it closely before turning to Peace. 'Is this yours?'

Peace nodded, his mind on the more important question of survival.

'What is this coloured band for?'

'That's the colour control. Rotate it and the pen will write in any colour you select.'

'Amazing! But where does the ink come from?'

'There isn't any ink,' Peace said wearily, wondering if it would be possible for him to escape via the toilets – a manner of exit he was not fond of, but which he had found useful in the past. 'The tip alters the molecular structure of any writing surface by mere contact, so it will never run out. And you can write on anything. Butter, ice, glass, chrome – it doesn't matter.'

Alf sniggered. 'Who would want to write on butter?'

Gooble moved closer to Peace and lowered his voice. 'Is this a new American invention?'

'I suppose you could say that.'

Gooble gripped Peace's shoulder and drew him away from the others. 'Warren, I'll give you a hundred guineas for this pen, here and now, provided you let me have the name and address of the manufacturers.'

'Those details are on the side of the pen, but hold on a second. How long would a hundred whatsits keep me in food and lodgings?'

'Ten or twelve days.'

That timespan seemed like an eternity to Peace in his present emergency, especially as the pen was a mass-produced throwaway job. 'I'll take it.'

'Good man!' Gooble fumbled in his pockets, then crammed

some large currency notes and coins into Peace's hand. 'Let's keep this between ourselves, eh?'

'Suits me.' His thirst suddenly restored, Peace returned to the bar and drained his tankard. He was in the act of setting it down when the landlord popped up from behind the counter as though spring loaded. The carving knife was back in his hand, and there was murder in his eyes.

'Now then, m'lad,' he snarled. 'You're going to pay for your drinks in blood.'

'Really?' Peace managed a calm smile as, with a casual gesture, he flicked one of the banknotes on to the counter. 'Wouldn't you prefer currency of the realm?'

Cherry seemed to shrink a little. 'But . . . But you told me you had no money.'

'I meant *serious* money. I always carry a hundred or so in my pocket for odds and ends.'

'Sorry, Warren,' Cherry said as he stooped and put the knife out of sight. 'But what with things getting a bit tight recently . . .'

'Think nothing of it,' Peace said. 'Let me have another pint of your finest ale, plus the same for my friends here. And while you're at it,' he added grandly, 'have something for yourself.'

'Thank you, thank you.' Cherry moved away to pull the fresh drinks.

'And what about this 34.4 then?' Josh demanded.

'Did you divide by the number of fingers on one hand?' Peace said, dearly wishing that Josh would drop dead.

'Yes, five.'

'You must have strange hands,' Peace replied, now in desperation. 'I've only got *four* fingers on mine. Your thumb isn't a finger, is it? Ha, ha!'

'I get you.' Josh frowned at his beermat. 'Let's see now – 172 divided by four is . . . um . . . 43.' His eyes suddenly widened. 'Swipe me! How did you do that?'

'Do?' Peace said weakly. 'Do what?'

'You got my age dead on! I was 43 last month! Come on, Warren, how did you do it? You started by judging the size of my feet, is that right?'

'Aha!' Peace tapped a finger against the side of his nose, a gesture he had only seen in ancient movies and had never quite understood. 'You have to work that out for yourself.'

'Here we are!' Cherry hoisted more tankards on to the counter, slapped some change down beside them, and raised his own drink. 'Good health and good fortune to all!'

Peace, beginning to feel the benign effects of alcohol, happily joined in the toast. His pleasure abated somewhat when he noticed that the change he had been given, from a £10 note, was only a few coppers. Even if the landlord was up to his notorious tricks with money, the sum Peace had received for his pen was not going to last very long if he could blow almost a tenth of it on one round of drinks. Perhaps Gooble was the real sharpster in the group.

It next occurred to Peace that the Great Britain of the variable-c universe, stuck in protracted Victorian conditions, might not have developed much of a social security system. If he wanted to live in any sort of comfort he would have to find employment soon. But what kind of work could he get? Even in his own universe, where he knew all the ground rules, his tendency to become involved in accidents had rendered him virtually unemployable. What was going to become of him in this alien territory?

'You know, Warren,' Cherry said, leaning across the bar in confidentiality, 'I wasn't joking when I said money had been tight with me of late. People think you're well off when you have a pub, but they don't know the half of it. Sometimes I feel like packing the whole business in and moving down to Manchester, where all the easy money is.'

Peace was immediately on the alert. '*Easy* money?'

'Fred is quite right,' Hector Gooble said, positioning himself beside Peace at the bar. 'Armstrong and Whitworth's is the place. They're always on the look-out for technical people and tradesmen of any kind. Can't get enough of them.'

'What does this outfit do?'

'You mean you don't even . . .!' Cherry looked astonished, then his expression cleared. 'I forgot that, with you coming from the States, you wouldn't have heard of Armstrong and

Whitworth. They're the biggest manufacturers of spaceships in Europe.'

'Spaceships, eh?' Peace took a long and satisfying drag on his pint as he considered the new information. Even though he was at a disadvantage in the variable-c universe, the fact that he had a background in really advanced space technology was bound to even things up for him or give him an edge. He could become a senior executive in no time at all, pulling in a huge salary, living a life of luxury in idyllic, unspoiled surroundings . . .

'Tell me,' he said, keeping any sign of eagerness out of his voice, 'how far is it from here to Manchester?'

Chapter 7

The train from Windermere to Manchester was a cheerful affair, with bright coachwork bearing the legend LMS on every door. It was drawn by a green and black steam engine which, with its gleaming brass details and hand-embellished cranks, looked like something from a nostalgia show. The briskness of the cold air enhanced Peace's perceptions, adding a sparkle to everything he saw. He took his seat in a carriage that was almost empty and brought out a newly acquired packet of cigarettes. They were called Summer Clouds and were so strong and flavour-laden that in his own universe they would almost certainly have been confined to some kind of museum of toxicology. He lit one and puffed contentedly on it until, with much tooting of various kinds of whistles, the train moved off. He gazed at the passing scenery with interest as the train made its way down a pretty autumnal valley, then along the shore of a large bay opening on to what Peace took to be the Irish Sea.

Actually, on the whole, in the final analysis, when all is said and done, taking the rough with the smooth, I've been rather lucky, he thought. *It's going to be a bit of a wrench never seeing my friends again, but, considering all the billions and trillions of nasty worlds in which I might have been stranded, this one isn't bad.*

His only possible source of worry at the moment was the supply of ready cash. The money Gooble had given for the pen had worked out at £105. At the time it had seemed a handsome sum, but after settling his bill at the Duck and Fiddler, then buying some necessary clothing and other items, he was left with a little more than £10 in his pocket. However, it was impossible to become depressed on such a gloriously sunny afternoon. Even with his feeble knowledge of British history, he knew that the north-west of the country was famous for the warmth and hospitality of its people. Characteristics like that would remain unchanged across the spread of universes. Admittedly, he had had a nasty experience or two with Fred Cherry, but the exception proved the rule and all that. All he had to do now was to show up at the headquarters of Armstrong and Whitworth, secure himself a good job, and then check into a decent nearby hotel.

The train had been on its way for about forty minutes and moved well inland when Peace began to notice a change in the quality of the light. A certain murkiness of the air was becoming apparent, and the level of brightness seemed to be falling. He squirmed closer to the window, got a partial view ahead and blinked as he saw a wall of grey cloud reaching far into the heavens, as though a dozen H-bombs had gone off close to one target. A minute later a kind of sooty twilight gathered on the landscape and raindrops began to streak the carriage windows.

'Excuse me, sir,' Peace said to the nearest passenger, a gnarled oldster who was glumly smoking a soggy roll-up, 'are we coming near Manchester?'

The old man fixed him with a rheumy grey eye. 'Can't tha bloody well tell?'

'Thank you, sir.' Peace took the reply as being in the affirmative. 'Does it often rain in Manchester?'

'Nay, lad. Only once a year.' The old man's shoulders shook with amusement. 'From August to th' following July.'

Several other passengers in the vicinity began to chuckle at the witticism. They all had a weather-beaten look about them, and Peace noticed for the first time that among their belongings in the luggage racks there were many raincoats and umbrellas. He deduced that jokes about bad weather were part of their everyday life, a kind of mental armour or waterproofing, and his spirits sank as the unnatural gloom beyond the carriage windows increased. The train seemed to be tunnelling into hell.

I don't think I could adapt to this, he thought, but then, determined not to lose his optimism, *I'll just have to do a bit of commuting after I get my executive post at Armstrong and Whitworth. That's all there is to it.*

Some minutes later the train slowed on the approach to a station and the passengers began struggling into heavy coats, putting on hats and caps, and testing the controls on their umbrellas. When the carriage had come to a halt the doors were thrown open to admit billows of reeking fog and smoke, copiously seeded with soot. Picking up the shopping bag which contained his belongings, Peace followed the others out on to a long platform. The glass roof was so grimy as to be almost opaque, the only light coming from gaps which also permitted rain to swirl down on the stoical travellers.

Peace was damp even before he reached the station's front doors and peered out at a bustling street where buses, trucks, cars and pedestrians went about their business in a dark grey, waterlogged environment. He had been told the A. and W. plant was only about a mile away, and had planned to conserve his cash by going there on foot, but the slanting and shifting downpour made that impracticable.

By the time he had crossed the open forecourt to a taxi rank and boarded a vehicle, the rain had penetrated his clothing and he was beginning to shiver. During the subsequent ride to the factory he perched uncomfortably on the taxi's rear seat, wincing every time a malicious rivulet abandoned his scalp and darted down his neck. His mood was not improved by the fact that with each passing minute the urban environment grew more seedy.

He had previously observed that the progress of civilization had been retarded in the variable-c world, but this part of Manchester seemed to be an extreme example. From what he could see, by rubbing small holes in the condensation which screened the taxi's windows, it had much the appearance of an eternally preserved Victorian slum. The corner shops and pubs were uniformly gloomy, and the sidestreets lined with cramped terrace houses receding into the smog and pitiless rain.

Peace was in a chastened and thoughtful frame of mind when the taxi dropped him near the entrance to a three-storey redbrick office building. Beyond it, looming up out of the mist,

101

were huge gantries which he would have considered more appropriate to a shipyard. A large notice board beside the double door was headed VACANCIES. Peace scanned the list and was reassured to see several entries referring to different grades of design staff. Realizing he was now becoming soaked, he sprinted up the curving stone steps and into the building. The entrance hall was a marble-clad cavern in which yellowish gas lights put up a feeble resistance to the encroaching gloom of the afternoon.

A blue-nosed man in commissionaire's uniform emerged from a small kiosk on the right and gave Peace a stare which was noticeably lacking in friendliness. 'What's your business?'

'I've come about a job,' Peace replied.

The commissionaire ran his gaze over Peace's bedraggled clothing. 'If it's semi-skilled or casual labour you should have gone to the works entrance in Craven Street.'

Up yours, Peace thought. 'I'm considering a position on the engineering design team.'

The commissionaire looked surprised. 'Which department?'

Peace, who had been expecting to be taken to a personnel office, was equally surprised. He was loath to admit to his inquisitor that he had no idea which branch of spaceship technology would be best suited to his talents. He floundered for a moment, then his eye was caught by a departmental directory on the wall immediately behind the commissionaire. There was an imposing array of disciplines from which to choose. Instinctively rejecting hydraulics, stress analysis, pneumatics, propellant chemistry, celestial computation and the like – all of which were too daunting – he plumped for structures. After all, a sheet of metal was bound to be just a sheet of metal, no matter what universe he was in.

'Structures,' he said. 'I'm a structures man from way back.'

'Wait here.' The commissionaire retired into his kiosk and closed the door. Peace saw him speak into a flexible tube which looked like a vacuum cleaner attachment. He nodded a couple of times, set the tube down and came back to Peace.

'Mr Bumguard will see you now,' he said. He studied Peace for a few seconds and a more kindly look came into his eyes.

'I'll give you a tip, young fellow. If you want to get a job here don't even blink when he introduces himself. Whatever you do, don't pass any comments about his name or you'll be out on your ear before you can say knife.'

'His *name*?'

'Yes. He's a Methodist and you know what they're like about vulgarity. He's very sensitive about his name, is Mr Bumguard.'

'Thanks for the warning,' Peace smirked. 'When I hear it I'll try not to be cheeky.'

The commissionaire shook his head. 'That's exactly the sort of remark I'm warning you about. Better take heed, lad. Go through the third door on the left and follow the signs for Structures 1. You can leave your bag here.'

Peace did as instructed and found himself in a long corridor, on both sides of which were dozens of offices screened by frosted glass. As he moved along it the office workers he encountered glanced at him incuriously. It occurred to him that security was non-existent for a major defence establishment: he had been allowed to walk into the place without identification. Then he remembered that in this case the enemies were putative Martians and Venusians. Apparently, the mere fact of his being human was all the security clearance he needed.

He went through several sets of doors into a region where the corridor ceiling was replaced by a sloping glass roof, the panels of which were almost as grimy as those of the railway station. It seemed that he had left the administrative offices behind and was now in the less salubrious quarters housing the firm's engineering staff. The corridor he was following had many offshoots, each a dwindling perspective of doorways, and it was only by paying close attention to signs that he was able to keep himself on the right track.

The employees he was now passing were predominantly male. A few were dressed in conservative suits and the rest were wearing tweed sports jackets, flannel slacks and neat collars and ties. Most had white rectangular objects, about the size of chocolate bars, projecting from their breast pockets.

103

Peace had noticed about fifty of them before it dawned on him what they were.

Slide rules, he thought in dismay. *Bloody antique slide rules!*

Electronic computers and calculators were unknown in the variable-c universe, he recalled, which boded ill for a would-be engineer who had trouble counting his small change. The mood of depression which had been growing within him since he reached Manchester abruptly deepened. His former confidence had all but vanished when he reached a door which had STRUCTURES 1 stencilled on the obscured glass. Not giving himself time to brood, he opened the door and went through into one of the largest rooms he had ever seen.

Rows of desks with angled drawing boards stretched into the distance. There was no ceiling, merely a series of bare roof trusses supporting a roof of corrugated asbestos and the inevitable grimy skylights. The smog which enveloped the city had even penetrated the long building and was drifting visibly among the rafters. It was intensified by a pall of cigarette and pipe smoke which made it difficult to see the far end of the drawing office. On Peace's left was a small half-glazed enclosure forming a separate office, and seated in it was a severe-looking man, presumably Mr Bumguard, who wore a black suit and had watered-down hair and a narrow face. He looked up from his paperwork with a morose expression as Peace tapped the door and entered.

'I take it that you're Mr Peace,' the man said with a strong Scottish accent. 'I'm the chief draughtsman here. My name is Bumguard.'

'How do you do, sir?' Peace put on what he hoped was a winning smile.

Bumguard scowled fiercely. 'So you think that's funny, do you?'

Peace hastily quit smiling. 'Not at all! I think that Bum— I mean . . . I don't know what you mean, sir.'

'I'm asking you if you think my name is funny.'

'No, *sir*! I don't see anything funny about it.'

'Then why did you grin?' Bumguard demanded. 'Answer me that.'

'I didn't mean anything by it, sir. When I'm nervous I'm inclined to be a bit of an . . .' Peace felt a surge of panic as he stifled the word *ass* – this was exactly the kind of situation in which the accident-prone side of his nature took a malicious pleasure in tripping him up. 'I mean, I smile all the time.'

'You don't look like you've got much to smile about,' Bumguard said suspiciously, eyeing Peace's wet and rumpled clothing.

'I just don't believe in mooning around when I'm – '

'Mooning!' Bumguard slammed down his pen. 'You *are* trying to be funny!'

'I assure you I'm not being fanny . . . I mean funny. My own name is a bit odd and I've been the butt . . . I meant to say subject . . . of too many fanny lines . . . I mean funny loins . . . oh God . . .' Peace broke into a light sweat as he felt his mouth go out of control. 'Please, I just want a job.'

Bumguard had half-risen from his chair and looked as if he was about to attack Peace, but he made an obvious effort to calm himself and sank down again. 'What qualifications have you got?' he said, dabbing his brow with an unsteady hand.

'Loads of them,' Peace lied as he strove to invent some authentic-seeming certification. *American Register of Structural Engineers? No – terrible acronym. This is awful! How am I going to rectumfy the situation? Try to chill out and get all the rotten puns out of your mind. Yeah, that's what to do! Hum the London derrière. Another rotten pun! Not to say ancient. Am I losing my mind? Do I need an anusthetic? God, there's another one! This interview is going to go down in posteriority . . .*

'Well?' Bumguard said, showing impatience.

'The trouble is,' Peace said slowly, nerves jangling as he tried to vet each word in advance, 'that all my diplomas are back in the USA.'

'You could send for them.'

'Yes, but the . . .' *God, I nearly said* bottom *line.* 'The fact is that I need a job right now because I'm flat broke. And I do know a lot about the design of spaceships.'

'Yankee sardine cans, more like!' Bumguard seemed to

regard American-designed spacecraft as an affront to the tradition of Scottish engineering excellence. 'I've heard that some of their armour plate is less than three inches thick. May the Lord preserve us against a Martian attack! Those glorified dinner pails you call ships won't be much help – one direct hit from a three-pounder is all it would take to blow one to smithereens.'

Peace gulped as, using the information just gained, he tried to visualize a British spaceship. Armour plating and artillery?

'Still, I suppose we could instruct you in the proper way to do such things,' Bumguard went on. 'Are you competent in mathematics?'

'Brilliant,' Peace said, then remembered the slide rules. 'Fairly brilliant. I mean, quite good.'

'You don't seem too sure.' Bumguard gave Peace a penetrating stare. 'Can you even demonstrate Pythagoras's Theorem?'

What in the name of Jehovah's jockstrap has that got to do with space flight? Peace thought as he vainly tried to dredge up some shred of reliable knowledge of classical geometry.

'Good old Pythagoras,' he said, feigning enthusiasm. 'One of my favourites! Wasn't he the geezer who was always going on about the square on the long side of a triangle?'

'A right-angled triangle.'

'Yes, the long side of a right-angled triangle.'

'The hypotenuse.'

'That's right. Hypotenuse. Lovely word. I've always had a soft spot for that word. It has a kind of poetry to it, don't you think?'

Bumguard pushed a jotter and pencil across his desk. 'Go ahead and demonstrate the theorem.'

Peace remained standing near the door, at a prudent distance from his inquisitor. 'The thing which always bothers me about Pythagoras's Theorem isn't whether or not it's true, but whether or not it's likely.'

'*Likely?*'

'Yes, likely,' Peace said, desperately trying to sound like a creative mathematician of the highest order. 'Just think about it. There must be millions of right-angled triangles all over the place. Perhaps billions of them. Is it *likely* that they would all have squares on their hypotenuses? I mean, where are all these squares supposed to come from?'

There was a fraught silence before Bumguard spoke. 'Mr Peace,' he said gravely, 'I believe you are what is known in my part of the country as a tumphy.'

Peace ventured a hopeful smile. 'Does that mean a creative mathematician of the highest order?'

'No. It means a blockhead.' Bumguard's narrow face became even more dour. 'Now go away and stop wasting my time. There's no job for you here.'

'But . . .' Peace became indignant. 'But I was told that A. and W. were desperate for engineers and draughtsmen.'

'Who told you that?' Bumguard said, somehow managing to combine a sniff and a sneer.

Peace had to think very hard to retrieve the name of his informant in the lakeside inn. 'Gooble. Colonel Gooble.'

'Gooble!' Bumguard's expression altered to one of surprise. 'But he's one of the military advisers to our board of directors. How did you meet him?'

'*Meet* him!' Sensing a change in his fortunes, Peace hid his own surprise and became airily casual. 'I don't think that's quite the right word for weekending with an old friend up in the lakes. Oh yes, old Hector and I go back a long way – a very long way.' Peace smiled reminiscently, savouring non-existent memories. 'It was when I happened to mention to him that I was temporarily embarrassed – no secrets between old chums, you know – that he told me about this place.'

'But why didn't you say that at the start?'

'I'm a man of high principle,' Peace said. 'I prefer to be judged on my own merit.'

'You? Merit?' There was a lengthy silence during which it was apparent that Bumguard was struggling to resolve an inner conflict. He had formed a low opinion of Peace, but at the same time was worried about doing himself a disservice by crossing someone who had influence up top. His face had a wan and introspective look – like, Peace thought gleefully, that of someone who has had an ice cube slipped into his anus and been ordered to retain it. When he spoke again his voice was strained.

'On thinking the matter over,' he said, 'I'm prepared to offer you a position as a draughtsman.'

'Thank you, sir,' Peace said, congratulating himself on his good luck. 'I'm sure you won't regret it.'

'Report here at eight sharp in the morning and my secretary, Miss Formby, will sort out all the formalities.'

'I'll be here at eight on the dot.' Peace was turning to leave when he remembered his dire shortage of funds. 'By the way, sir. I'll have to find some accommodation in Manchester, and, as I said, I'm flat broke. Can I have an advance?'

Bumguard looked puzzled. 'A what?'

'An advance. On my salary.'

'Are you saying that you want some money? Before you've even picked up a pen?'

'That's the general idea,' Peace said, nodding. 'I could do with say . . .'

His words trailed off as he became aware that something strange was happening to Bumguard's face. The bony wedge of countenance had begun to twitch and contort alarmingly, and with each spasm long greyish teeth came into view, only to be concealed again as Bumguard forced his lips to close. From the midst of the muscular turmoil Bumguard's yellow-stained eyes regarded the universe helplessly, in what seemed to be abject terror.

'Don't . . .' he finally wheezed, '. . . make me laugh.'

Peace, who had been convinced his prospective boss was having some kind of a seizure, was relieved to hear the real cause of the display. Bumguard was only laughing. It seemed that his Scottish Methodist upbringing forbade such sinful pleasures, hence the facial trauma. All was well – except that the tortured mirth had been triggered by Peace's request for money. Things did not look too promising in that respect, but it was too early to give up hope.

'Sir?' Peace said as soon as Bumguard's features had been restored to what passed as normal. 'Have you thought any more about my advance?'

'Throughout the entire history of A. and W. no employee has ever had money in advance – and you certainly won't be the first.' Bumguard paused to quell some residual twitching of his upper lip. 'Furthermore, we don't permit our staff to borrow money from *any* source. Just remember that being in debt is a sacking offence. I'll see you in the morning, Mr Peace.'

Out in the street the rain was coming down steadily in fine vertical lines, looking as eternal as ever. The cloud ceiling was so low that it appeared to sag between the roof tops. Peace stood in a doorway, smoking one of his dizzy-making cigarettes and watching the smoke he exhaled blending with drifts of smog. The stone slabs of the footpath near him were black and shiny with moisture, and dappled with greenish blobs of phlegm deposited by passers-by. Gutters and downpipes murmured fitfully and unceasingly as they discharged their quotas of soot-laden rain.

Peace tried not to feel depressed.

At least I've got a good job, he told himself. Thoughts of soon being able express his inborn artistry in the design of spaceships stiffened his resolve. Accommodation in a plush hotel was out of the question for the present, but surely he would be able to find cheap and friendly digs close by. After a week or two he would be on his financial feet again, then he would start making the most of his new life.

He smoked two more cigarettes in quick succession and, with his head spinning on fumy nicotine, set out to find suitable lodgings. Davy the commissionaire, proving to be quite a sympathetic character, had directed him to Jubilee Road. It was less than a mile from the A. and W. offices and was said to contain a number of boarding houses which were popular with white-collar workers.

Jubilee Road turned out to be a canyon of three-storey redbrick terraces fronted by tiny gardens and iron railings. To Peace it looked pretty dismal, but not as dismal as some of the streets he had glimpsed on his way from the railway station. He decided to give it a try. Of its popularity he was soon left in no doubt because the first dozen or so boarding houses he inspected all had NO VACANCIES signs in the windows. By this time he was soaked to the skin and the delicate flower of his optimism had wilted. Even his shopping bag was disintegrating, exposing his spare clothing to the rain.

The more mute rejections he received the more desirable Jubilee Road began to seem. In his mind it became the only place in the city worthy of consideration, and cruel fate had seen to it that he was to be excluded. A paranoiac gloom was settling over him when, at last, he reached a house, inexplicably named Park View, which advertised that it still had room. It looked a little shabbier than the others, but to his re-educated perceptions it was beautiful. He was not going to let a few decayed window frames deter him from taking up residence in the most coveted thoroughfare in the country, possibly in the whole world.

Three paces along the red-tile path took him to the front door. He set his bag down and knocked gently, anxious to create a good impression from the beginning. After a minute had passed without any response he knocked again, firmly this time. When there was still no result he began knocking harder and harder, until he was pounding on the door with all his strength and rapidly developing a conviction that the place was deserted. As well as the rain that was descending on him from the sky, huge drops were coming from a faulty overhead gutter, unerringly finding his cranium and impacting on it with audible smacks.

Finally the unfairness and sheer misery of it all became too much for him and he lashed out at the door with his foot. The kick had the unexpected effect of stoving in a panel of the age-weakened wood. Peace was gaping at the damage with a mix of savage satisfaction and dismay when the door suddenly swung open. In the aperture, staring intently at him, was a plump, sallow-complexioned young woman. She was wearing a flowered button-down dress which was not quite equal to the task of containing her generous bosom.

'Hell, hell, hello!' Peace stammered. Hoping to divert the woman's thoughts from the broken panel, he grabbed her hand in both of his and pumped it up and down. 'I'd like to come and live with you. I mean, I'm looking for lodgings in this area.'

To his relief the woman smiled, showing slightly prominent teeth. 'We do have a vacant room,' she said, her eyes locked on his, maintaining the somewhat unnerving direct gaze.

'That's just fine,' Peace said, releasing his grip on her hand. 'May I look at the room?'

'Come in and I'll show—'

'Betty!' Another woman's voice boomed out of the dimness behind the door. 'Who's ya talking to?'

'A gentleman wants lodgings, Mam,' Betty said, glancing over her shoulder. A few seconds later an enormous woman hove into view. The new arrival was wearing a tent-like dark blue dress and had a slabby, red-hued face which would have looked more at home on a hard-drinking stevedore. Her eyes, which were like tiny beads of jet, surveyed Peace's dripping figure from head to toe and did not like what they saw.

'Gentleman?' she bellowed. 'Huh!'

'Good afternoon, madam,' Peace said politely, disguising his immediate dislike of the woman. 'I believe you have a—'

'There's a deposit of twenty pounds. That means you pays it now.'

'I don't need you to tell me what a deposit is,' Peace said, his antipathy starting to gain the upper hand. 'But, as it so happens, I find myself temporarily in ... ah ... straitened circumstances as regards finance.'

'That means you ain't got the twenty quid.' The monster tapped her daughter on the shoulder. 'Get shut of him, Betty.' With a last venomous glance at Peace she disappeared into the gloomy reaches of the house.

'Well, I guess that's that.' Trying to preserve what was left of his dignity, Peace picked up his bag. The bag promptly separated itself into a soggy upper half and an even soggier lower half, spilling his belongings on to the path. He gathered the lot into his arms, bowed to Betty, and was turning to leave when she caught his arm.

'Don't go,' she whispered, fumbling in a pocket of her dress. 'Here! Here's the twenty pounds you need.'

'But . . .' Peace gawped at the four blue banknotes which had been thrust into his hand. He then entered a state of confusion, one in which the events of the next few minutes passed him by without fully imprinting themselves on his mind. There was the recall of the monster . . . learning that she was the widowed Mrs Thora Thistlethwaite . . . giving his own name . . . Thora's beady-eyed surprise on discovering that Peace did have some money, after all . . . her snatching of said money . . . the climb up the narrow stairs leading to the top of the house . . .

All at once Peace found himself alone with Betty in a slope-ceilinged attic bedroom. He gazed at her in puzzlement and gratitude blended with a burgeoning affection. It was true that her complexion was not great, but he no longer saw it as sallow: it had become an intriguing romantic pallor. It was true that she was too heavy, but most of the extra weight was in the best places. It was also true that her teeth were just a little prominent, but Peace had always thought of slightly prominent teeth as being sexy. She was breathing deeply after the climb, and with each airy intake little diamond-shaped gaps appeared between the buttons of her dress, providing glimpses of black underwear. Peace felt his affection for Betty mature into adoration.

Still looking directly into his eyes, Betty said, 'You would like to go to bed with me, wouldn't you, Warren?'

Peace swallowed to ease a sudden dryness in his mouth. 'How did you guess?'

'It was the way you responded to my signals when I opened the front door.'

'Your signals?'

'Poor, simple male.' Betty smiled knowingly. 'I'll bet you don't even realize what you did.'

'Ah . . . no.'

'When we shook hands you put your other hand over mine and pressed it. You were unconsciously reacting to my sexual signals.'

'Is that what happened?' Peace forbore to mention the

kicked-in door panel and his efforts to distract her attention from it.

'Yes. And you made a Freudian revelation when you said you would like to come and live with me.'

'I guess I did, at that.' Peace decided not to disclose his tendency to choose wrong words when under a strain. There was a time for being forthright – and a time for keeping one's trap shut.

Betty went to the bedroom door, slid home a small brass bolt and returned to him. She put her arms around his neck, renewed the intense eye contact, and nuzzled her belly against his.

'Take me, Warren,' she urged. 'Take me now.'

Chapter 8

The first thing Peace noticed when he was setting off to work was that the weather had improved. Rain was still falling – he could not imagine it *ever* stopping – but now it was diffuse, hanging in the air like the spray from an atomizer, and there were a few breaks in the clouds. The gaps revealed nothing more than higher levels of cloud, but the portents seemed optimistic – in keeping with the general improvement in his mood and outlook.

He had not, until meeting up with Betty Thistlethwaite, realized how much he had been missing regular dollops of good, uncomplicated, vigorous sex. Betty had proved to be a gifted and expert lover, ministering to him far into the night. Long after he had begun to flag, she had revitalized him time after time with an extensive repertoire of tricks and techniques. And now, in spite of having had less than four hours' sleep, he felt relaxed both mentally and physically. The only negative aspect of the whole business was an extreme tenderness of the genitals, which forced him to proceed with a stooping gait to reduce chafing from his underwear.

The breakfast served up by Thora Thistlethwaite had been substantial, if somewhat greasy, and had introduced him to a spicy fried delicacy known as black pudding. He had thought of asking how it was made, but instinct had warned him that it might be better to remain in ignorance. Despite some misgivings about the fattiness of the meal, he had eaten his fill, grateful for the energy replenishment.

Walking as part of the horde converging on the A. and W. plant, with all his appetites pleasantly sated, he could turn his mind to the prospect of his first day working in a spaceship design office. The ships of his own universe were ugly rectangular boxes, with nothing about them to inspire a creative engineer, but it was bound to be a different story when one was dealing with reaction-propelled jobs which had to bore through the atmosphere. In his mind Peace practised drawing curvatures, graceful yet imbued with power, streamlined yet cloaking enormous mass. Yes, designing spaceships was going to be a stimulating challenge – one which could very well provide the intellectual fulfilment he had been seeking all his adult life.

The first hint of disillusionment came shortly after he met Madge Formby, the chief draughtsman's secretary. She was about sixty, thin, with grey-blonde hair and rimless glasses, and projected an air of efficiency which was somehow enhanced by the cigarette which always hung from her lower lip. Peace liked her at once because of her dry humour and the liberal sprinkling of tobacco ash on her knitted pullover.

'Your starting rate will be ninety pounds,' she said, in answer to the question he had overlooked during his interview with Mr Bumguard.

'Sounds reasonable,' Peace said. 'How much does that come to in an average week?'

'Ninety pounds. That's your pay per week.'

'*What?*' Peace was aghast. 'That's not much for a top-flight designer.'

'No, but it's all right for a tumphy – which is how the boss describes you.'

'But my digs alone come to sixty a week.'

'That means you'll have thirty to play with, less income tax, of course.' Madge sent out a plume of smoke and ash. 'I only wish *I* had that much.'

'You said ninety was my starting pay – perhaps it will soon go up.'

Madge shook her head. 'It's more likely to go down. It will *definitely* go down if old Arsefender picks any holes in your work.'

'This isn't what I expected,' Peace muttered, mentally saying goodbye to his mansion in the country. 'Where do I go for my medical?'

'Medical? What's that?'

'The medical examination. You know – for my insurance and sick pay and all that sort of stuff.'

The fall-out from Madge's cigarette grew heavier. 'Son, I don't know what it's like in America, but if you take sick here *you'll* be the one who pays. Yours wages will be docked, and if you're off more than three days you'll be shown the door. Now go up to the top end of the office and find your section leader, Alf Grindley. Old Rumpshield thinks you've been in here too long as it is. I can see him giving you the evil eye.'

Peace looked into the adjoining enclosure and quailed as he saw Mr Bumguard, half-risen from his chair, staring in his direction through the glass partition.

'I'd better get out of here.' Peace stood up and went to the door.

'Just a minute, son,' Madge said. 'Why are you walking funny like that?'

Peace resisted an impulse to adjust his underpants. 'I've got a bit of back trouble.'

'Be careful with it. Remember what I said.'

Peace nodded, went out into the vast misty perspectives of the drawing office and began the long trek to the far end. *Perhaps money isn't everything*, he told himself as he passed the ranks of tilted boards, where hundreds of men were much engrossed in their work. *What really matters is the satisfaction I'm going to get from the job, the outlet for all my creative abilities.*

By the time someone had pointed out the right person to him, his good spirits were returning and he was able to smile as he approached the section leader. Grindley was a small ginger-coloured man whose long nose and pear-shaped body made Peace think of a kangaroo.

'Good morning, Alf,' he said cheerily. 'I'm the new man – Warren Peace.'

'It's Mr Grindley to you,' Alf replied. 'We'll have none of that Yankee buddy-buddy stuff around here. You'll treat me with proper respect.'

Up yours, Peace thought. 'Of course, sir.'

'Now, your assessment isn't very good – I don't know why all the dross gets dumped on me – but we'll put you to work somehow. Come over here.'

Grindley led the way to a vacant desk and drafting board. Attached to the board by brass drawing pins was a large sheet on which were several cross-sections through what Peace took be a spaceship. It resembled a fat artillery shell standing on its base and magnified to the size of an office block. There were dozens of decks and hundreds of compartments.

'This is the general arrangement of the Type 42 destroyer,' Grindley said, tapping the drawing. 'Do you get the picture all right?'

'I think so.' To Peace the ship was a bloated monstrosity, almost as ugly as those he was used to, and the prospect of working on it was immediately repellent. 'I think I should tell you, Mr Grindley, that I'm mainly interested in finding an outlet for my creative abilities.'

'That's good,' Grindley said, 'because I'm going to *give* you an outlet. Here it is, right here.' He placed a fingertip near the nose of the ship and with it followed a very thin and squiggly line which ran almost to the bottom level.

'What's that?'

'It's what you wanted.' Grindley looked happy. 'It's the outlet from the wash basin in the assistant chief astrogator's room. The pipe is two inches outside diameter, and you'll be responsible for the correct positioning of a two-and-a-half inch hole in every deck plate, flange and—'

'Wait a minute!' Peace cried. 'I can't do that kind of work!'

'Really? In that case you'd better bugger off out of here and stop wasting my time.'

'I mean . . .' Peace had meant that he *refused* to stoop to such an unutterably boring task, but he had to consider the consequences of trying to make a stand. No money . . . eviction from his lodgings . . . wandering Manchester's drab streets in the eternal rain . . . starvation . . . perhaps pneumonia . . . He glanced around, feeling trapped. Men at nearby desks, who had been following the conversation with evident interest, made no attempt to hide their amusement.

117

'Well?'

'I meant I can't do *enough* of that kind of work.'

'Don't let me hold you back.' Grindley waved magnanimously at the drawing board, then ran a critical eye over
Peace's much taller frame. 'Why are you all stooped over like
that? Is there something wrong with you I should know about?'

'Just a little back trouble,' Peace mumbled.

'Huh!' Obviously believing he had been landed with someone
who was both mentally and physically defective, Grindley
resumed his own work, apparently forgetting that Peace even
existed. Peace stared at the sectional drawings of the spaceship
in front of him, nonplussed by their complexity. What was he
supposed to do now? How did one even make a start on such a
miserable and uninspiring chore? Fishing out his pack of
cigarettes, Peace lit one and inhaled deeply, hoping the toxic
smoke would spur his brain into action. All it did was precipitate a bout of giddiness.

'What's the matter, mate?' The whispered words came from
an amiable-looking, red-haired young man at an adjoining
desk. 'Are you stuck?'

'Stuck?' Peace tried to appear amused by the question. 'Me?
Stuck? No, I'm simply taking a minute or two to assess the
general aspect of the job, establish the parameters, weigh up
the various . . . um . . .'

'You mean you're stuck.'

Peace gazed for a moment at the other's freckled countenance and decided to take a chance. 'Stuck is hardly the word
for it. I haven't a clue what to do next. I might as well clear
out of here right now before I get thrown out.'

'Keep your voice down or old Alf will hear you,' the young
man husked, glancing in Grindley's direction. 'Did I hear
right? Is your name Warren?'

'Yes.'

'I'm Harry Hoole. You look tall enough to be a basketball
player, Warren. At least you would be tall if you stood up
straight, like. Can you play basketball, Warren?'

'I used to play a bit.' Peace was pleased at being able to

speak truthfully about his past for a change, but felt he was losing the drift of the conversation. 'Why?'

'The section team is hard up for good players this year. If you'll turn out for us – regular, like – the rest of the lads and me will cover for you in here. Till you get the hang of the job, like. What do you say?'

'That sounds great.' The proposition did indeed sound great to Peace, offering him a readymade social life as well as a means of staying in employment. 'Count me in.'

'Good man!' Hoole said warmly. 'There'll be a training session at eight tonight in the sports club. I'll see you there, Warren.'

'That's a date.' Peace caught Hoole's arm just in time to prevent him returning to his own desk. 'Harry, what about my work here? I wasn't kidding when I said I'd no idea how to start an engineering drawing.'

Hoole gave a reassuring shake of his head. 'You won't need to *start* any drawings, Warren. At least, not too many. The first drafts for most of them were done soon after the design of the Type 42 was started back in 2346.'

'In 2346!' Peace did some mental arithmetic. 'But that was over forty years ago!'

'It takes time to design a big ship, Warren. The job can't be done overnight, like.'

'But *forty years*! Why, that's an entire working life.'

Hoole nodded. 'Job security, Warren. You can't beat it. Old Ted Coppley, who was at your desk before he retired last month, spent about thirty years on Ablutionary Discharge Pipe 103 alone. He was a real character, was old Ted.' Several nearby draughtsmen smiled in agreement.

'He must have been a slow worker,' Peace said faintly, new concepts of boredom teeming in his mind.

'Not old Ted! He was a good grafter, was old Ted.'

'I'm afraid I don't understand all this. You said all the original drawings were done forty years ago, and yet my predecessor, old Ted, put in thirty years on a single waste pipe. I don't get it.'

119

'Ah, but you're not allowing for the RMs,' Hoole said. 'You've got to allow for the RMs, Warren.'

'The RMs?'

'Retrospective Modifications,' Hoole explained patiently. 'Drain pipes from wash basins and toilets and the like have a very low priority compared to hydraulics and pneumatics lines and so forth. So when a change is introduced to a weapons system, like, or a control system, like, it's usually the sodding old drain pipe that gets moved. And when that happens every drawing showing the position of the drain pipe hole has to be revised. That takes time, Warren.'

'I see the point,' Peace said, beginning to feel unwell, 'but I still think that thirty years is a hell of a long . . .'

'Then there's the copies. Don't forget about the copies, Warren. No component of a spaceship exists in isolation, like, so when a drawing is changed copies of it have to be sent to all the other sections and departments and subcontractors that'll be affected. As often as not the draughtsman has to make upwards of a hundred copies. Sometimes *two* hundred!'

'That's quite a chore, I admit, but surely it can't take all *that* long on a good photocopier.'

'Photocopier?' It was Hoole's turn to show puzzlement. 'What's a photocopier?'

'You must know,' Peace said unhappily, sensing that he had reached the edge of a new and more fearsome mental abyss. 'A machine that runs off copies of—'

Hoole interrupted him with a bark of amusement which was shared by the nearby draughtsmen. 'You might have all kinds of fancy gadgets like that in Yankee-land, Warren, but they're as scarce as rocking-horse manure around these parts. All our copies of drawings have to be made by hand, Warren. Like, I mean, like – what do you think a draughtsman is *for*?'

Peace dragged a high wooden stool towards him and sat down on it. This was worse than he could have expected. Much worse. He had always lost interest very quickly in any task which failed to offer variety and excitement, but in this case he was stultifying before the job had even begun.

'All right,' he mumbled, 'how do I start?'

'I never had much to do with ablutionary discharge pipes. I'm a high-pressure steam conduit man,' Hoole said with evident pride, 'but I know there was an RM on ADP 103 at the back-end of last year. It was re-routed between Deck 14 and Deck 18 to make room for the extra munitions hoists to Fore Turret 9B. Let's see how far old Ted had got before he packed up, like.'

Hoole slid open the top drawer in the desk to reveal a small stack of record books which had multi-coloured marble patterns on the edges. There were also sheafs of complex charts and forms, most of them interleaved with flimsy black material which after a moment's thought Peace identified as carbon paper. After a minute of delving and flicking, Hoole looked up with an enthusiastic grin.

'You're in luck, Warren, my old son! Ted was down to Deck 16. The master schedule calls for only eighty copies of the floor-plate plan, and Ted had already done ten of them. That means you have only seventy copies to make, like. That's dead easy work and while you're doing them you'll have loads of time to learn the rest of the system, like. You've really landed on your feet this time, Warren.'

'Oh joyous day,' Peace replied, trying to look similarly enraptured.

For the next few hours, under the gleeful gaze of Hoole and several other draffies, which was how the design office workers styled themselves, he struggled with an unexpected first hurdle in his new career – learning how to draw lines. His difficulties arose from the fact that he was required to work in ink, using a pen which resembled a surgical instrument. It had two blades whose separation, and thus the width of the line, was adjusted by a tiny screw. Although basically simple, the device was supercharged with the enmity which all machinery habitually displayed towards Peace. When he tried to draw a thin line the ink flowed only intermittently, if at all; when he tried a thick line the whole of the ink surged on to the paper in a single malignant blob, involving him in sessions of blotting, drying and scraping with a razor blade. At times the pen spontaneously sprang from his grasp, indelibly marking his hands, clothing and anything else that happened to be close by. Even the parquet floor in the vicinity of his desk became dappled with black starbursts.

By lunchtime he had completed six straight lines of his first copy drawing and was in a state of nervous debility.

In the afternoon, stupefied by a canteen meal consisting mainly of fried egg, sausages and more black pudding, he progressed to lettering by hand and the drawing of circles. As he had expected, using needle-pointed compasses proved not only difficult but dangerous – and specks of blood were as troublesome to erase from the absorbent paper as the blobs of indian ink.

As darkness gathered above the grimy skylights, numerous gaslamps were turned on throughout the huge office. Their wan yellowish glow created haloes in the invasive mist, adding to the shadowy vastness of the place. The fumes from the lamps mingled with the drifts of tobacco smoke, producing an odorous fug which Peace, already suffering from mental exhaustion and an overloaded stomach, found highly soporific. His eyes kept closing of their own accord and he began swaying slightly on the stool, with consequent deterioration of his drafting abilities.

The mutilation he was inflicting on the drawing sheet brought some amiable joshing from nearby draffies, but he was able to accept it without rancour. Even to his own eyes his work betrayed a certain lack of promise. He dreaded Grindley coming over to check on his progress, but the section leader seemed too busy with his own affairs, and it was with profound relief that Peace joined his neighbours in an orderly exodus at six o'clock.

The rain-seeded darkness outside was like a slap in the face, bringing him wide awake for the walk back to Jubilee Road, during which he had ample time to mull over his fate. Being a spaceship designer with A. and W. was boredom as he had never known it, misery as he had never envisaged it, and yet he could see no escape route. A lifetime dominated by the meanderings of Ablutionary Discharge Pipe 103 stretched out before him, and it was hardly a prospect to be relished.

His only recourse, it seemed, was to like it or lump it – after all, the other men in the office seemed quite happy and content with their lot. Perhaps, came a new thought, the harrowing first day at the drawing board was clouding his judgement. Perhaps a bite to eat and an hour's rest before the basketball practice would enable him to see things in a new light.

Pleased at having introduced a positive note into his thinking, Peace tried to shuck off his weariness and speeded up his step. If he got back to his digs quickly he might have *more* than an hour's rest.

'Warren! Your clothes are *soaking!*' The note of concern in Betty Thistlethwaite's voice as she met him in the hall was comforting to Peace.

'Afraid so,' he said. 'I guess I'll have to save up for some kind of raincoat.'

'I'll get you one at the Co-op tomorrow and you can pay me when you have the money.' Betty kissed him full on the lips and snuggled against him, heedless of the moisture that was soaking into her dress, then drew him towards the stairs. 'Come on. We'd better get you out of those wet things.'

'But what about your mother? Won't she . . .?'

'She's at bingo.'

'But what about my dinner?'

'I'll bring it up to you on a tray.' She showed her slightly prominent teeth in a meaningful smile. 'Later.'

Immediately they entered his room she bolted the door and set about the job of separating him from his clothes. Peace was both flattered and aroused: she was wearing a different dress, but it had the same kind of provocative diamond-shaped peepholes between buttons in the region of bosom and hips. The only problem as far as he was concerned was that he was quite exhausted and craved a period of rest.

'I . . . I've been invited to join the section basketball team,' he said as she was draping his shirt on a chair.

'That's good, Warren. Sport helps to keep a man strong and virile.'

123

'But I have to go to a practice session this evening.'

'What time?'

'I said I'd be there at eight o'clock.'

'So why are you looking so worried?' Betty tugged open his belt and began to undo his pants. 'That gives us a full hour before you have to leave.'

The basketball practice was held in an overheated, under-ventilated hall, and consisted of two solid hours of running and jumping – activities which had no appeal to Peace at the best of times. On this occasion they were made a nightmare by the abnormal tenderness of his private parts. When he had gone home for dinner they were just beginning to recover from the drubbing received on the previous night. Now, after the fresh encounter with Betty, they were in a state of throbbing hypersensitivity.

The point-scoring leap, so peculiar to basketball, might have been designed to exacerbate his problem. The act of springing into the air and swinging the right arm caused his underpants to grab his pudenda with the ferocity of a sadistic JCB. Each time it happened he froze at the peak of his trajectory and emitted a loud gasp before landing on one leg in a strangely Eros-like posture. He then hopped frantically in a circle, sometimes concluding the manoeuvre by collapsing on the floor.

The team's coach, a grim-faced oldster by the name of Ed Clutterbuck, watched his performance with growing incred-ulity and distaste. Disdaining to speak directly to Peace, he kept taking Harry Hoole into a corner and remonstrating with him. His words were too low to be heard, but Peace could tell he was expressing displeasure at having a physical and mental defective brought into the squad. Hoole reacted by shaking his fist at Peace each time their eyes met, and refusing to listen to his explanations about a sudden worsening of his back trouble.

At the end of the training session there was a general movement towards the communal showers. Peace, in spite of being drenched with perspiration, took the opportunity to pull on his clothes and make his escape from the hall. On the way back to his digs he passed numerous pubs and felt a strong craving for beer, but they looked the sort of places in which a stranger would scarcely be welcome – particularly one with a crouching, low-legged gait and powerful body smells.

By the time he reached the house in Jubilee Road he was worn out. It had been a long, boring, humiliating, stressful and exhausting day, and all he could think about was falling into bed and losing consciousness. He hobbled up the front path and rang the doorbell, cherishing the knowledge that his malodorous condition would be enough to repel any woman, even the nymphic Betty Thistlethwaite.

'Hi,' he said, slumping against the jamb as she opened the door. 'What a night I've had!'

Betty drew him into the dim hallway and at once threw her arms around his neck. 'I've missed you so much, Warren,' she breathed, pressing her face to his chest.

He allowed a few seconds for his personal fumes to have their full effect. 'I'm not always as overripe as this. The showers were too—'

'I just want to know one thing,' Betty cut in, eagerly caressing his throat with her tongue. 'Are you *always* going to come home covered with sweat – or is tonight my special treat?'

As his days at Armstrong and Whitworth turned into weeks, and the weeks into dreary months, Peace discovered the value of short-term goals. He found he could endure any period of misery or boredom by breaking it up into manageable chunks, by firmly focusing his thoughts on whatever break in the routine was coming next. At the start of each day in Structures 1 the first anticipated diversion was the mid-morning break, during which he had strong tea and a bacon sandwich. As soon as it was over he began concentrating on the prospect of lunch, then on the afternoon break, then on dinner, then on supper. The artificial fixation on meals developed into a real craving for fatty foods, and he embraced the local belief that a man needed 'a good lining' in his stomach to withstand the rigours of work and weather. A diet of fried bacon, fried sausage, fried egg, black pudding, pork pies, sausage rolls, fish and chips, steak and kidney puddings, suet dumplings, fried bread and mushy peas – often augmented by calorific currant-filled delicacies known as Eccles cakes – had a disastrous effect on Peace's waistline. Far from curbing his appetite, the thought that he could be indulging in slow suicide actually encouraged him to cram more food into his burgeoning belly. Death seemed quite a reasonable alternative to the monotony of his rain-soaked existence.

Other short-term goals were the basketball training sessions, which became quite bearable after he was dropped from the roster of players and appointed assistant team manager. The job consisted mainly of stitching torn nets, repairing punctures in the balls and making tea, but he tackled it willingly because it got him away from Betty Thistlethwaite several times a week.

His other diversion – this one a genuine high spot of the week – was the Friday after-work visit to a pub with five or six other draffies from Structures 1. Propped up against a high wooden counter, he downed countless pints of ale, bags of oily potato chips, peanuts and truly astonishing concoctions which went by the name of pork cracklings. These appeared to be fragments of the hide of very old pigs, fried in batter and thickly rimed with salt, and Peace, convinced they had to be the unhealthiest food in the universe, devoured them at every opportunity as part of his suicide plan. In the early stages he had entertained hopes that the reek imparted to his breath by cracklings and beer would be repugnant to Betty, but it turned out that to her the smell was 'right masculine' and a powerful aphrodisiac.

In work his progress was very slow in spite of assistance from his friends. He learned to handle the strange drawing instruments with some competence, and the floor near the desk ceased resembling a photographic negative of a star field. He even acquired some understanding of what he was doing within the complex and vastly cumbersome A. and W. design system, but at all times he was impeded by the dead weight of boredom. Facts which an interested person would have absorbed without effort bounced off the leaden screen surrounding his mind. Grindley, furious at having been saddled with an apparently hopeless dolt, only spoke to him when he thought of fresh sarcasms with which to amuse the rest of the section.

'I wish I had your gift of creativity, Peace,' he would say. 'I would never have been creative enough to put a one-inch rivet through a half-inch hole, the way you've just done – so creatively. Would you mind explaining, for the benefit of us uncreative sods, exactly how to do it?'

The only thing which made existence at all bearable for Peace was the discovery that he was permitted to visit the construction shops to carry out physical checks on dimensions. Instead of increasing his effectiveness, however, this freedom reduced his output almost to zero. He took to disappearing from the drawing office for hours on end so that he could roam the shops and repair yards, where the monstrous, bullet-shaped spacecraft reached into the sky. The vast structures, studded with gun turrets and exhaust tubes, had all the aerodynamic grace of a cast-iron stove, but Peace had stopped concerning himself with aesthetics. It was enough for him that the ships, especially the ones surrounded by scaffolding and cranes, made excellent hiding places.

He would position himself in secluded nooks, tape measure in one hand and a cigarette in the other, staring out at the rain and nostalgically thinking about his days as an Oscar. What wonderful times they had been! He must have been insane to reject that adventurous life – with its immunity to hunger, thirst, fear, sexual domination, pain, weather, doubt, insecurity and all the other features that made up his present existence. And hopelessness. That was an item he had left out of the catalogue of gloom. He had no hope of returning to his own universe, nor even of having a decent look at this one. The spaceships of the retarded variable-c universe were scarcely capable of reaching a nearby planet, let alone exploring the galaxy. There were times when he suspected that the governments of the world secretly knew that the threat from

127

Mars was non-existent, and were maintaining the global defence programme as a means of creating employment.

Thinking about space travel usually reminded Peace that he should be spending more time on board the prototype of the Type 42 destroyer. It was not a good place for a contemplative smoke because it was too full of A. and W. design people, and there was a chance of his being spotted and reported to Alf Grindley for slacking. The hull and principal internal load-bearing members of the vessel were virtually complete, but much of the remainder was a mock-up fabricated in plywood and plastics which could easily be altered to suit modifications in the design. Peace had once tried to follow the capricious Ablutionary Discharge Pipe 103 through all decks of the Type 42, but had given up in disgust, deciding it would have been easier to trace the source of the White Nile.

So predictable had his life become that he regarded the arrival of the pimples as a major occurrence.

His complexion had always been clear, but three months of fatty foods had played havoc with his system and he began to develop unsightly spots on his face and neck. He had never considered himself a vain person, but the pimples got on his nerves. When the pre-breakfast inventories revealed they were on the increase he became deeply concerned and set out to find a remedy.

On his first visit to the local chemist he was overjoyed to find that Germolene was available in the world of null-c. He rushed home with the precious pink ointment, applied it liberally and stood at the mirror, waiting for the pimples to vanish. When they were still flaunting their presence after a full hour he was forced to conclude that null-c Germolene was inferior to the variety he had always known, which could vanquish leprosy in ten minutes. After experimenting unsuccessfully with several other treatments he resorted to growing a beard to hide the offensive blemishes.

He quite liked sporting a beard and had often grown one in his pre-Oscar days, striving for a conquistadorial look in the hope that it would impress women friends. A drawback had always been the itchiness of the early phase. In the present case it was made worse by the reaction of the pimples which, sensing they were in some kind of peril, retaliated by becoming redder and angrier. One particularly malevolent zit established itself behind his right ear, where it took pleasure in making him yelp with agony when accidentally touched by his comb.

He persevered with the beard, despite joshing from his clean-shaven comrades, and in a few weeks was reasonably content with its cosmetic effect. After some initial reservations, Betty Thistlethwaite decided that it was 'right masculine' and a powerful aphrodisiac.

On days when he was too weary for clambering around cold and draughty spaceships, Peace would leave his desk on a pretext and wander the corridors of the technical division. The endless tunnels with their frosted-glass partitions, burbling gaslamps, innumerable doorways and peripatetic staff made an ideal environment in which to lose himself. And he occasionally did exactly that, thanks to the lack of obvious landmarks.

One afternoon, when it was growing dark early and rain was drumming on the skylights, he realized he would be late for the tea break and tried a shortcut. He thought he knew exactly where he was going, but suddenly found himself passing a door on which was a sign which read: COMPUTER ROOM.

He halted abruptly, staring at the plaque. Computers in the variable-c universe? Surely that was an impossibility. He looked up and down the corridor, baffled. He was fairly sure he had passed this way a number of times previously, but how could he have failed to notice such an intriguing sign? The more he scrutinized the corridor the more doubtful he was about having seen it before. The place was oddly deserted, the glow of the gas flames weaker and more fitful than usual, and all at once there was a suggestion of eeriness in the surrounding gloom.

This is weird, Peace told himself as fantasies began to

whisper in his mind. Were there so many linking passageways in the design complex that they had achieved supradimensional connectivity, making it possible to reach a location without crossing the intervening space? Or was this a magic corridor which only appeared at certain times, luring the unwary into dangerous regions of the unknown?

Slowly, in the grip of a strange compulsion, Peace went to the enigmatic door and tapped on its varnished wood. The door was opened immediately by a tall, white-haired man wearing an immaculate black suit and a silver tie. His face was grave, the grey eyes wise and serene.

'What can I do for you, young man?' he said in a courteous, unaccented voice. 'My name is Eldridge.'

Peace gave a shaky laugh. 'For a moment I thought you said Eldritch.'

'It's curious how many of the people who come to my door make that mistake.' Eldridge's eyes glinted briefly. 'Now, how can I be of service?'

'Ah . . . I'm new to the firm . . . just getting to know my way around,' Peace said. 'Do you really have computers in there?'

'Of course.'

'I mean *real* computers. Programmable ones. The sort that can handle long computations.'

'Any other sort would be of precious little value. Am I not correct?'

'You're dead right.' Peace became aware that the room behind Eldridge was very bright compared to the norm at A. and W. and that there was a *modern* quality to the radiance.

'Electricity,' Eldridge explained, noting the direction of his gaze. 'I couldn't do my work without it. Supplies are a bit troublesome, but I believe that one day there will be electricity in every home. What do you say?'

'I agree.' Peace felt a longing to see one of Eldridge's computers for himself. 'Would it be possible for me . . .?'

'To have a look around my department? Are you interested in computers, Mr . . .?'

'My name is Warren Peace, and I'm absolutely fascinated by computers.' Peace's pulse quickened as, out of the blue, he glimpsed a possible escape route from the misery of his life in Structures 1. 'In fact, it's my ambition to work on computers some day.'

'Well, well,' Eldridge said, opening the door to its full extent. 'You know, I might be able to offer you a position in this very office – provided you show the necessary aptitude, of course.'

'You'd have nothing to worry about on that score,' Peace said, his breast suddenly full of joyous optimism as he walked into the L-shaped computer room. The illumination came from very large filament lamps suspended from the ceiling.

'And you'd have to be in very good physical condition,' Eldridge added, inspecting Peace from head to toe. 'Are you physically fit, Warren?'

'Fit as a flea.'

'Then why are you walking all stooped over like that?'

'Just a bit of back trouble,' Peace muttered, inwardly cursing Betty Thistlethwaite. 'It'll soon pass.'

Eldridge smiled. 'That's good. As you must already know, Warren, operating a computer is no job for a weakling.'

'Too true!' Peace said, wondering what Eldridge meant.

'I have a long calculation here which has been sent over by the Stress Analysis department. It's to do with recoil forces in Aft Gun Turret 17.' Eldridge took a sheet of paper from a desk. 'Would you like to watch while I run it through the computer?'

'That would be great!' Grinning enthusiastically, unable to believe his good fortune, Peace walked around a corner with the older man and into the main part of the office. The only thing in it was a massive contraption, as tall as himself and about four metres wide, supported by heavy steel stanchions which were bolted to the floor. It was made up of perhaps two dozen horizontal strips of white plastic, each graduated with black lines and numbers. Peace's grin froze into a grimace of horror as he realized he was looking at the biggest and most complicated slide rule in the observable universe. The pocket versions used by the other draughtsmen were something of a mystery to him; this monstrosity was beyond all comprehension.

'Well, here we go!' Eldridge went to the machine, and with

much consultation of the paper in his hand, began sliding various strips to the left or right. They were attached to an arrangement of robust coil springs, and with each adjustment tension built up in the system and the slides became progressively harder to move. Within a very short time Eldridge had grown red in the face and was sweating profusely.

'Now you see why I need the electric lights in here,' he panted as he aligned ultrafine graduation marks on adjacent strips with a trembling hand. 'This work is hard on the eyes.'

As he continued with his labours the resistance in the system of coils accumulated and it took all his strength to move each slide and peg it in place. The entire machine began to quiver with pent-up energy. Peace grew increasingly nervous as he listened to the twanging of springs and the creaks of the metal framework.

'That's it!' Eldridge finally exclaimed, grasping a large lever which protruded from the side of the machine. 'Stand well clear, Warren!'

He pulled the lever, there was an appalling burst of sound and, amid a shower of pegs, the slides went into a spring-loaded frenzy of readjustment. As they clattered to a halt a loose washer fell out of the works and rolled away across the floor. The computer went on vibrating for several seconds before lapsing into quiescence.

'That's all there is to it, Warren. All we have to do now is read off the result,' Eldridge said, triumphantly mopping his brow. 'I'll wager you're dying to try your hand.'

Peace backed away, shaking his head. 'I'm sorry ... I've made a mistake ... I ... I only came to sweep the chimneys ...'

'But you seemed so *interested*,' Eldridge pleaded, coming after Peace with outstretched hands.

Peace turned and fled the room. He sprinted the length of the magic corridor, reached familiar territory and got back to his own office just in time to grab a mug of tea and an extra bacon sandwich. As he gulped the strong tea, trying to steady his nerves, Harry Hoole came to stand beside him.

'What's the matter, Warren?' he teased. 'You look a bit flustered, like. Did Alf spot you skiving out in the yard?'

'As a matter of fact, I've just been offered a better job,' Peace replied airily, annoyed by Hoole's attitude. 'In the computer room.'

'You mean you've just run into old Slipstick Sid?' Hoole emitted a loud guffaw which attracted the attention of other draughtsmen. 'No wonder you look flustered – you were lucky to get out of there with your virginity, like.' He paused and gave his audience a sly grin. 'At least, I *presume* you got out with your virginity . . .'

Peace, wondering how he could have been naive enough to imagine that his lot could ever improve, picked up one of the greasy sandwiches and began boosting his cholesterol levels.

Spring of the year 2388 manifested itself in two different ways. There was a slight increase in the temperature of the rain, and a very slight decrease in the number of blobs of phlegm decorating the wet pavements – but by then Peace had become too apathetic to take much heed of the majesty of the seasons.

His main solace in life was the fact that his stomach had become such a burden that climbing a couple of flights of stairs made him quite breathless. Encouraged by what he saw as a possible harbinger of an early death, he increased his consumption of the toxic Summer Clouds to sixty a day. This brought about a promising rattle in his lungs, but there was a drawback in that the added expense left him permanently short of cash.

His lifestyle was such that in general he had no great need for money, but the disadvantages of being poor were brought home to him on the night of the showdown with Betty Thistlethwaite.

The day had begun badly, with the announcement that Ablutionary Discharge Pipe 103 was on the move again. The reason given in the all-department memorandum was that it had been deemed necessary to install an improved fuse crimper near one of the lifeboats on Deck 16. As the new model was larger than the one to be replaced a number of lower-priority services, including ADP 103, were being diverted.

The change meant that every drawing Peace had done in the previous six months was obsolete and had to be scrapped. He took the news stoically enough – having managed to complete only five usable drawings in that period – but the indignation shown by colleagues prompted him to overdose on pork cracklings, of which he kept a plentiful supply in his desk. By the time he got back to his digs he was suffering recurrent bouts of nausea, and decided to take to his bed immediately. He had been in it for less than ten minutes when Betty came into the attic room.

'You're a sexy beast, Warren,' she said in mock-reproval, beginning to undo her buttons. 'You just couldn't wait for me to get into bed, could you?'

'Don't bother to take off your dress,' he said weakly, struggling up on to one elbow. 'I'm out of action for the time being.'

She paused, frowning, gibbous bosom partially unleashed. 'What do you mean?'

'I mean what I just said. I'm a sick man, Betty. I'm too pooped for any bonking today.'

'You can't be pooped – not with all the good nourishing food my mam gives you.'

'I tell you I'm whacked,' Peace said. 'I've got to get some sleep.'

'You only *think* you're tired,' she replied, slipping out of her dress as she came to the side of the bed. 'I'll soon have you sitting up and taking notice.'

He shrank back. 'Don't touch me.'

'You're just being silly,' Betty said in a brusque voice. 'Stop playing games, Warren.'

'I *have* stopped playing games,' he cried, stung by her tone, by his realization that at every moment of his life – even on a bed of sickness – he was subject to the dictate of others. 'I've stopped playing all games, and that includes yours. From now on you and I are going to be landlady and lodger – strictly that and nothing more!'

Betty's eyes hardened. 'Is that really the way you want things to be, Warren? Strictly business?'

'Yes.'

'Very well.' She held her hand out to him, palm upwards. 'Let's have it.'

Peace blinked at her. 'Let you have what?'

'The two hundred pounds you owe me.'

'*What*? Two hundred!' He attempted a sneer. 'How did you arrive at that ridiculous—'

'You got twenty pounds off me the day you moved in here,' Betty snapped. 'Then there was your raincoat. And your new shoes and shirts and underwear. *And* all the money you keep borrowing for cigarettes.' Betty jiggled her hand impatiently under his nose. 'Come on, Warren, pay up!'

Peace decided not to crumble. 'And what, pray tell, do you propose to do if I simply say I haven't got two hundred?'

Betty filled her lungs. 'I propose to tell my mam – and she'll hammer the tripes out of you and fling you out on the street on your arse; then I'll go and tell your boss – and he'll give you the sack; then I'll go and tell the cops – and they'll put you in prison. You seem to think it's a hard life in the spaceship factory, Warren – but just wait till you see what the jails are like around these parts.'

Peace decided to crumble.

'That,' he said, 'is a very fetching little bra you're wearing . . .'

The fact that Peace spoke with a foreign accent, and was therefore bound to be educationally suspect, was a useful cover-up on those occasions when he betrayed his ignorance of recent history. Events in the null-c world, he learned, had closely paralleled those of his own universe up until the beginning of the twentieth century. It was only when the question of the speed of light had begun to affect science and technology that the two world-paths had diverged.

Once, when he had managed to rouse himself from his general apathy, he had gone to a public library and done a little reading on the matter. He found that World War I had taken place roughly as scheduled – its causative factors too well established to allow humanity a reprieve – but from then on things had been different. The name of Adolf Hitler did not appear in the encyclopaedias, and there had been no World War II. Nor had nuclear energy been developed, although Peace did find one reference to Albert Einstein in a biographical dictionary:

Einstein, Albert, 1879–1955, American engineer and inventor; b. Germany; recognized as a major innovator in modern plumbing. He made a fortune from his invention of the combined ballcock and air purifier which revolutionized WC design. In later life he achieved some success as a writer of scientific romances, most of them set in fantastic imaginary universes where the speed of light was constant. This obsessive feature of his writing was disparaged by literary critics and he died in relative obscurity, an embittered man.

Skimming through almost four centuries of history, Peace was impressed by the extent to which the non-appearance of electronics had helped preserve the old world order. The great powers of the Victorian era had continued on their traditional ways, complacent and in balance. Many sciences, particularly astronomy, had stagnated. There had been no exploration of the solar system by unmanned probes, and the lack of progress with observational instruments had allowed belief in the canal systems of Mars to persist. Somehow, this delusion had escalated into a global conviction that Mars was a military menace to Earth.

Ludicrous though it all seemed to a dimensional outsider, there had been benefits to mankind in that the common threat had had something of a unifying effect on nations. War had been less common; and international travel was virtually unrestricted. Peace's own case was relevant. It had been possible for him, although perceived as a foreigner, to take employment in England with no need of paperwork and with no snooping by the establishment.

He was thankful for the latter, already having to contend with enough snooping from Grindley, Bumguard and various other bosses who were coming to realize that his work potential was close to zero. They had begun watching his movements closely, with the result that he was now getting into trouble for even the slightest breach of the rules.

A crisis arrived one afternoon, precipitated by nothing more than his discovery that his hair was greasy. He would normally have waited to get back to his digs to wash it, but his facial spots had been playing him up all day and the feel of lank, oily hair seemed an intolerable extra burden. Setting his pen down, he slipped away to the cold, gloomy chamber which housed the toilets. Tea break was at hand and therefore the place was empty, but Peace knew from past experience that if he failed to get every last molecule of soap off his scalp he would have dandruff to add to his other afflictions. That necessitated multiple rinsing, so he would have to work quickly in case someone came in.

He went to the line of six wash basins, put in the plugs and turned on all the hot water taps. As soon as the basins were full Le whipped off his shirt, dipped his head into the first and lathered up with A. and W. soap. That done, he rinsed his hair, pulled out the plug, took a quick sidestep to the second basin and had another rinse. He then lathered up again before hurriedly moving on.

This, he congratulated himself, pleased with the illicit excitement and the delicious sense of danger, *is going to be the fastest shampoo in history*.

Now building up a good speed, he darted along the row of basins, rinsing and unplugging, rinsing and unplugging. The sound of the drain pipes, belching in unison, became thunderous. Turning away from the sixth basin, blinded with suds, he grabbed for the nearest roller-towel – and knew at once that something was wrong. The towel felt too stiff. Furthermore, it was warm. He opened his eyes and found he was holding the front of Mr Bumguard's waistcoat.

'Peace!' Bumguard's narrow face was twitching with fury. 'What do you think you're doing?'

Peace released the garment and leaped backwards. 'I'm . . . ah . . . it's . . .' Lost for words, he resorted to a line he had heard in old movies. 'Mr Bumguard, this isn't what it seems.'

'It seems to me that you're washing your hair on company time. Is that not correct?'

'Well, yes . . .' Peace strove for new inspiration. 'But I've got a good reason.'

'Out with it!'

'Ah . . . Itchy scalp! I had a terrible itch in my scalp and it was distracting me from my work.'

'But you don't *do* any work! You haven't done any work since you came here.' Froth appeared at the corners of Bumguard's mouth as he warmed to his subject. 'In fact I doubt if you've done any work in your whole life. You're the worst loafer and scrounger I ever met.'

'Steady on!' Peace began to feel indignant. 'I wouldn't say that.'

'No, but I would,' Bumguard snarled. 'I've been keeping an eye on you, Peace, and I've come to the conclusion that you're a total chancer. I don't think you've got a single whit of design experience. Not one! And I'll tell you something else – I don't think you're a friend of Colonel Gooble at all. I believe you bluffed your way into this firm. What have you to say to that?'

'I suppose every man's entitled to his opinion,' Peace said huffily and then shivered, becoming conscious of the water that was trickly down his bare torso. 'Mr Bumguard, do you mind if I dry my hair? I don't want to drip all over my desk.'

'You can set your mind at rest on that score.' Bumguard gave a snort of malign satisfaction. 'You and your desk are about to part company for good, Peace. You're fired!'

Peace gaped at him. 'You can't sack me like that.'

'What way do you want me to do it?' Bumguard said, his face going through the alarming contortions which showed he thought he had said something funny. 'Put your shirt on and cover up that disgusting paunch – it's obscene in a young man – and then collect your belongings and get off these premises before—'

He stopped speaking as Alf Grindley, looking more like a

kangaroo than ever, came bounding into the toilets. Ignoring Peace, Grindley went straight to Bumguard, cupped both hands around his ear and began whispering with every appearance of urgency. Bumguard listened for a moment, his face growing pale, then turned and sprinted out of the room.

'What was all that about?' Peace said.

'You'll find out soon enough.' Grindley examined Peace with a morose eye. 'Christ, that's some gut you've got there, lad. No wonder you've got a bad back, carrying a thing like that around with you.'

'Why is everybody so obsessed with my stomach?' Peace snatched his shirt from its wall-hook and struggled into it.

'Maybe it's because we're not used to seeing pregnant men in these parts.'

'Well, you won't have to put up with the sight of me and my stomach for much longer.'

'Why? Are you going back to Yankee-land?'

'I might be going to the poorhouse or even to jail, for all I know,' Peace replied, suddenly choked up with self-pity. 'Old Arsefender has just given me the boot.'

'Nah, there's no need for you to worry about losing your job,' Grindley said, with an uncharacteristic note of kindliness. 'The government has just declared a state of emergency, and as a defence worker your employment is secured.'

'Emergency?' Peace said. 'What kind of emergency?'

'I'm not supposed to blab about this, but there'll be an announcement pretty soon anyway.' Grindley placed a hand on Peace's shoulder, elevating him to the status of a comrade, and spoke in solemn tones. 'Son, we've just received word that the Martian invasion has started.'

Chapter 9

The following day's newspapers all carried stories about the huge Martian warship which was slowly approaching Earth.

It had been detected by telescopes on board a Defence Force cruiser, which had promptly reported the discovery, using the primitive continuous-wave radio which enabled the military to communicate by means of dot-and-dash code. Estimates of the warship's size varied widely because, in the absence of radar, there was some doubt about its distance from Earth. Everybody agreed, however, that it was *big* – and that it would be in the vicinity of Earth in nine or ten months.

Peace read the stories and listened to the ensuing conversations with frozen incredulity. He *knew* that Mars was uninhabited, but to tell people exactly how he knew would be asking them to accept something infinitely less likely than their belief in interplanetary invaders.

To add to his personal dilemma, there were moments when his confidence wavered. He had to admit that there was *something* out there – the news bulletins were coherent and very persuasive – and the fact that Mars was a dead planet in his universe did not give any real guarantees for the null-c continuum. How could he be absolutely certain that this local version of the Red Planet was not teeming with hostile aliens? His common sense told him that such a thing was impossible, but even in his short life he had more than once seen common sense confounded. The great mystery remained: what *was* the huge object slowly spiralling in towards Earth?

In the Armstrong and Whitworth technical division the state of emergency brought about some major changes in the working routine. Everybody was required to put in four extra hours a day – a scheme which, by Peace's reckoning, might get the first Type 42 destroyer operational in ten years' time instead of fifteen.

All the draughtsmen were exhorted to give of their best and, if possible, to double their output. There was a definite we're-all-in-this-together feeling abroad, and Peace noticed that people passing each other in the corridors had begun exchanging thumbs-up signals. Alf Grindley persisted with his new practice of addressing Peace as 'son', while at the same time urging him to abandon his slothful ways and put his back, bad though it was, into the war effort. Peace was uneasy about the new relationship, especially as dodging work now laid him open to charges of being not only unpatriotic but unfilial into the bargain.

On the first day of the productivity drive Grindley had brought all the draffies in his section together for a pep talk. While stressing the need for them to double their output he had looked at Peace with a wry twinkle and said, 'That shouldn't be much of a problem for you, son – because twice bugger all is still bugger all.'

Peace had afterwards been subjected to banter from Hoole and the others, some of it rather pointed, and he realized that his workmates were no longer amused by his attitude to the job. As a result of the psychological pressure he felt obliged to make more of an effort, and thus it came about one morning that, having announced his intention to take some on-site measurements, he visited the prototype of the Type 42 destroyer.

The multitudinous levels of the ship were swarming with welders, riveters, fitters, carpenters and other tradesmen whose activities filled the vast shell with echoing sounds. Wreaths of smoke drifted in the open spaces, coiling in the glare of arc lights, and amber sparks occasionally blossomed like meteor showers in the upper reaches. None of the elevators had been commissioned as yet, so Peace was obliged to ascend to Deck 14 by means of companionways and ladders which had been temporarily lashed in place.

By the time he reached his destination he was panting raucously, thanks to his excess weight and abused lungs. The compartment in which he was interested, host to a section of Ablutionary Discharge Pipe 103, was deserted. The pipe itself projected up through a plywood floor plate for about two feet, ending in a flange which would enable it to be joined to the next length, which would eventually come through the deck above.

Peace eyed it with distaste and decided he was entitled to a rest and a quiet smoke before starting to work. He sat down on the floor beside the pipe, lit up a Summer Cloud and luxuriously inhaled a chestful of poison. It immediately made him feel relaxed. Outside the compartment was a world of noise and frenetic industry, but he had found a little oasis of peace where he could briefly put aside the cares of existence. One just had to have one's little escapes, he decided, otherwise life would be unbearable.

He was puffing contentedly on the cigarette when, happening to glance out through a porthole, he noticed something unusual. Ever since he had joined A. and W., five older spaceships had been visible in distant parts of the yard, looming out of the mists, their outlines blurred by scaffolding and cranes. He had been told they were undergoing major refurbishments to bring them up to modern Defence Force standards, but they had looked so solid and settled that he could not visualize them ever going aloft again. He would not have been surprised to find moss and creepers growing up their sides.

Now, however, something had changed. One of the ships had been stripped of its scaffolding and there seemed to be a great deal of activity around its base. Intrigued, Peace decided to go over to the porthole for a better look. He set his half-smoked Summer Cloud on the top flange of Ablutionary Discharge Pipe 103, heaved himself upright with difficulty and stooped to retrieve his smoke. His chronic maladroitness, not having been in evidence for some time, chose that instant to stage a comeback. As a result his fingers dislodged the cigarette, and it seesawed for a moment before disappearing down the pipe.

Peace stared after it in disquiet for a second, then gave a dismissive shrug. *No harm done*, he assured himself. *There*

*can't be any risk of fire from a measly little butt like that. It's
bound to drop into a sewage tank or something similar.*

He had taken one pace towards the porthole when, from
somewhere below, there came a hoarse shriek. The sound, loud
enough to cut through the pervasive industrial clamour, was
suggestive of surprise, agony and rage – and it made Peace's
blood run cold. He clapped a nervous hand to his mouth, and
was looking around for a place in which to hide when footsteps
vibrated the ladder leading up to the compartment.

A moment later a very small, undernourished man in greasy
overalls bounded into the room. 'Did you do it?' he demanded
angrily. 'Did you throw a lit fag down that pipe?'

'I . . . I'm sorry,' Peace stammered. 'I didn't mean to do it.'

The little man was not appeased. 'Sorry, are you? Well, it's
no bloody good being sorry, you gormless-looking berk! Idiots
like you should bloody well be locked up. You deserve a good
kick up the balls, you do!'

Peace decided he was taking too much abuse over a trivial
accident. 'Is that so?' he sneered, emboldened by the man's
lack of height and breadth. 'Perhaps you'd like to *try* kicking
me up the balls.'

'Oh, *I'm* not going to do it,' the little man said. 'It was my
mate who swallowed the fag end.'

'*Swallowed* it?' Peace began to feel queasy. 'But that doesn't
seem poss— How did he manage to do a thing like that?'

'We thought there was a blockage in the pipe and he was
blowing up it. To get it clear, like. Then the fag end went down
his throat. He's lying down on Deck 16 at this very minute,
spewing all over the place.'

'That's terrible,' Peace said contritely. 'I'll have to go down
and apologize to him in person. What's his name?'

'Psycho Sam.'

'Psycho Sam?' Peace gave an uncertain laugh. 'That's a
funny nickname.'

'Nothing funny about it,' the little man said. 'He's not right
in the head, is Sam. Those blind rages of his . . . Why, I've seen
him put a man in hospital – just for knocking over his tea
mug. In and out of jail all the time, he is, and one of these days

143

he's bound to go up for murder. To tell you the truth, I'm a bit worried about Sam.'

'You're worried about *him*!' Peace headed for the door of the compartment. 'Look, you'll have to apologize to Sam on my behalf – I've just remembered I have to attend an important meeting in the . . .'

His voice faltered as the ladder outside began to bounce and creak violently, to the accompaniment of heavy breathing and low-pitched growls. He watched in horror as the doorway filled from the bottom upwards with a bristle-headed apparition which had to be Psycho Sam. It consisted of a face which would have made a Neanderthal wince, surmounting a pyramid of muscle and sinew. The tiny eyes, almost lost in bony caverns, fixed Peace with a glare of hatred.

'Youse,' the apparition announced as it entered the room, 'is gonna die.'

'Now, now,' Peace cried, cowering back against the wall, 'don't get carried away.'

'Youse is the one that's gonna get carried away – in a box.' Sam's eyes flickered balefully as he savoured the witticism. 'A wooden box.'

'You don't want to land yourself in bad trouble with the law.' Peace turned in desperation to the small man. 'You're Sam's friend – advise him what to do for the best.'

The small man nodded. 'Beat his frigging head in, Sam.'

'I'm *gonna* beat his friggin' head in,' Sam growled, continuing his advance on Peace. 'With these.' He brandished his massive fists in Peace's face, giving him plenty of time to read the words LOVE and HATE printed on the knuckles.

Peace, now hemmed into a corner, realized his only hope of survival lay in diverting the ogre's attention. 'That's a pretty weird thing to have tattooed on your hands,' he said, feigning genuine puzzlement. 'VOLE and HEAT. Why have you got VOLE and HEAT written on yourself?'

'LOVE and HATE, youse stupid twat!' Sam bellowed. 'Can't youse even read?'

Peace shook his head. 'Sorry, that's not what it says from where I'm standing.'

'Huh?' Sam turned his fists inwards and his brow corrugated as he tried to proofread his own knuckles.

Peace seized the opportunity to dart past him and sprint for the door. The small man made no attempt to bar his way, but Peace, needled by the matter of the friendly advice, punched him on the nose as he went by. Howling with pain, the small man clapped his hands to his face and staggered into the path of Sam, who was now in snarling pursuit. Their collision gave Peace a few extra seconds in which to increase his lead. He slid down the ladder to the next deck and, regardless of the gripping pains caused by his underpants, ran at speed for a nearby metal stair.

His progress down through the ship was impeded because he kept bumping into or having to go around other people. The mountainous Sam had no such problem – workmen either scattered out of his way or were hurled aside – with the result that he gained on Peace deck by deck. By the time they reached the lowest levels he was close enough for Peace to hear him chanting a kind of homicidal mantra, *I'm gonna scupper youse, I'm gonna scupper youse, I'm gonna . . .*

The build-up of sheer terror in Peace's mind was so great that he had begun to moan aloud with every breath. He skidded around a corner into a loading bay and saw before him a large open-top crate. It was shoulder high, but with his muscles on adrenalin boost he was able to vault over its side with dream-like ease. The thistledown sensation came to an abrupt end when he landed astride a large diesel engine. Clenching his teeth, he lay in silence along the back of the machine and listened intently, wondering if Sam would descend on top of him at any second.

A full minute went by before he could accept that neither Sam nor any other worker had witnessed his vanishing act. *I'm safe in here*, he thought, profoundly relieved. *I've been very lucky, really. It was a good thing for me that this crate was sitting here, ready to save my life. All I have to do now is lie low for a few minutes to let the heat die down, especially in Sam's throat, ha ha, then when I'm sure it's safe to do so I'll head back to the office and have a nice strong mug of . . .*

145

His self-congratulatory reverie was disturbed when everything suddenly began to go dark, to the accompaniment of loud slithering noises.

He glanced up and saw a wooden lid being slid into place above. As he lay in the blackness, wide-eyed with alarm, there came the sound of nails being hammered, then the crate tilted and he felt it begin to move. Peace clung to the big engine during a series of sickening swings and lurches which ended with a solid thud. An automobile motor roared into life, the crate started to jounce, and he realized it had been loaded on to a truck and was on its way to an unknown destination.

This is terrible, he thought miserably, cursing his bad luck at having been lured into the crate. *Perhaps I'll be in here for days. Perhaps I'll be in here for weeks. Or months! Perhaps one day they'll find my desiccated corpse and wonder who I was, and perhaps some sensitive and tender-hearted woman – not an oversexed type like Betty – will look down at my pitiable remains and shed a quiet tear. Perhaps she'll see to it that I get a decent burial, and perhaps every now and then she'll come and kneel by my grave and place a few simple flowers of the field at my headstone, and perhaps there'll be a look of ineffable regret on her lovely face as she dreams of things that might have been if only fate had been kinder and allowed us to meet at an earlier time, before—*

Peace was beginning to enjoy the melancholic scenario when, only two minutes after it had set out, the truck jolted to a halt. There was a loud clanking of chains and more swinging sensations, followed by another thud, and he knew he had been unloaded. But where? After such a short journey the vehicle must still be in the A. and W. yard, but he had no idea which part. Wondering about his chances of getting back to the design office without too much fuss, he strained his ears for clues as to his whereabouts.

'Well, sir, that's the replacement power unit for the midsection blast screens.' The speaker seemed to be just outside the crate, his voice muffled by the timber partition.

'So the stores had one, after all,' another man replied.

'No, sir, but I managed to commandeer . . . I mean *requisition* . . . this one from the Type 42 prototype.'

'Good work, lieutenant. That's everything, isn't it?'

'Yes, sir. We can take off at any time.'

'In that case we'll seal up the ship and depart without any further delay. I can't wait to give those damned Martians a taste of good British shrapnel . . .' The voice faded into the background noise as the speaker moved away.

'Hang on a minute!' Peace called out in sudden alarm as full understanding of his new predicament came to him.

He was on board the warship which had drawn his attention earlier – the unusual activity surrounding it had been an indication that it was preparing for blast-off – and soon he would be on his way to do battle against the Martian invaders. It was true that he had been praying to escape the dreariness of his life in Manchester – but not like this! He would not have entrusted his safety to one of A. and W.'s primitive ironclads at the best of times, but the prospect of going on some half-assed emergency expedition was unbearable. Even if the ageing pile of metal did manage to get into space intact, the Martian weaponry was bound to annihilate it in the first instants of the engagement . . .

'What am I saying?' Peace demanded of himself. 'There *aren't* any Martians. Or are there? Who *says* there aren't any Martians? I'll bet the whole solar system is knee deep in them. *Help! Help!*'

Driven by fresh panic, he clambered down from his uncomfortable resting place in the blackness and began pounding on the side of the crate with his fists. The sound was drowned out by a blaring of klaxons which in turn was obliterated by the growing thunder of rockets. Vibrations shook the crate and its contents as the rocket exhaust swelled far beyond mere thunder, becoming a mind-numbing, heart-stopping tumult which seemed to tear reality itself apart.

Peace slowly sank to his knees, giving way to despair and the accelerative increase in his weight.

*

The next two days – or it may have been three – passed very slowly for Peace. Even if he had possessed a wristwatch he could not have read it in the darkness, and therefore had to assess the passage of time by means of the ship's bells. The difficulty with that was his inability to make sense of the old nautical signals for changing the watches. Mercifully, soon after take-off the sound of the rocket motors had faded to a continuous low growl, enabling him to snatch a little sleep, but the spells of unconsciousness had only added to his uncertainty about the hours and days.

The loading bay containing his new home was, apparently, one of the least popular areas of the ship. After he had been in quiet isolation for what felt like a month, his fears about starvation began to return. A search of his pockets for anything edible yielded one bag of pork cracklings. He had resolved to eat just one of the salty morsels, which now seemed delicious, every hour or so, but hunger had got the better of him and he had devoured the lot in a single burst of gluttony.

Eventually he lapsed into a fatalistic torpor, spending long periods dreaming about his idyllic existence as an Oscar, and as a result was quite startled when there came the sound of crowbars attacking the top of the crate. The lid was drawn aside in a matter of seconds, admitting a dazzle of yellowish light. Profoundly relieved that his incarceration had come to an end, Peace, already composing words of gratitude, stood up and looked over the side of the crate. The four crewmen who had effected his rescue leaped backwards in fright, almost becoming airborne in the fractional gravity. One of them actually collided with a wall of the compartment and dropped his crowbar.

'Look here, sir,' another called out. 'A stowaway!'

A young lieutenant, obviously in charge of the working party, lowered an engineering drawing he had been consulting and gave Peace an accusing stare. 'It's no good your trying to hide in there any longer,' he said tersely. 'Come out at once.'

Peace gaped at him. 'I wasn't *hiding* in here. Well, I guess I did hide at the start, but that was only because I was trying to get away from a homicidal apeman who was—'

'Are you going to come out of your own accord, or will we have to haul you out by the scruff of the neck?' the lieutenant cut in. 'We don't take kindly to stowaways in the Defence Force.'

'I tell you I'm not a stowaway,' Peace said, beginning to lose his patience. 'Who in his right mind would want to stow away in this rusty old heap of—?'

'All right, men. Drag the stowaway out of his lair,' the lieutenant ordered. 'Use as much force as you have to. Don't worry about putting a few bruises on him.'

The four crewmen nodded happily and started forward with crowbars at the ready.

'There's no need for any unpleasantness,' Peace said in an attempt to preserve a modicum of dignity. Although weakened by hunger and thirst, he made quick work of scrambling over the side of the crate, aided somewhat by the low gravity. Two of the crewmen grabbed his arms and the others, eager for a slice of the action, went behind and forcibly laid hold of his collar and the seat of his pants. Peace, now feeling like a trussed chicken, realized that his attempt to preserve the elusive modicum of dignity had not been a success.

'I warn you, as soon as I see your commanding officer I'm going to have words with him about this,' he said to the men.

'You won't have long to wait.' The lieutenant replaced a speaking tube he had snatched from a recess in the wall and nodded to his men. 'Captain Hardacre-Smith wants the stowaway brought to him right now. Get him up there – on the double!'

Peace, who had always thought that 'on the double' merely meant walking quickly, felt that his captors were showing an excess of zeal when they lifted him clear of the deck and bore him away. In spite of his struggles and protestations, he was carried up through many levels of the ship, drawing curious stares from what seemed the entire crew, and taken into a large room in which stood a group of men in imposing uniforms. His porters deposited him in the centre of a wide floor and moved back.

'Good work, lieutenant,' said a pink-faced, keen-eyed man wearing captain's insignia. 'Stand by.'

'Sir!' The lieutenant saluted and rejoined his stalwarts, leaving Peace alone in the open space.

'So! What have we here?' Captain Hardacre-Smith ran his penetrating gaze over Peace's dishevelled figure. 'Tell me, young man, what did you hope to gain by stowing away on board DFS *Firebrand*?'

Peace shook his head. 'I'm getting pretty sick of saying this, but I'm *not* a stowaway.'

'You can't deny that you concealed yourself in a packing case.' Hardacre-Smith's mien became even more severe. 'Are you aware there are stiff penalties for unlawfully entering a Defence Force vessel, especially one on active service?'

'What's the matter with everybody around here?' Peace demanded of the group of top brass facing him. 'I tell you I was only . . .' His voice faded, stilled by an upheaval far down in his consciousness. Three of the officers were dressed in what he recognized as Defence Force uniforms, dark blue with a minimum of embellishment, but the other two wore scarlet tunics, Sam Browne belts and black trousers which were reminiscent of the old Canadian Mounted Police. They could have been members of some joint forces staff. The taller of the pair, middle-aged and very upright in his bearing, had a squarish, weathered face which somehow looked familiar.

Peace rummaged through his memory, wondering where he might have seen the man before, and felt prelusory stirrings in his brain. They were enhanced by the fact that the officer seemed to be reciprocating, eyeing *him* with special interest. And, suddenly, the neural connections were made. Gooble! He was looking at none other than Colonel Hector Gooble – the man he had met and befriended on his first evening at the inn beside Lake Windermere.

On the instant of identification, Peace saw Gooble give a slight start and he knew that the recognition had been mutual.

'If I may put in a word at this point, Captain,' Gooble said immediately. 'I have met this man before. His name is Warren

Peace – and you are quite wrong in thinking he is a common stowaway.'

Peace nodded vigorously, his eyes prickling with gratitude. Good old Gooble! He had popped up just at the crucial moment to avert a serious misunderstanding, one which could have landed Peace in jail for a long time. There *was* some justice in the grand scheme of things, after all.

'You say you actually know the man, Colonel?' Hardacre-Smith looked surprised. 'Well, if he isn't a stowaway, what is he?'

'This man,' Gooble announced, 'is a Martian spy!'

That's a lie! Peace had intended to shout the words, but his throat seemed to have seized up and all he could do was emit a series of feeble bleats. He had to hope they would be sufficient, for the nonce, to convey his feelings of shock, scorn, indignation and righteous anger.

'A spy!' Some of the pinkness left Hardacre-Smith's face. 'Have you any evidence to support such a serious charge?'

'A great deal of evidence, captain,' Gooble said. 'One evening last autumn I chanced to visit the Duck and Fiddler tavern at Windermere, and there I encountered this man who calls himself Warren Peace – an alias, if ever I heard one. He was behaving in a very odd and shifty manner, and claimed to be an American whose cruiser had just sunk in the lake. Those present accepted his story, although I must say that it didn't ring quite true to my trained ear.

'It was only after he had left the area that we heard reports from local people of a huge meteorite plunging into the lake, only a matter of minutes before Peace appeared – *dripping wet*, mark you – at the tavern. In retrospect it is perfectly obvious that the so-called meteorite was in fact a Martian spy ship, now cleverly concealed in the waters of Lake Windermere.'

Peace, alarmed by the case being built against him, redoubled his efforts to speak, but only succeeded in raising his bleats to a higher pitch. Captain Hardacre-Smith frowned at him and motioned for Gooble to continue.

'During the course of the evening,' Gooble said, 'Peace asked me many questions about the organization of the Interplanetary Defence Force, and I also overheard him obtaining information from the landlord about the location of the Armstrong and Whitworth yard.'

'That's a load of bull,' Peace cried out, managing to break his verbal blockade. 'The man's off his head.'

Hardacre-Smith eyed him gravely. 'Do you deny that your name is Warren Peace? Do you also deny showing up at the Duck and Fiddler tavern, and claiming you had sunk in Lake Windermere, and meeting Colonel Gooble and questioning him about the Defence Force, and obtaining information from the landlord about the A. and W. yard?'

'No, but . . .' Peace lapsed into a frustrated silence, finding himself in the now-familiar bind – the truth about his situation would sound too preposterous to be given even a moment's serious consideration.

'But what?'

'But . . .' He glanced around the assembly in desperation. 'Do I *look* like a Martian?'

'Possibly,' the captain said, obviously unimpressed by the logic behind the question. 'We have no way of knowing what a Martian looks like. Besides, you don't have to *be* a Martian to spy for them. Perhaps they recruited you. *Bought* you. You could be a traitor to your own species.'

The suggestion brought an ominous murmur from the men standing behind Peace.

'That's a nutty suggestion,' he said at once. 'Look, I freely admit that I asked questions about the A. and W. yard, but that was because I was broke and looking for work. I then travelled down to Manchester and got a job in A. and W.'s technical division. What's wrong with that?'

'What kind of a job?'

'Draughtsman.'

'On which project?'

'You're checking to see if I really do know my way round the firm,' Peace said confidently. 'For your information, I work on the structure of the Type 42 destroyer.'

'So you've been learning all about our latest and most

advanced warship.' Hardacre-Smith gave Gooble a significant stare and leaned closer to address him. 'It looks as though you've got something here, Colonel. The evidence against the prisoner is piling up.'

'Evidence my backside!' Peace shouted. 'Look, all I did was go to Manchester and get a job with A. and W. It was all perfectly open and above board.'

'Is that so?' Gooble chimed in with a sneer of disbelief. 'Well, if everything was so open and above board, as you want us to believe, perhaps you would care to explain why you have adopted a disguise. Were you afraid you would bump into me at A. and W.'s and be recognized?'

'Disguise?' Peace was baffled. 'What are you talking about?'

'That beard, of course! It fooled me when you were first brought in here, but not for long.' Gooble nudged Captain Hardacre-Smith with his elbow. 'I think he's wearing a false stomach into the bargain, trying to alter his whole appearance. It just doesn't look natural, stuck on to the front of him like that. If you ask me, it's a strap-on job.'

Hardacre-Smith stroked his chin thoughtfully. 'I think you're right.'

'Less of the personal remarks,' Peace said indignantly, trying to pull in his belly.

'With your permission, captain, I'll take a better look.' Gooble came forward to Peace and, while inspecting his beard at close range, spoke in a low voice. 'You thought you were so clever over that business with the pen, didn't you, Peace?'

Peace, who had almost forgotten about selling his super-stylus to Gooble, replied in equally low tones. 'Was there a problem with it?'

'You know there was a problem, you dirty crook. The manufacturer's address on the side of it has never existed. I want my hundred guineas back.'

'So that's why we're whispering – you don't want your top-echelon buddies to hear all about your shady wheeling and dealing.' Peace smiled thinly, savouring the moment. 'You can forget about your hundred guineas, colonel. I haven't even got a hundred pence on me.'

'You don't seem to realize how serious your position is,' Gooble persisted. 'You're in deep trouble, Peace, but if you tell me where the money's stashed I may be able to make things easier for you . . . perhaps put in a plea for clemency.'

'I'll be able to prove my innocence when we get back to the works,' Peace said, 'so you know where you can stick your plea for clemency.'

'Colonel, what are you whispering about?' Hardacre-Smith put in impatiently.

'Just interrogating the prisoner.' Gooble gave Peace a look of purest malevolence. 'I will now check his stomach.'

He made good his word by forcefully jabbing Peace's midriff with stiffened fingers. Peace winced and responded by kicking Gooble on the shin, an action which drew an even more ominous rumble from behind him. Gooble betrayed no pain, but when he turned and walked back to the other officers his dignity was marred by a curious low-gravity limp.

Watching him depart, Peace felt a glow of self-esteem. It would have been easy to curry favour with the colonel by pretending to have money somewhere and giving a fictitious location for it, but for once he had put honour and pride before all else. He could now face the inquisitors with his head held high, knowing that even if he were to be locked up for the duration of the flight he had retained something far more precious than freedom – his self-respect.

'Well?' Hardacre-Smith said to Gooble.

'I tried offering the prisoner leniency – hoping to get him to confess – but you saw the viciousness of the man for yourself. I suppose I should have known better. What can one expect from a wretch who is prepared to sacrifice the lives of every man and woman and sweet innocent little child on Earth for thirty pieces of Martian silver?'

During Gooble's intemperate burst of oratory Peace gazed calmly at Hardacre-Smith and the other officers, a half-smile playing on his lips, his hopes bolstered by the fact that the colonel had gone over the top. No intelligent people were going to be swayed by such an obvious attempt to play on their emotions.

'He's a cool customer, I'll grant him that,' Hardacre-Smith commented. 'Not many men could remain so composed when about to be convicted for spying and treachery.'

Gooble snorted with rage. 'I'll wipe the damned insolent smile off his face, just see if I don't! There can be only one penalty for treachery in time of war . . .' He fumbled with his holster and pulled out a heavy revolver. '. . . and that penalty is *death!*'

Oh God, Peace thought, shocked into immobility as Gooble levelled the weapon, *maybe I should have offered him a cheque for his forking hundred guineas.* He heard the men behind him, obviously not suffering mobility problems, scattering out of the line of fire. Inconsequential thoughts continued to blitz his mind: *Perhaps the old ratbag would have agreed to instalments. I could probably have managed a fiver a week, even on the pittance A. and W. pay me . . .*

'Colonel Gooble! What do you think you're doing?' Captain Hardacre-Smith, moving with commendable speed, grasped the revolver's barrel and forced Gooble's hand downwards. 'Have you gone out of your head, man? We don't *do* things like that in the Defence Force. Pull yourself together!'

Peace gazed at the captain with gratitude and burgeoning respect. He had sensed all along that Hardacre-Smith was one of the old school of gentleman officers – an authoritarian who could be stern on occasion, but unswerving in his devotion to the principles of justice, scrupulously fair in all his dealings.

'I . . . I'm afraid my patriotic anger got the better of me,' Gooble said. 'I'm sorry.'

'And so you should be,' Hardacre-Smith went on severely. 'Have you forgotten that, as captain of the *Firebrand*, I am in supreme command here?'

Good old Hardy, Peace thought gleefully, enjoying the spectacle of the colonel's discomfiture to the utmost. *You tell him!*

Gooble looked downcast. 'I think it was the contemptuous sneer on the scoundrel's face that drove me over the—'

'That's no excuse,' Hardacre-Smith cut in. '*I'm* the captain of this ship – and when anybody is going to pronounce a sentence of death around here *I* will do it.'

Gooble stopped looking downcast. 'Does that mean you're going to have Peace executed?'

'Of course! He's a traitor, isn't he?' Hardacre-Smith turned towards Peace, cleared his throat importantly and said, 'Warren Peace, you are adjudged guilty of spying for the enemy and accordingly I sentence you to summary execution. May God have mercy on your soul.'

When first accused of being a traitor Peace had been too stunned to speak; when menaced by Gooble's revolver he had been too frightened to move; now, on hearing his death sentence, he was too shocked and dispirited to do *anything*. He stood perfectly still, unable even to blink, surrendering to the superior forces of fate. What, he asked himself, would be the point of struggling any further? He had fought against bad luck all his life, and every time he had extricated himself from one trap it had only been to walk straight into another, one which had been more carefully laid and was even more deadly. The end result had always been inevitable – it was just that he had never admitted it before . . .

With Peace's newfound fatalism came a sense of placidity and resignation, almost of relief. The feeling was akin to the one when he thought he might starve to death in the crate, but this time it was more profound. He had an even stronger urge to compose his own eulogy, to fantasize about the regrets others would feel after he had died, and, above all, to make a beautiful and heartrending farewell speech. He had always wanted to hold an audience in the palm of his hand and, things being the way they were, he was unlikely to get a better chance than the present one. Now quite reconciled to dying, he began the first mental draft of his panegyric.

The change in him was initially noticed by the lieutenant and same four crewmen, now assigned to guard him while the ship's chaplain was being located. They were wary of him at first, obviously expecting trouble of one kind or another, but in the face of his quiet composure their hostility faded and was replaced by a thoughtful unease.

'Are you really a spy?' the lieutenant, whose name was Denby, whispered to him during the wait.

'No more than you are,' Peace replied. 'And I wouldn't try to hide anything at this stage, not when I'm about to meet the One who sees all.'

'I had no idea this would happen when we got you out of that crate. Now I feel . . . responsible.'

'Don't let it bother you, son.' Peace smiled sadly. It was the first time he had ever addressed a man that way and he liked the feel of it. 'Life has been a heavy burden for me of late, and now I'm going to lay the burden down. So, you see, you've actually done me a favour – and I thank you for it.'

'Oh God,' Denby said, furtively knuckling his eyes as he turned away.

Even the chaplain, a chubby Commander Lockett, appeared to be impressed by Peace's aura of acceptance and serenity. 'It will be extremely quick,' he said, in answer to Peace's question. 'You will be placed in an airlock. The inner door will be sealed, the outer door will be opened immediately, and you will be . . .' He stopped speaking, embarrassed.

'Exhausted is the word I think you're looking for,' Peace said with a wry twinkle. 'An appropriate term, really. I'm already quite tired – of my sojourn in this vale of tears.'

'You're a brave man,' Lockett said, and he too was furtively knuckling his eyes as he turned away.

When it was time for him to be marched to the execution chamber a blue-jowled bosun called Rigby approached Peace and tied his arms behind his back. The four crewmen who were his original captors took up positions beside Peace, but instead of hoisting him clear of the deck they permitted him to walk with dignity. The metal-walled corridor along which they progressed was empty, possibly because orders had been given to keep uninvolved personnel away. Peace's escorts were quiet during the short walk, the only conversation coming from the rear of the procession, where Gooble, Hardcastle-Smith and the other top brass held a lively discussion about flower arrangements in the officers' mess.

When the group reached the airlock door bosun Rigby went forward with a large bunch of keys and unlocked it. He then rotated the dogging wheels and slid the massively ribbed door aside on greased tracks. Beyond it, harshly illuminated by arc lights, was the grey-painted shape of a lifeboat resting on semi-circular cradles. Peace eyed it with some surprise.

'Don't waste what time you've left dreaming up any clever ideas,' Rigby said to him, not unsympathetically. 'I keep all the lifeboats locked up tighter than a duck's rear end.'

'Thanks for the advice – I know you mean well.' Peace went to the airlock doorway unbidden and slowly stepped over the threshold, holding himself straight, head high. He felt he had his valedictory address just about ready to roll. It still had a few rough edges here and there, the odd phrase which perhaps could have done with a polishing touch, but not enough to spoil the overall effect. Determined to extract the maximum amount of egoboo from the tragic moment, he turned to face the men in the corridor.

'So this is how the story ends,' he said in pensive tone, addressing himself mainly to Denby, Lockett and the four crewmen, all of whom were gratifyingly ashen-faced and sad of eye. 'I suppose it's not a bad way to go . . . one brief bright moment of pain . . . and then the ultimate freedom . . . the final EVA. This frail body of mine will be dispatched to drift in space for ever . . . at peace . . . at one with the splendours of the universe . . . with a billion blazing suns to light its lonely way. No sad lilies for me, no pale and wilting blossoms – in their stead I will have a wreath of stars. Yes, it's not a bad way to go.

'Do not grieve for me, my friends. It is you who remain behind that are to be pitied. While you continue to suffer the slings and arrows of this mortal coil, with all its fears and uncertainties and transient delights that become as wormwood in the mouth, I will slumber on the bosom of the stellar deep. Age will not harm me, nor . . .'

'Oh, get on with it,' Hardcastle-Smith snapped impatiently at the bosun. 'Eject the idiot before he bores us all to death.'

'But I haven't finished yet,' Peace said indignantly. 'Kindly show some consideration.'

'You've had too much consideration already,' Gooble put in, gesturing for Rigby to get on with the job. 'We're not listening to any more of that claptrap.'

'Sorry about this,' Rigby said to Peace as he began to slide the airlock's inner door into place.

'I'll give you one of the good bits,' Peace said, speeding up his delivery. '. . . Slings and arrows of . . . no, I've already done that part . . . time for mature reflection on the eternal verities. Speaking as one who is about to cross the fateful threshold of the palace of eternity, it behoves me to hand on to you the flickering torch of—'

'Captain! Captain!' An officer Peace had never seen before came bounding into view and collided with Hardcastle-Smith as he tried to halt in the low gravity.

'What's the matter with you, Reardon?' Hardcastle-Smith demanded as he pushed the officer away. 'Can't you see I'm busy?'

'It's an emergency, sir.'

'What kind of an emergency?'

That's what I'd like to know, Peace thought, exasperated by yet another interruption.

'It's the Martian battleship,' Reardon cried in obvious panic. 'It's dead ahead of us at close range. Only a few thousand miles away!'

'That's impossible,' Hardcastle-Smith said. 'It will be weeks before we come anywhere near the enemy.'

'I tell you, sir, the sighting has been confirmed. The ship has appeared just ahead of us.' Reardon spoke in shocked wonderment. 'It's almost as if the Martians can jump through space. Instantaneously. Oh, sir, what are we going to do?'

'Do? *Do?* We're going to fight the Martian swine, you fool.' Hardcastle-Smith shoved Reardon back in the direction he had come. 'Sound the call to action stations. Follow me, men. We're going to *war*!'

Within a second the captain and all the others had disappeared from view, leaving Peace totally without an audience. He stood for a moment, undecided about how to react. Having resigned himself to the next world, he was having difficulty in coming to grips with the problems of the present. He stepped back over the airlock threshold into the corridor, which was now deserted, and flinched as klaxons began to blast with ear-punishing ferocity.

Peace frowned as he tried to think logically in spite of the din. If the Martians, or some other lot of extraterrestrials, had mastered warp technology – and it sounded that way from what Reardon had said about their ship jumping through space – their weaponry should be equally advanced. That being the case, the DFS *Firebrand* and everybody on board were likely to be molecularized, atomized or even quarkized at any instant. He had already had good reason to get away from the ship in a hurry, and now there was infinitely more urgency – but what action could he take? It was not as if some well-wisher was going to hand him the key to the lifeboat . . .

Lost in thought, he had been staring at the large bunch of keys dangling from the airlock door for several seconds before he realized he was staring at a large bunch of keys dangling from the airlock door. In the panic over the Martian sighting the bosun had forgotten all about them.

My God, I've got a new chance to live! Peace thought. *It means all that effort I put into my valedictory going down the drain, but I suspect it needed a bit more work on some of the metaphors. Anyway, I don't think I really wanted to die – not with a couple of old pervs like Gooble and Hardacre-Smith getting off on it.*

Suddenly galvanized, he began struggling with the cord that bound his wrists. The knots, hardly intended to restrain him for very long, loosened rather easily and in a moment his hands were free. He grabbed the keys, went back into the airlock and closed the door from the inside, shutting out the insistent clamour of the klaxons. He glanced around and at once became aware of a new problem: nowhere could he see a control panel which would allow him to open the huge compartment's outer door.

Reassuring himself that the ship's designers were bound to have made such provision, he renewed the search and his gaze was caught by an odd-looking mechanism projecting from the deck immediately behind the bullet-shaped lifeboat. It resembled an enormous frying pan, with its circular portion covering the lifeboat's single exhaust tube, and its handle running down into a box from which several hydraulic pipes spread along the deck.

'Not bad,' he murmured admiringly. 'The old frying pan over the exhaust tube trick.'

He ran to a door in the side of the boat, found the key to open it after several attempts, and climbed inside. On settling himself in the pilot's seat near the prow he looked at the controls and nodded as he saw they were absolutely basic, designed to be operated by an inexperienced person in an emergency. Praying that he had not misunderstood the workings of the pan-like device, he closed the ignition and fuel pump switches and thumbed a button marked START.

Behind him a rocket motor burbled into life and he visualized its exhaust impinging on the pan and pushing back the supporting lever. The airlock's outer door, visible ahead of him through the view panel, promptly slid aside and he saw the spangled blackness of space. He pulled back on the throttle column and, with a thunderous roar from its engine, the lifeboat surged forward like a live creature seeking its natural environment.

Peace gave vent to a cry of exultation as he realized he was free.

The clustered lights of the *Firebrand* dwindled in the aft-view mirrors. Peace turned his head to the left and looked at the Earth–Moon system. The sun lay in the same general direction and he had to narrow his eyes to pick out the two slim crescents, considerably shrunken by distance. He smiled and had actually begun to swing the lifeboat's nose around in the direction of home when several unhappy thoughts occurred to him in quick succession.

In the excitement of the escape from the mother ship he had been thinking, when there was time for thought, as though he were still in his own familiar universe. In that universe, with its superb space technology, any craft, even one as small as a lifeboat, could go anywhere in the galaxy at any chosen speed, any multiple of the velocity of light.

But things were vastly different in the null-c cosmos.

Here, the space traveller had to contend with factors such as fuel limitations, reaction mass, inertia, distance and relative velocities. And the message for Peace – couched in those dry-as-dust technical terms – was that he would *not* be going home.

The *Firebrand* had climbed out of Earth's gravitational well at around ten miles a second, and had maintained a mild but constant acceleration ever since. Peace was unable to do the computations in his head, but he knew that by the time he had broken away from the big ship it was some millions of miles from Earth and travelling *fast*. Although the lifeboat appeared to be at rest it was actually retreating from the home planet at the speed the *Firebrand* had imparted to it. He could aim the boat's nose at Earth and burn fuel until its tanks ran dry, and all the while – despite the evidence of his senses – he would be travelling backwards. And, when his motor eventually coughed itself into silence, he would have achieved nothing more than a slight reduction in his outward speed.

In a theory discussion he had once heard the predicament described as the Black Destroyer catch. He could no longer remember how the term was derived, but this was no occasion for memory games – for he had not yet summarized all his current troubles.

His unexpected stay of execution had come about because the alien battleship had materialized 'a few thousand miles' ahead of the *Firebrand*. That figure had to be some kind of a guess, perhaps a wild one, but at the speed the *Firebrand* was going the precise distance was unimportant. It was likely to meet up with the alien at any minute, any *second* – which meant that Peace's tiny, unshielded craft would do the same!

This is terrible, he thought. He instinctively glanced to his right, wondering just how much time he had in reserve, and his jaw sagged as he found himself looking straight at the Martian battleship.

He had not expected to pick up anything untoward with his unaided vision, because the intruder must have been detected originally by the *Firebrand*'s powerful telescopes.

But there it was!

In spite of the bright sunlight falling on it, the alien ship was quite difficult to see. It registered on the eye as a dark circle lurking in the background of stars – strange, unearthly, totally unlike anything fabricated by humans. The menace it exuded was enhanced by its dull purplish hue and a livid flickering, probably reflections on force shields, which occasionally passed across its surface.

The terrifying spectacle was increasing in apparent size as Peace's craft bore him towards it at tremendous speed. He stared at it, mesmerized, waiting for the hellish flash of a radiation weapon which would be the last thing he would ever see. Then an odd thought occurred to him. The disk of the alien *was* growing larger, but at a more leisurely rate than he had expected. The process of enlargement had been going on for quite a few seconds now without any dramatic consequence, which meant the alien was much farther away than he had supposed. That, in turn, meant that it was very much larger than he had supposed – with a diameter of some hundreds of miles! Could any ship, even one built by extraterrestrial warlords, be that big?

Wait a minute. Peace studied the disk afresh and his mouth went dry as recognition flared in his mind. *That's not an alien battleship. That's an aubergine hole!*

His limbs twitched, part of the body's primitive response to newly perceived danger, but he was too dumbfounded to take any constructive action. Stellar physics had never been one of his strong points, but he could recall that an aubergine hole was one of the family of interdimensional extensions of a puce hole. At its heart was something called an overdressed singularity – a theoretical impossibility – for which it tried to compensate by alternating between two states of existence, one of them fairly likely, and the other highly improbable. In the latter state it usually expelled matter instead of attracting it. The energy losses thus incurred meant that it could exist for only a year or two, during which time it made random short-range jumps in space. These leaps were accompanied by shrinkage through a series of progressively weaker phases, until it became a rather feeble entity, known as a chartreuse hole, after which it ceased to exist altogether.

Peace's heart began to pound as he realized that the aubergine hole he could see from the lifeboat window had to be a degenerate cousin of one of the puce holes which had swept him into the variable-c universe in the first place. When he had emerged it must have been in its gentian hole phase – the next step down from puce. Since then it had been expelling matter at a furious rate, until it had been forced to make the quantum leap into the aubergine hole phase. As fortuity would have it, the accompanying spatial leap had brought it into the heart of the solar system, where it might exist for just a few days before undergoing another change.

The important thing, as far as Peace was concerned, was that he was being given not only a new chance to live, but to return to his own universe. It was a slim chance, one that only a desperate man would even consider taking, but it was all he had. And for that he was grateful.

He brought the lifeboat around until its nose was aimed at the purplish disk, then pulled the throttle back to its full extent. His head was pushed back against the high seat as the little craft responded with maximum acceleration. In the blackness off to his right the lights of the *Firebrand* were suddenly lost in the flare of its own rockets. Peace visualized the scene on the mother ship's bridge.

Captain Hardacre-Smith and his officers must have been busy with their slide rules and, having deduced that they were heading for an enemy 'ship' the size of a small moon, decided against being too hasty. Peace was glad they had made the decision early enough, given the *Firebrand*'s engine power, to swing clear of the aubergine hole. He would have been more than happy to have Hardacre-Smith and Gooble slide down its throat into God-knows-where, but a lot of decent people would have gone with them. As it was, they would all live to spin tales to their grandchildren about the Defence Force's first taste of interplanetary warfare.

Peace wished he had a similar guarantee about his own prospects. He groped in his jacket pockets and found a single fragment of pork crackling. There was rather a lot of grime and fluff clinging to its greasy surface, but food poisoning was the least of his worries at that moment. He ate the fragment, then lit up a Passing Cloud and puffed it anxiously as he watched the purple disk slowly expand to receive him.

Chapter 10

The greatest single achievement of twentieth-century scientific thought was the realization, expressed in Bell's theorem, that a purely objective universe could not exist. Peace's grasp of physics was not good, and he rarely troubled himself over all the philosophical implications, but Bell's theorem gave him something extra to worry about as the lifeboat dived towards the heart of the aubergine hole.

He would soon be passing close by the singularity at its core, and in the vicinity of any singularity, particularly an overdressed one, the laws of physics no longer held good. For a time he would enter a wrap-around cosmos where illogicality ruled supreme. It was bad enough knowing that he would exist briefly in a mad universe, but the fact that he – as its sole observer – was going to affect that universe powerfully with the contents of his mind was alarming in the extreme. In the past he had found ways to bring disaster down on himself when given very limited scope, in a simple bathroom, for example, so how was he going to fare with a whole universe at his disposal? Especially one in which events could be influenced by his own unruly subconscious?

The aubergine hole now filled the entire view ahead, and Peace felt queasy as the lifeboat began a series of *squirming* movements which would not have been possible in only three or four dimensions. It was moving at tremendous speed, undulating through gravity layers like a snake, plunging into realms where the probable was improbable, and the impossible quite commonplace.

I'll have to control my thoughts, Peace told himself as he fought to subdue his fears. *I'll have to think logically, discipline my conscious mind, keep an iron grip on the rotten old subconscious in case it tries anything funny . . .*

*

'Warren Peace!' the schoolmaster thundered, his narrow face livid with anger. 'Why are you late again?'

Peace froze in the entrance to the classroom. 'I'm very sorry, Mr Bumguard. I overslept.'

'Would you care to explain exactly *why* you overslept?' Bumguard glanced around the other pupils and they tittered in expectation of some fun. 'Is your bed so warm and luxurious, the mattress so pliant, the covers so downy soft, that you simply couldn't bear to extricate yourself from it?'

'No, sir.'

'Then perhaps there was a pea under the mattress, and – like the princess in the story – you are so sensitive that the presence of this leguminous intruder quite spoiled your night's sleep?'

'No, sir.' Peace shot a look of hatred at his classmates who were quaking with amusement. 'I had to stay up very late last night, sir.'

'I'm very sorry hear that, Peace,' Mr Bumguard said with exaggerated sympathy. 'And what lengthy undertaking delayed your retirement? Were you, perhaps, counting the spots which so strikingly adorn your countenance?'

Peace felt the redness of embarrassment flood into those areas of his face which were untouched by acne. 'I was trying to finish my homework, sir.'

'Oh yes, that would be your three-page synopsis of *The Merchant of Venice*. Well, don't be so modest – grant me the privilege of seeing your masterpiece, Master Peace.'

Peace had to wait until the class had stopped laughing at the well-worn joke. 'I didn't get it finished, sir. There was my geography homework as well. It was too much.'

'Your excuse is not acceptable, Peace. All your fellow students managed to complete their assignments.' Mr Bumguard rapped on his desk to let the class know that the entertainment was over. 'Perhaps a few hours' detention will spur you to greater efforts, Master Peace. You will report to me here at ten o'clock on Saturday morning.'

'But I'm supposed to turn out for the basketball team on Saturday morning, sir.'

'They'll just have to manage without you,' Mr Bumguard said severely. 'Now take your seat and try to pay *some* attention to your studies. Today you will be introduced to the delights of Pythagoras's Theorem . . .'

Peace seethed inwardly for the remainder of the school day. He was the star of the form's basketball team and had been looking forward to Saturday's game. While walking home in the late afternoon, with a fresh burden of homework in his satchel, he brooded on the unfairness of life in general, and on his difficulties with schoolwork in particular. He could make an adequate showing in the few academic subjects which interested him, but his problem was that he found most of the work so *boring*. English literature was one of the worst subjects, especially Shakespeare; all areas of mathematics, geometry prominent among them, were excruciatingly dull when expounded by Mr Bumguard; and Peace's natural interest in the geography of his own world had been smothered under lists of the exports and imports of South American republics.

There's just too much to learn, he decided as he took a short cut through Hadley Woods. *If old geysers like Euclid and Shakespeare had only realized the misery they were going to inflict on future generations of school kids they wouldn't have produced all those boring plays and propositions. Why, I'll bet that even Columbus would have turned back before he reached the Americas if he had known he was practically doubling the amount of boring geography in the world.*

The novel thought took a powerful grip on Peace's young mind as he made his way through the wood. If only he could jump back in time and warn Euclid and Columbus and Shakespeare about the future consequences of their activities the quality of life for millions of children would be vastly improved.

It was when he neared the other side of the wood, and saw the familiar path leading to his Uncle Trevor's house, that the really exciting part of his idea clicked into place. He *could* go back in time and put his scheme into action! Uncle Trevor was the world's greatest inventor – a genius who could make literally anything – and if asked nicely he would be only too happy to provide a suitable time machine.

I'll do it! Peace thought gleefully. *I'll go and explain my plan to Uncle Trevor right now, then I'll be able to make the world a better place for generations of overworked school kids – myself included.*

Grinning with anticipation, Peace set off along the path to his uncle's house. He had covered only a short distance when his steps faltered and his grin became uncertain. In some recess of his mind there flickered a strange and disturbing vision. It was of a man, bearded and plump-bellied, in a tiny spacecraft which was falling through layers of shifting luminosity and colour. The man, who seemed oddly familiar, was shaking his head violently, and from his mouth there came a faint, faint cry, the echo of an echo: *This is too ridiculous for words. I refuse to be the author of such a farcical universe. My God, I've got to bring my subconscious under control before this rubbish gets out of . . .*

The inexplicable vision was gone in an instant, however, and young Peace continued cheerfully along the path. A few minutes later he came to his uncle's stone cottage and went into the large and cluttered workshop at its side.

'Hello, young Warren!' Uncle Trevor, a white-haired man with pebbly glasses, looked up from his workbench with a welcoming smile. 'What brings you to this neck of the woods?'

'Hello, Uncle! I remember you telling me how you hated doing homework when you were a boy at school, so I was wondering . . .' Peace went on to outline the problems he was having with Mr Bumguard and home assignments, and the solution he had dreamed up. 'So you see,' he concluded, 'everything would be just wonderful if you would build me a time machine.'

'No need to build you one, my boy,' Uncle Trevor beamed. 'I've got one right here in the shop, already built. I had to take it back from a client last week.'

'I don't want one that has something wrong with it.'

'Relax, my boy. No need to be so suspicious.' Uncle Trevor tousled Peace's hair. 'The machine is fine. Biggs, the man I

169

built it for four years ago, was short of ready cash and he asked for time to pay. I agreed for him to do it in forty-eight monthly instalments – but you'll never guess what the idiot did next. He got into the machine, set it to jump ahead four years and pressed the button! As far as I was concerned the machine simply vanished for four years, then it reappeared in the same spot last week. You'd hardly credit this, but when Biggs came out of it again he expected – just because four years had passed – to find the machine already paid for! You should have seen his face when I asked him who he thought had been making the payments in the meantime.'

Uncle Trevor laughed at the memory, then brought Peace across the workshop to a corner where there stood an artefact resembling an old-fashioned telephone kiosk.

'Is that it?' Peace said, somewhat disappointed. 'Isn't it supposed to be made of shimmering rods which meet at funny angles and give you a wrenching sensation in the eyes when you try to follow them?'

'You just can't get decent shimmering rods these days – they aren't making them any more – and the price of wrenching angle connectors has gone through the roof.' Uncle Trevor's bespectacled eyes clouded for a moment, then brightened again. 'Anyway, it doesn't really matter what the chassis looks like. The years you're aiming at, specially for Euclid, are so far back that the machine will have to operate in its hotrod mode.'

'What does that mean?'

'Stripped right down, Warren. Minimum mass transfer. The machine won't materialize along with you at the targets. You will pop out of thin air – or that's how it will appear to anybody who happens to be watching – and then when the power reserves start to fade the machine will snatch you away again before you get stranded. At the sort of ranges we're talking about you'll probably have only two or three minutes at each place.' Uncle Trevor paused to give Peace an amiable nudge. 'You'll have to do some fast talking, but that shouldn't be much of a problem for you.'

In a short while, after obtaining dates and locations from an encyclopaedia, Uncle Trevor had the time machine fully programmed and ready to depart. Peace stepped inside it and, suddenly feeling quite nervous, pressed the activator button. There was a loud throbbing sound and everything outside the booth, including Uncle Trevor, dissolved into unstable zigzag patterns. Peace's sense of wonder was aroused as he realized he was zooming through time and space.

He was beginning to enjoy the experience when, unaccountably, the vision of the bearded spaceman again trembled in his mind. *This is no way to run a universe*, the man seemed to be saying, fretfully, in the falling leaf of his ship. *This is more like some comic book story I once read, and it's stuck in my subconscious. I've got to get a grip on myself . . .*

The mind-mirage faded almost as soon as it had formed, and Peace had no time to ponder its implications because he felt a giddy *whooshing* sensation and all at once he was standing in a small, marble-walled room. Through the single window he could see a building with many fluted columns, conveniently positioned to establish that he was in Ancient Greece. In the room was a table at which was seated a gloomy-looking man who was studying a parchment covered with annotated diagrams. The man, apparently too dispirited to be shocked at the sudden materialization of a stranger, gazed at Peace with dull eyes.

'Is your name Euclid?' Peace said to him.

'What's it to you?' the man asked in fluent, meticulously precise but oddly accented English.

'My name is Warren Peace, and I bring you a message from the distant future.' Peace spoke quickly, aware that his time was sharply limited. 'All this work you're doing on axioms and propositions and boring old stuff like that is making things tough on—'

'What's that thing sticking out of your pocket?' Euclid cut in, his face showing the first signs of animation. 'Is it some kind of aid to computation?'

Peace scarcely glanced at the slide rule projecting from the breast pocket of his school blazer. 'Future generations of children are having their lives made miserable by—'

'Let me see that.' Euclid snatched the rule from Peace's pocket and excitement flared in his eyes as he moved its slide and cursor. 'I *see* how the instrument works! With the aid of this marvellous device I'll be able to solve all the problems which have perplexed my mind for so long. My contributions to geometry and other branches of mathematics will be increased ten-fold at least!'

'Hold on a minute,' Peace protested. 'This isn't the way things were supposed to—'

His words were cut short as the surroundings dissolved into dancing prismatic zigzags. There was another moment of giddy dislocation, then he found himself standing in a tiny, wood-panelled room which was obviously a cabin in an old ship. A burly man was slumped over a desk which was littered with maps, almanacs and several brass chronometers. His face was buried in his arms and he was sobbing quietly.

'Excuse me,' Peace said timidly, 'are you Columbus?'

'It is my misfortune to be none other,' the man replied, raising his head and speaking in fluent, meticulously precise but oddly accented English. He seemed too distraught to feel any surprise over the presence of a stranger on his ship.

'My name is Warren Peace, and I've come from the distant future to ask you a favour,' Peace said. 'You see—'

'I'm in no position to grant favours,' Columbus cut in. 'I will soon be in disgrace with the queen, because I have no choice but to turn my ships around and abandon this voyage of discovery.' His voice quavered and tears coursed down his cheeks. 'And to think I believed I would be a famous figure in history! Why, I had even composed a rhyme to help school children remember my great deed. In fourteen hundred and ninety-one; Columbus sailed the ocean dun.'

'Shouldn't that be ninety-*two*?' Peace said.

'Of course not,' Columbus snapped. 'Don't you even know what year it is?'

Peace, momentarily forgetting about his time travelling, glanced at the date panel on his watch, and in the same instant his mind was once again invaded by the bearded spaceman. *I recognize that watch*, he seemed to exclaim. *It's the one I gave to the landlord of the Duck and Fiddler. This is getting too ridiculous for words. 'Ocean dun' indeed!* The vision was abruptly dispersed as Peace felt Columbus tear the watch from his wrist.

'What a wonderful miniature timepiece!' Columbus said, his face transformed with joy. 'Why, I see it is even calibrated in seconds and *fractions* of a second. With this Godsend, this splendid chronometer, I will henceforth be able to calculate my longitude with the utmost precision. I don't have to turn back to Spain, after all. Oh joyous day!'

'Hold on a minute,' Peace protested. 'You don't seem to realize that I came here to—' For the third time everything about him splintered into geometric patterns and the universe itself seemed to lurch.

When his surroundings finally steadied he was in a small room with whitewashed walls, leaded windows and low ceiling beams. A balding man with a pointed beard was seated at a desk, disconsolately staring at an inkwell and quill pen. All around him, even on the floor, were sheets of paper disfigured by scrawls and blots.

'Are you,' Peace said, somewhat in awe, 'Mr Shakespeare?'

'Shakespeare, Wagstaff, Wavepike, call me what you will,' the man replied sadly. 'What's in a name? No great lustre will ever attach to mine, for here, at the very outset of my career, I have decided to lay down my pen and make no further attempts to write.'

Peace was tempted to leave well alone, mindful of how he had scored own goals with Euclid and Columbus, but he found himself touched by the intense melancholy in the young Shakespeare's eyes. It would do no harm to cheer the poor guy up a bit, give him a therapeutic shot of egoboo.

'Sir, you will always be a great writer in my eyes,' he lied as he went towards the desk, taking his pen out of his inside pocket. 'In fact, I would be honoured if you would give me your autograph.'

You fool, the chimeral spaceman whispered from the wings of his mental stage. *That's my superstylus – the one I sold to*

Gooble. Haven't you worked out why old Shakey has decided to quit the writing lark? Just wait till he claps eyes on . . .

'I am the one who is honoured,' Shakespeare said with evident gratitude. He took the pen, experimentally drew a few squiggles on a scrap of paper, then began to quiver with manic excitement. 'This is the most splendiferous writing implement I have ever seen. I had wearied of my chosen craft because of the hardship and tedium of trying to set down my thoughts with nibs that break and blotch – but see how this peerless pen wings its way across the page! Henceforth, plays and sonnets without end will flow from my liberated hand.'

'Hold on a minute,' Peace protested. He tried to snatch the pen from Shakespeare's grasp, but he was too late – his surroundings again dissolved into glowing, throbbing patterns. There was a lurch, a thud, a sudden silence, and he found himself once more in Uncle Trevor's familiar workshop.

'How did it all go?' Uncle Trevor beamed. 'May I take it that your mission to the past was a great success?'

Too upset to relate his misfortunes, Peace brushed past his uncle in silence and headed for home. He spent the whole evening brooding, unable even to look at his homework, and lay awake long after going to bed. Consequently he was later than usual when he arrived at school the next morning to face the daily inquisition.

'I just wasn't able to get *through* the homework, sir,' he said in answer to Mr Bumguard's inevitable question. 'There was too much work for me to cope with.'

'You should be ashamed of yourself,' Mr Bumguard replied severely. 'You will never amount to anything, Peace. Have you ever considered how fortunate you were not to have been born long ago? Great men of the past, figures such as Euclid and Columbus and Shakespeare – just to choose a few random names from your recent studies – succeeded in earning their places in history, and *they* didn't have all your fancy modern aids and gadgets. Have you ever thought about that, Master Peace?'

'Yes, sir,' Peace said, with an expression of bitterness ill suited to one so young. 'I think about it quite a lot.'

*

The first intimation that he had re-entered normal space-time came when he saw star fields weaving dynamic patterns all around the lifeboat.

Realizing the craft was tumbling, he stabilized it by means of the steering jets – moving like an automaton – then set himself the task of coming to grips with reality. Part of his field of vision was occupied by a disk of pinkish purple which he identified as a magenta hole, an object which was one step down the energy scale from an aubergine hole. It was expelling him at high velocity, hurling the lifeboat into what might or might *not* be a galaxy of his home universe. With no navigation computers to help, he would have to try orienting himself by sight alone.

It was an exercise which demanded the utmost concentration, but his brain was not yet functioning as it should and his thoughts kept straying to the juvenile Warren Peace and the preposterous adventure with the time machine. Had it all been nothing more than a crazy dream? Or had he, during his dangerous flirtation with the overdressed singularity, actually moulded an alternative universe from the raw materials of his own subconscious mind? If so, he felt quite sorry for the younger alternate version of himself.

That poor kid is even better at walking into trouble than I am, Peace thought, shaking his head in rueful sympathy. *At least I sometimes manage to look ahead and see what's coming in time to take avoiding action.*

In the instant of completing the thought he happened to look straight ahead of the lifeboat. His eyes widened as he saw the blocky outline of a spaceship directly in his path, then they closed of their own accord as he realized there was no time to take avoiding action.

Chapter 11

The crash came almost immediately – a deafening metallic clamour, a twisting collision which threw Peace forward into the lifeboat's control console. He lay on the sloping surface clutching his nose, which seemed to have borne the brunt of the impact, and in the midst of the pain came wonderment over the fact that he was still alive.

He opened his eyes and, through the transparencies of the cockpit, saw grey-painted walls on all sides. The walls were plentifully adorned with conduits, hatches and flat boxes with stencilled lettering – all the familiar paraphernalia of a spacecraft interior. It slowly dawned on Peace that the lifeboat had been captured and engulfed by a much larger vessel. The powerful sense of relief which welled up within him was enhanced as he saw, in spite of the tears blurring his vision, that the equipment signs were in both English and Esperanto. He sobbed aloud with relief. Not only had he survived the transit of an aubergine-magenta hole interdimensional coupling, but he had arrived back in his own universe or one very similar.

He felt the lifeboat settle to the deck in the grip of force-field clamps, and a few seconds later green lights began to glow at various locations on the walls surrounding it, an indication that the huge hold had been flooded with air. Still numb and bemused with shock, he pried himself away from the control console and stumbled to the lifeboat's door. Its lock mechanism defied his attentions at first, but then it glided away from him with a magical ease which told him it was being opened from the outside. He watched in frozen fascination as the aperture swiftly enlarged.

'Warren!' said the golden giant who was standing beyond the doorway. 'We were starting to get worried about you.'

Peace gorged his eyes on the sight of the Oscar and felt his knees begin to wobble. He knew he was going to faint, not least from pure happiness.

'Hec! Hec Magill!' His words were indistinct, partly through emotion, partly because of his physical weakness, but mainly because he was still clutching his damaged nose. 'I love you, Hec.'

When Peace regained consciousness he was lying on a comfortable divan in what appeared to be the ship's sick bay. Two Oscars were standing close to his bed, and several others waited quietly in the background. All Oscars seem identical to the human eye, but with his special perceptions Peace was able to recognize the nearby pair as Magill and Ozzy Drabble.

'Hec and Ozzy, Ozzy and Hec,' he said in a feeble voice, 'you don't know how glad I am to see you.'

'We're glad to see *you*,' Magill replied by means of the speech converter at his waist. 'But why didn't you respond to our radio signals, Warren? It was quite a tricky job for us, matching velocities with that funny little ship you were in.'

'No radio. Where I've been they don't have much in the way of radio communications.' Peace became aware of a throbbing in his now-bandaged nose. 'And forgive me for mentioning it, but you didn't match velocities very well. I must have hit the back wall of that hold at some speed.'

Magill glanced indignantly at Drabble. 'That's the gratitude we get.'

'I'm sorry,' Peace said in hasty contrition. 'I've been through so much recently that I'm not thinking properly. You guys have saved my life and I can't thank you enough. If you hadn't been there, waiting for me, I would probably have been lost for good in the . . .' He paused as realization of the full extent of his good fortune sank in. 'How *did* you manage to pick me up so soon?'

Drabble shrugged, highlights flowing on his massive gold shoulders. 'It wasn't too difficult. One of our group leaders is pretty hot on stellar physics and he said that if you had survived going through a puce hole there was a chance you would emerge from a gentian hole in another universe. All you had to do then was hang around for a while until the gentian hole degenerated into an aubergine hole, then drive your ship into it and pop out through a magenta hole in *this* universe. There was only one magenta hole in this part of the galaxy, so all we had to do was keep an eye on it. Our main worry was that the magenta hole might prematurely lapse into the heliotrope or even the hyacinthine hole phase which, as you know, isn't far off the terminal chartreuse hole state, in which case—'

'Stop!' Peace cried, his brain foundering in the flood of advanced terminology.

'Anyway,' Drabble concluded, 'we knew it would be easy enough for you to get back here. The only things we haven't been able to figure out are what took you so long and why you decided to swap your perfectly good star cruiser for that crummy little iron tub.'

Peace's nose, apparently deciding to serve as an emotional barometer, suddenly intensified its throbbing. 'You think it was *easy* for me to come back! Just let me tell you what I went through while I was—'

'Yes, Warren?'

'Some other time,' Peace said dispiritedly, realizing the impossibility of trying to portray the full misery of his life in the null-c universe in less than a day.

'And there's something else, Warren,' Magill came in.

'Well?'

'You're in pretty bad shape, Warren. You've put on about ten kilos around the middle and, to be quite frank, you look sort of debauched. Were you living it up on some ritzy pleasure planet? Is that why you took so long before deciding to come back?'

'Ouch!' Peace gave the involuntary cry as his affronted nose began a savage and painful pounding.

Magill leaned forward anxiously. 'What's the matter?'

'My nose hurts.'

'Don't worry about your nose, Warren. I smeared it with

Germolene as soon as we got you into the sick bay – that'll put it right in no time.'

'You're very kind.'

'And while I was at it,' Magill added, 'I shaved off that ridiculous beard – it didn't really suit you, you know – and I put some Germolene on your spots. They've all gone now.'

'Very good of you.' Peace felt he should have been consulted about the beard, of which he had grown rather fond, but he had no complaints about the banishment of his pimples.

'You can't have been living a healthy life to get a bad complexion like that, Warren,' Hec Magill said, his persistence providing Peace with an annoying reminder of why he had found life with the Oscars so irksome in the first place. 'I only hope you weren't indulging yourself in saturated fats.'

Peace, who could hardly remember the last time he had eaten, felt a sudden craving for a bag of pork cracklings. 'Is there any food around here?'

Drabble nodded vigorously. 'Lots of it! Lots of good nourishing, health-gving food just for you, Warren. We've got to get you fit and well again as soon as poss—' He broke off as Magill elbowed him in the ribs, an action which produced a sharp ringing sound.

'What's going on?' Peace said, suspicions aroused.

'Nothing.' The brazen giants exchanged furtive glances. 'Nothing at all, Warren.'

'Out with it!' Peace stared into the ruby lenses of their eyes. 'Why are you in such a hurry to get me fit and healthy again?'

'Fact of the matter is,' Magill said, 'that we've got a mission planned for you.'

'What kind of a mission? Is it dangerous?'

'There'll be plenty of time to talk about things like that later on,' Magill said in incongruously motherly tones. 'The important thing now is for you to get lots of rest and proper food. We just want you to relax and concentrate on getting yourself back into shape.'

'How the hell do you expect me to relax when . . .?' Peace allowed the sentence to tail off as, seemingly in response to some covert signal, all the Oscars abruptly vacated the room – leaving him alone with his uneasy thoughts.

The first two days were quite pleasant.

Peace was transferred from the huge area command ship to a standard star cruiser and flown to a planet which seemed, from what he saw of it, to be covered entirely with gentle hills, gentle grassland and gentle streams. There, in a prefabricated chalet, he was checked by Oscar medics and encouraged to do little but eat and sleep. The food was of the healthy variety, but it was appetizing enough and very well presented, so his only real source of dissatisfaction was the unavailability of cigarettes. His Oscar mentors would not even allow him a pack of the insipid modern Helth-E-Puffs, claimed by the manufacturers to dispense vitamins in gaseous form. He spent hours wishing he could light up a rank Summer Cloud and inhale its heady toxins. When his feelings of deprivation became too strong he assuaged them by dreaming of a future in which he had returned to and was living on the planet Ulpha, a world he had visited during his early days in the Space Legion, where the surface was covered with tobacco plants and small volcanoes, and the atmosphere consisted of aromatic smoke.

On the third day the Oscars, having decided that Peace was sufficiently rested, began rehabilitating him in earnest.

His aversion to physical exercise was well known to them, so they devised a crude but effective method of getting around it. Each morning he was put on board a skimmer, flown to a point a long way from base and dumped out on the grass. The skimmer then departed, leaving Peace with a meagre ration of food and a direction finder. To obtain more food and a bed for the night he had to walk all the way back to the chalet, a distance which was increased daily until it reached a gruelling sixty kilometres.

After a week of the regimen he had a deep suntan and was pleased to discover that his paunch, which seemed to have been mostly retained fluid, had all but vanished. His endurance had greatly increased into the bargain, and he might even have started feeling grateful to the Oscars had it not been for his old enemy – boredom. Enjoyment of solitary trekking calls for special character traits; Peace had none of them, and was never going to acquire any.

Walking on featureless prairie twelve or fourteen hours a day made his spell on the A. and W. design team seem like a Mardi Gras, and he soon reached a state in which he almost looked forward to his impending mission, regardless of how dangerous it might be. Magill, Drabble and the other Oscars were preserving total secrecy over the mission – something which he saw as a bad omen – but *anything* was preferable to the monotonous slog from one green horizon to another.

So intense was the ennui that the rediscovery of the zit behind his right ear was something of a major occasion in his life. The spots on his face had faded at the first benign touch of Germolene, but when anointing them Magill must have failed to notice the one on the mastoid bone. Peace was unable to view it directly, but he could tell by touch that it was a fine specimen, a shining example to its erythematic fellows, a prince among pimples. It was also extremely clever. All of Peace's other zits had made the mistake of adopting the standard pustule form, which made them vulnerable to popping, but this one had chosen to manifest itself as a quite pliable and ill-defined bump which was highly resistant to pressure.

Peace became aware of the pimple and its sterling attributes one day while sitting on a grassy hillock, resting after a spartan lunch of oat cakes and carrot juice. He decided to shorten its life, using the method favoured by acne sufferers throughout history, and was mildly surprised when it refused to yield. Accepting the challenge – no other pastimes were on offer – he tried stepping up the pressure. The zit retaliated with unexpectedly severe stabs of pain which brought tears to Peace's eyes. Gritting his teeth, he renewed his efforts, moaning in anguish as he employed both hands to exert maximum force, but after several minutes of self-torture he was forced to admit defeat. The pain had become unbearable and the zit was still secure in its stronghold behind his ear. Far from being debilitated by the struggle, it seemed to have doubled in size.

Thereafter, at least once a day when he was in need of a diversion, he returned to the fray, but the only result was that the zit continued to grow and become even more adept at unleashing bolts of agony when disturbed. He developed for it the kind of grudging respect that a combatant can feel towards a resourceful enemy, and even gave it a name – Zorro. At any stage of the relationship he could have chosen the ultimate sanction represented by Germolene, but it always seemed to have slipped his mind by the time he got back to the chalet at night. More than once it occurred to him that his forgetfulness could have been inspired by an instinct for fair play, a subconscious feeling that for the sake of honour he ought to defeat Zorro in straight combat.

However, the battle of the blemish and all such trifles were driven from his thoughts on the day he was told exactly what kind of mission he was being asked to undertake . . .

When Peace walked into the conference room he saw eight Oscars at the long table, and the fact that they were seated told him something really serious was afoot.

Oscars normally had no use for chairs, being immune to tiredness, so he knew they were attempting to put him at ease. The attempt was not a success. He had been somewhat edgy to begin with, and the spectacle of the group of Oscars trying to be tactful made him highly apprehensive.

'Good morning, gentlemen,' he said brightly, disguising his alarm as he went to the sideboard and began pouring himself a cup of bio-coffee. 'There was no need for you to sit down, you know. I wouldn't have minded you doing a bit of looming over me. What are friends for if they can't have a nice quiet loom among themselves every so often? In fact, only last night it occurred to me that one of the things wrong with modern life is that people simply just don't do enough loom—'

'Sit down with us, Warren,' Hec Magill said. 'There's no need to be nervous.'

'What makes you think I'm nervous?'

'I'm not sure. It might be something to do with the way you're pouring bio-coffee into the bio-sugar bowl.' Magill's voice, issuing from the speech converter strapped to his waist, had a certain dryness which made Peace suspect the golden giants were laughing at him. It was hard to tell with Oscars. Their subetheric voices, which enabled them to converse among themselves even when thousands of kilometres apart, were inaudible to the human ear and for all he knew jokes at his expense were flying round the table thick and fast.

It wasn't like this back in good old Manchester, he told himself as he redirected the stream of bio-coffee. *At least you knew where you stood with those guys. It wasn't a bad life back there, now that I weigh it up – a few restful hours at the office, into the pub with the lads afterwards, a few good laughs, a few pints of ale, a few decent ciggies, a few packets of cracklings, a brisk walk home in the refreshing rain, into the sack with good old Betty . . . What made me want to leave that place?*

His ruminations were interrupted as the Oscars jumped to their feet and gave the circled-fingers-around-the-eyes salute to Brown Owl who had just come into the room. Brown Owl sat down at the head of the table, motioning for the others to be seated again, then turned his ruby eyes towards Peace.

'Come and sit with us, Warren,' he said through a speech device he must have donned just for the occasion. 'There's no need to be nervous.'

'What makes you think I'm nervous?'

'I don't know. It might be something to do with the way you're pouring bio-coffee into the bio-cream jug.'

The other Oscars stirred slightly and this time Peace was sure they were laughing at him. Abandoning the idea of having a drink – the insipid bio-decaff was not to his taste anyway – he took the single remaining chair, at the opposite end of the table from Brown Owl. For quite a while the only sound in the room was that of furniture creaking under the weight of massive gleaming bodies. Peace's uneasiness increased.

'There's a box on the table in front of you, Warren,' Brown Owl finally said. 'Open it.'

Peace, who had not noticed the small rectangle, eyed it with some reserve. 'What's in it?'

'Just a little token of my personal esteem for you.'

'If this is another medallion . . .' Peace raised the lid of the box and his jaw sagged as he saw that it contained, nested in crimson velvet, what appeared to be a twenty-pack of Summer Clouds in pristine condition. 'How . . . ? What . . . ? But this is . . . Who . . . ? Why . . . ?'

'I knew you'd be pleased,' Brown Owl said indulgently. 'Go ahead and light up, Warren. Enjoy yourself.'

'I don't understand this. Where did they come from?'

'There was an empty packet in your jacket and one half-smoked butt in the lining. It was easy enough to have everything copied. The only difference between those cigarettes and the originals is that those are self-igniters.' Brown Owl gave a gracious wave. 'Help yourself, Warren. Puff away to your heart's content.'

Peace took a cigarette in trembling fingers and sucked it into life. He inhaled deeply, rapturously, sending the room into a wavering spin.

'I can hardly believe what I'm seeing, Brown Owl,' Ozzy Drabble said in a scandalized voice. 'Giving Warren *cigarettes*!'

The commander was unperturbed. 'Don't be such an old prig, Ozzy. Warren saved us from that pryktonite meteor, remember, and the least we can do is let him enjoy a smoke if he feels like one.'

'That's all very well, Brown Owl, but what about the harmful effects on the rest of us? What about the passive smoking? I've read that inhaling second-hand smoke is worse than—'

'How can you inhale second-hand smoke or any other kind of smoke when you haven't any lungs and don't even breathe?' Brown Owl cut in.

'I forgot about that.'

'It's a pity there's no such thing as passive thinking, Ozzy,' the commander said. 'It would do you good.'

That's a nice one, Peace thought. *Passive thinking!* He took a second luxurious drag, wondering why he had never appreciated Brown Owl's tolerance before. Then he recalled that Brown Owl had never *had* any tolerance before. The commander had reached his position of eminence because he was the most straight-laced of the lot, a stickler among sticklers. Could there be something symbolic in the gift of cigarettes? There was, after all, no point in worrying about carbon monoxide levels in the blood of a man who was facing a firing squad.

'About this proposed mission,' Peace said, carefully casual, his enjoyment of the cigarette diminishing. 'Is there . . . um . . . much to it?'

'Much to it!' Brown Owl paused for dramatic effect. 'We're only going to rid the galaxy of its ultimate villain, the most evil creature that ever lived. *That's* all there is to it. You know who I'm talking about, don't you?'

'Jeeves?'

'Correct, Warren.'

'Jeeves, eh?' Peace's memory held only a vague image of the benign-looking, silver-haired, cuddly man, and he suddenly realized that during his exile in the null-c universe he had never thought about Jeeves, who had done his utmost to kill him. Perhaps it was something to do with the method Jeeves had employed, the puce hole sandwich. Attempted murder by stabbing or strangulation was highly personal, the sort of thing a person could brood over and take umbrage at, but assassination by astronomy seemed more like an act of God. Peace knew that he should hate Jeeves, and yet the only emotion he could summon up was a vague antipathy mingled with a certain amount of curiosity. Perhaps too many people had tried to kill him at various stages of his life; perhaps one became blasé about such things after a while.

'Yes. Jeeves.' Brown Owl repeated the name with venom and loathing. 'The ultimate criminal mastermind.'

'What's he been up to recently?'

'Sammy Wooton is the chief of our records bureau – he'll bring you up to date.'

Wooton nodded to Peace from across the table. 'We have just received confirmation that one of Jeeves's gangs has been active on Mitsu. That's a planet which was originally colonized by the Yokahama Manufacturing Company, so it has a dedicated market economy. The television service is run by the government and has at least forty minutes of product commercials to the hour.'

'But surely the people wouldn't watch any television,' Peace said.

'They *have* to,' Wooton replied. 'The law requires every person over the age of two years to watch television for a minimum of seven hours a day, and the penalties for disobedience are severe.'

Peace was aghast. 'But that's terrible! If Jeeves has a hand in that sort of thing something certainly ought to be done to—'

'Jeeves has nothing to do with that part of the set-up. It's the way the planet has always been run. The Oscar Ethics Council disapproves, naturally, but we don't interfere with Mitsu's internal affairs. Jeeves's involvement came about in connection with video recorders.'

'I should have guessed that one,' Peace said. 'If I lived in a place like that *I'd* want a recorder. Then I could fast-forward the commercials when I was watching the programmes.'

Wooton shook his brazen head. 'The fast-forwarding of TV commercials is highly illegal on Mitsu. Their video machines are designed and manufactured in such a way that when anybody tries to fast-forward on them they melt down and at the same time send a felony alert to the police.'

'I'm ahead of you now! Jeeves's mob is smuggling normal recorders into Mitsu and selling them on the black market!' Peace gave an appreciative chuckle. 'That may be illegal, technically speaking, but personally I don't regard it as a crime.'

'That's *not* what's happening. There's a worldwide electronic surveillance system which can detect the emanations from *any* recorder, domestic or imported, which is being fast-forwarded – and the penalties are even harsher than those for mere nonviewing.'

Peace frowned. 'Then I haven't grasped the problem.'

186

'I *know* you haven't grasped the problem,' Wooton shouted. 'And the reason you haven't grasped it is because you won't forking well listen! I'm sitting here trying to explain it to you and you keep opening your big mouth and interrupting.'

'No need to lose your temper, Sammy,' Brown Owl said reprovingly.

'I'm sorry, Brown Owl, and I apologize for using strong language, but this idiot gets on my nerves the way he won't shut up and listen.'

'I'm very sorry I'm sure,' Peace said to Wooton. 'I won't butt in again.'

'Are you sure?'

'Cross my heart.'

'Well, all right then. What Jeeves's men were doing was to . . .' Wooton paused to glare at Peace, seeing if he would dare to cut in, and only continued when it felt safe. 'Was to smuggle in gadgets which they claimed could fast-forward any video machine without it being detected. They sold them to gullible people in their millions and cleaned up an absolute fortune, but the gadgets were not what they seemed.'

Peace, now intrigued, began to ask the obvious question, but was quelled by an ominous brightening of Wooton's crimson lenses. He closed his mouth.

'Not by a long chalk,' Wooton added, staring directly at Peace, perversely daring him to speak. Peace, refusing to take the bait, waited in silence.

'Not by a very long chalk,' Wooton persisted.

Peace studied his fingernails.

'Not by a *very* long chalk,' Wooton went on. 'Not by the longest darn chalk you ever—'

'Oh, get on with it!' Brown Owl snapped.

'But he's not even listening,' Wooton cried, pointing an aggrieved finger at Peace.

'I'm getting tired of this!' Brown Owl thumped the table, creating a fist-shaped dent in its metal surface. 'What *were* these damned gadgets?'

Wooton flinched. 'They were introverter time machines.'

'Time machines!' Brown Owl sounded truly shocked. 'You

187

mean that when the viewers thought they were fast-forwarding their video recorders they were actually—'

'Fast-forwarding themselves,' Wooton confirmed. 'The Mitsu government clamped down as soon as they found out what was going on – people's lives were being shortened, their consumer potential whittled away – but the damage was widespread by that time. It hardly bears thinking about.'

'I trust you've heard enough,' Brown Owl said to Peace, his voice solemn. 'Quite apart from your own personal stake in the matter, you can appreciate that – for the well-being of every decent citizen of the galaxy – this fiend Jeeves simply has to be dealt with. It's your duty to all of humanity to accept the mission.'

Peace nodded slowly. 'I can see that, but why have *I* been singled out for the job?'

'Because you're the only member of the Oscar brotherhood who looks like a human being. Who *is* a human being, I mean. The rest of us haven't the remotest chance of getting through Jeeves's rings of bodyguards.' Brown Owl's voice shook with fervour. 'You've *got* to do it, Warren. You've got to bring Jeeves's criminal career to an end – for ever.'

'Hold on a minute.' Peace puffed worriedly on his cigarette. 'I know that Jeeves deserves to die, but I don't think I could bring myself to kill a man in cold blood.'

'We're not asking you to *kill* him,' Brown Owl exclaimed, sounding quite shocked. 'Oscars have never condoned murder, no matter what the circumstances might be. Had you forgotten? I'm surprised you could think such a thing, Warren.'

'I apologize.'

'I should hope so! The very idea!'

'It was a pretty nasty thing to say,' put in Wooton, who had been smouldering in the wings of the conversation.

'Why don't you . . .' Peace, who had been about to ask Wooton to shut his mouth, was thwarted by the realization that Wooton did not possess a mouth and diverted the remainder of the question to Brown Owl '. . . tell me what you *do* want done to Jeeves?'

'It's quite simple, Warren. We want you to get close to Jeeves and then . . . use the psychostat on him.'

'The psychostat?' Peace said, none the wiser. 'Is that some kind of paralysis gun?'

Brown Owl's speech converter emitted a chirp of amusement which was echoed around the table. 'No, Warren, it's a highly sophisticated piece of electronic equipment which our research lab has developed specially for this mission. It won't harm Jeeves in any way – in fact, it will do him a lot of good.'

'I don't understand.'

'Here's the situation,' Brown Owl said. 'As you already know, Jeeves has a dual personality, one of them evil, the other saintly. That's part of the reason he's been able to stay in business so long. On the few occasions when we did manage to corner him, and might have put paid to the monster for ever, he reverted to his good personality. When he's like that he has no memories of his evil deeds, no knowledge of his other self at all, and no Oscar could contemplate roughing up a saint. Otherwise, our Mr Jeeves would probably be two metres under the soil right now.'

'I thought you said you don't condone killing.'

'I said we don't condone *murder*, Warren. It's perfectly all right to use reasonable force when apprehending an evil-doer – and what seems reasonable to an Oscar in the heat of the action may not seem reasonable to the thug involved.'

Peace nodded. 'Especially if his arm has just come off.'

'I'm glad you haven't lost your sense of humour,' Brown Owl said. 'Anyway, the psychostat, as its name suggests, is a machine which will alter the neural chemistry of Jeeves's brain in a way that will permanently lock him into one of his two personalities. Naturally we want him frozen into the good personality, which he is in at present. Once that has been achieved the evil Jeeves will never reappear.'

'I like it,' Peace said, genuinely impressed. 'So all I have to do is get close to Jeeves, press a button or something on the psychostat, and the mission is accomplished.'

'It's not quite as simple as that. Unfortunately it was impossible to build a machine which would work instantaneously – the delicate chemistry of the brain has to be gentled along – so you will have to be in Jeeves's company for a few days. Five should be all right, six would be better, seven ideal.'

'Does that present problems?'

'Nothing too serious,' Brown Owl said encouragingly. 'We know that Jeeves's criminal henchmen like to keep a watch on him when he's in the good incarnation, so they can be all set for when he reverts, but I imagine it's not too strict.'

'And what about the psychostat itself?' Peace said. 'Is it easy to conceal?'

'No problem there, Warren. It's so small that it could easily be incorporated in almost anything you would normally carry around.' Brown Owl's eye-lenses glinted. 'Something like, for example, a cigarette case.'

'I should have *known*!' Ozzy Drabble pounded the table, creating another large indentation. 'You had me fooled, boss! I should have known you wouldn't let Warren wreck his health unless there was something to justify it.'

Huh! Peace thought indignantly. *It looks like I'm expendable all of a sudden.* He was about to voice a protest when it came to him that he was soon to be paroled from his term of ambulatory boredom. Another adventure lay ahead, the chance to encounter the greatest criminal mastermind in the galaxy and to go down in Oscar history as the man who brought his career to a close. There was bound to be a certain amount of risk involved, however, and it would have been gratifying if Brown Owl had shown even a little concern over that aspect of the mission.

'Gentlemen, let us not forget that there is a serious element of risk in the mission,' Brown Owl said gravely, his gaze fixed on Peace. 'One which I can't dismiss lightly.'

Peace sat up straighter, wondering how he could ever have doubted his leader's humaneness.

'My concern is about you, Warren,' Brown Owl said. 'And I won't even try to hide it.'

Peace blinked rapidly, a lump forming in his throat.

'I am concerned,' Brown Owl went on, 'in case you mess up the whole operation by doing something totally stupid and putting Jeeves in a bad mood. It only needs *one* of your feckless stunts to ruin all our—'

'Hold on a minute!' Peace cut in, wounded. 'What are you talking about?'

'I'm talking about the need to keep Jeeves in a good mood during the time you'll be with him. He's been in the saintly incarnation for about four months now, which is longer than usual, and he'll be like a time bomb. The slightest annoyance at this stage could trigger him into reversal, so if you start irritating him . . .'

'There you go again,' Peace said indignantly. 'What makes you think I might irritate the man?'

'It's just *you*, Warren. Everything you do seems to get on people's nerves . . .'

'I'll second that,' Wooton chimed in spitefully.

'. . . And nobody knows what crazy escapade you'll be off on next,' Brown Owl continued. 'It pains me to say this, but you're just not reliable, Warren. Look how long it took you to decide to come back into this universe! The delay has forced us to do everything in a rush, and at the worst possible stage of Jeeves's cycle.'

'If that's the way you feel about me,' Peace said in a strained Beau Geste kind of a voice, 'it might be best for all concerned if I decline to accept this mission.'

'You might have something there,' Brown Owl said, rubbing his chin with a metallic screeching which set Peace's teeth on edge. 'It could indeed be wiser to wait for Jeeves's *next* saintly phase. It would mean giving him extra time to perpetrate crimes, but on the other hand we'd have an extra nine or ten months to train you for the mission and discipline you and get you back into good physical condition. Yes, now that I weigh it up, the best policy could be to—'

'Strike while the iron is hot!' Peace, appalled by prospects of going back to his daily hikes, jumped to his feet and spoke in tones that were both urgent and earnest. 'I'm the first to admit that I might have gone off the beam a couple of times in the past, and that I'm a little accident prone now and again, but we owe it to every decent citizen of the galaxy to take action

against Jeeves without delay. I give you my solemn pledge
that no action of mine will irritate or upset Jeeves in any way
– and that you can trust me to bring the monster's criminal
career to its long-awaited end.'

This is going to be a cinch, he thought, congratulating
himself as he saw most of the Oscars begin to nod in approval.
*Even I can manage to stay out of trouble for a mere five or six
days.*

Chapter 12

The Tucker Hotel on Richmalia, Jeeves's home planet, was respectable and comfortable without being too expensive. It had been carefully chosen for those attributes, to complement Peace's new identity. He was using the name of Sebastian Graves, and was supposed to be a freelance writer of sociological studies and television documentaries. His cover story was that he had come to Richmalia in the hope of being given an extended interview with Jeeves, one that he could use as the core of a book about great humanitarians.

On checking into the hotel he had tried for an immediate appointment, but a press secretary had told him the first slot was not available until six days hence. Peace had no doubt that the time would be used to investigate his background. He had no worries on that score – the electronic fudging of his records was excellent – but it left him with six extra days to get through without putting a foot wrong in any way.

Inspired by the importance of the mission, plus a desire to prove Brown Owl wrong, he decided to remain in the safety of his room for the entire period, only emerging to eat in the hotel restaurants.

On the first evening he settled down on a couch to the accompaniment of undemanding music and began to memorize the data he had been given about Jeeves the Good. The notes were as boring as he had expected. It turned out that the saintly Jeeves was a tycoon who gave most of his earnings to charity and who devoted much of his time to worthy causes. He had a modest lifestyle, eschewing all worldly pleasures, and his only form of self-indulgence was a passion for things called fractal damasks.

Peace, who had never heard of them, looked up fractal damasks in his wristopaedia. They were relics of an ancient

Richmalian civilization, pieces of figured textile in which the patterns shrank and iterated through progressively finer threads, until at the final gossamer level they could only be seen with a low-powered microscope. They were almost impossible to reproduce, even with nano-technology, and examples of the incredibly delicate material changed hands for millions of monits. When Peace read that a fractal damask the size of a handkerchief could have taken a century to produce it reminded him of the misery involved in designing an A. and W. spaceship and what little interest he had in the subject promptly faded.

After another hour of studying notes he was practically stunned with boredom. The benign Jeeves, it appeared, loved everybody on the planet, and the feeling seemed to be mutual: an arrangement which led to an unutterably dull existence. Peace began to understand why it was that when Jeeves did a personality flip he became so villainous. It seemed a quite natural reaction. He felt he would have done the same thing himself.

Stretched listlessly on the couch, he was running an idle hand through his hair when suddenly he winced with pain. His fingers had accidentally come in contact with the angry pimple behind his right ear. *Zorro*, he thought. *Zorro the Zit! I had forgotten about you – but now your time has come!*

Pleased at the unexpected diversion, the prospect of a rousing hand-to-hand struggle, he threw his notes aside and, with a certain amount of trepidation, exerted some pressure on the pimple with his finger and thumb. He had been prepared for it to hurt, but the resultant pain was severe enough to wring a startled curse from his lips. Mustering his resolve, he increased the pressure, again without success. He then tried attacking from different angles, probing for a weakness, but the accompanying stabs were so fierce that they brought tears to his eyes – and still the pimple remained inviolate.

'All right,' he muttered savagely, 'if that's the way you want it.' He switched over to the two-handed mode, left arm bent awkwardly behind his head, and renewed the assault. Thus

194

contorted he fell off the couch and rolled around the floor, alternately swearing and moaning in agony as the zit resisted even his best efforts to breach its epidermal defences.

'I'll get you for this, Zorro,' he sobbed, wondering how long it would take room service to provide him with a needle or, ideally, a surgical scalpel. 'A touch of cold steel is what you need! We'll see how you like a—'

'Warren? Are you all right?' The voice, coming from the video communicator embedded in one of Peace's front teeth, had a buzzing, vibratory quality. It was, however, recognizably that of Brown Owl, who had decided that the mission should be under his personal control.

'I'm fine,' Peace said, wondering how he had managed to forget being under surveillance. 'Couldn't be better.'

'Thank God for that. We thought you'd been poisoned.'

'No, honestly, I'm fine.'

'It was the way you seemed to be in convulsions. Rolling about on the floor.'

'Exercise,' Peace improvised, clambering back on to the couch. 'Keeping myself in combat readiness.'

'Is that why you were talking to yourself?'

'Yes, sir. Psychological conditioning. It's all part of modern hi-tech warfare.'

'Really?' The buzzing voice sounded dubious, not to say sceptical. 'Threatening to bayonet somebody called Zorro?'

'I think I'll go to bed now,' Peace said. 'It's getting late.'

A few minutes later, lying in the darkness, he swore at himself for having once again conjured turbulence out of the doldrums. In spite of being completely alone in an ordinary hotel room he had, without even trying, found a way of bringing misfortune upon himself. He had succeeded in reinforcing the commander's low opinion of him – and all because of a zit behind his ear! The only sensible course of action, he decided, was to ignore the pimple altogether, have nothing more to do with it, let Mother Nature take her course. The pimple, no matter how large, red, resilient, angry and painful, was bound to fade away of its own accord in the fullness of time.

After all, he reasoned as he drifted off to sleep, *people with no arms don't have to go around covered in spots . . .*

When Peace got out of the robocab his first thought was that the computer controlling it must have made a mistake. He had expected to be set down at the entrance to a prestigious office building, one in keeping with Jeeves's mega-monit business empire. But before him was a modest shop, part of an undistinguished row, which seemed to sell homemade candies and children's toys. The sign above it read: HAPPINESS INC.

He checked the address – 333 Lancaster Avenue – and confirmed it was the one given to him by Jeeves's secretary. 'Are you there, Brown Owl?' he subvocalized, unsure about how to proceed and seeking guidance from his orbiting mentors.

'This is Hec Magill,' came the wasp-in-a-jar reply from one of his incisors. 'Brown Owl is having a rest right now. Do you have a problem?'

'I think so,' Peace whispered. 'This place doesn't look like any kind of headquarters building to me. How does it look to you?'

'I can't see it, Warren. How do you expect the camera to pick up anything when you have your mouth shut?'

'Sorry.' Peace bared his teeth in a smile he hoped would not make him appear too idiotic to passers-by.

After a brief silence Magill said, 'What's on your mind, Warren?'

'It's this *place*. I was told I'd find Jeeves here, but it looks like a candy and toy store.'

'It *is* a candy and toy store.' There was another silence, somewhat longer this time. 'Warren, haven't you bothered to read the notes we gave you?'

Peace's heart sank under a sudden weight of guilt. 'Of course I read the notes. Most of them anyway . . . I might have skipped a line or two in the boring bits.'

'If you'd read those boring bits you'd have learned that Jeeves owns the store and spends a lot of his time behind the counter in there.' Magill's voice had little of its usual friendliness. 'I have to tell you we're all getting a bit worried about you up here, Warren. Brown Owl is convinced you had some kind of seizure in your hotel room the first night.'

'I'm perfectly all right, Hec – believe me.' The realization that he might have damaged his relationship with Magill filled Peace with genuine concern. 'I've got to go in there now – it's almost time for my appointment – but I promise I won't let you down, Hec. Word of honour!'

'We're counting on you.'

Peace nodded, his breast swelling with resolve to win the lasting respect of Magill and all his golden comrades. He had completed six long days of waiting without much going wrong, apart from the one little bit of awkwardness with Brown Owl, and he was determined to make a memorable success of the next six days. The Oscars were going to be proud of him.

It was a fine spring morning in Brightland, Richmalia's capital city, and neat little clouds were drifting across a canopy of childhood blue. The peacock trees were in bloom and the brightly clothed pedestrians were relaxed and cheerful. To Peace the scene was a vignette of all that was good in modern civilized life, a reminder of what the Oscars stood for.

He took a deep breath, crossed a well-tended grassy strip to the entrance of the shop and went inside. The interior was larger than he had expected, seeming to extend right through to the other side of the block. The decor made much use of polished wood and bevelled glass, giving the place the antique air of a sepia photograph. In spite of the earliness of the hour there were lots of customers, mainly family groups with a high proportion of children.

Peace looked to his left, towards the candy section, and saw behind the counter a plumply cherubic man with a pink complexion and silver hair. His heart lurched as he realized he was looking at Jarvis Jeeves, part-time galactic villain, the saintly incarnation of the monster who had sworn to kill him. Jeeves was busy serving a group of small girls, all of whom were laughing as he pretended to haggle over the price of chocolate bars and was actually handing out far more than the bargain entailed. With his twinkly eyes and quirky smile he was benevolence personified, every child's vision of a kindly uncle.

Peace fingered the cigarette case in his pocket, with its built-in psychostat, and was profoundly relieved that he was not required to assassinate Jeeves. No matter how long the list of crimes perpetrated by Jeeves's alter ego, it would be unthinkable to direct a weapon against the jovial personality of Jeeves the Good . . .

'A very good morning to you, Mr Graves!' The greeting came from a smartly dressed, capable-looking woman of about fifty who was approaching Peace with outstretched hand. 'I'm Amanda Coogan, one of Jarvie's personal assistants.'

'Hello,' he said, shaking hands with her. 'How did you know who I—?'

'Oh, I know you very well, Sebastian,' she said, smiling whitely. 'We have to run security checks on everybody who comes to see Jarvie – that's how he likes to be addressed – so I know all about you.'

'Really?' Peace felt a twinge of unease as it occurred to him that the woman might be a caretaker for the criminal organization which owed its allegiance to the other Jeeves.

'Yes. It's a shame we can't take everybody on trust, as Jarvie would like us to do. He loves everybody, you see, but there are some very strange people going around these days, if you know what I mean. We have to be on our guards against psychopaths who might try to harm Jarvie just to make themselves famous.'

'I understand,' Peace said. 'You can't be too careful.'

'That's why I have to inspect the square metallic object you have in your right-hand pocket, Sebastian.' Amanda smiled again, ruefully. 'It's made of some unusual metal that our scanners can't penetrate. Do you mind?'

'Not at all.' Peace fished out his cigarette case and passed it over. 'The only dangerous substance in there is the tobacco. I'm afraid I indulge in the weed.'

'That's all right. Jarvie loves his cigars.' Amanda opened the case and examined it closely.

Peace watched her with a studied lack of concern. The circuitry of the psychostat was integrated with the molecules of the case, making it virtually impossible to detect, but here was an opportunity for his chronic bad luck to manifest itself in some unexpected way. *You can't foresee the unforeseen*, he thought, then pushed the would-be aphorism to the back of his mind to await some polishing. He kept a covert eye on Amanda while the inspection continued, and almost gave a sigh of relief when she snapped the case shut and handed it back to him.

'Thank you, Sebastian,' she said. 'Now I can take you across to meet Jarvie, but there's one more little formality. I hope I'm not trying your patience.'

'Patience has always been one of my strong points,' Peace replied, trusting there were no long-range lie detectors aimed at him.

'It's one of Jarvie's most endearing little foibles, one of his ways of getting more people involved in his charitable work.' Amanda cast a fond glance in the direction of Jeeves, who was now dispensing multi-coloured lollipops to a different group of youngsters. 'He will only give an autograph or grant an interview on condition that the recipient pays a visit to the blood donor stand here in the store.'

'I guess I can go along with that,' Peace said unhappily. He had always felt queasy about donating blood, but vaguely recalled that some famous figure of the past had a similar way of inducing people to part with theirs. 'Um . . . what sort of quantity is involved?'

'It's up to you really, but we feel that two litres is a reasonable amount.'

'Two litres!' Peace cried in consternation. 'But that's about half my supply! I'm not giving that much!'

To his surprise, Amanda began to laugh. 'We're not asking you to *give* blood, Sebastian. We want you to *receive* some – as a gift from the inhabitants of the planet Poople.'

'The planet Poople! Is this some kind of a joke?'

'It's no joke,' Amanda said seriously. 'The inhabitants of Poople are afflicted with a disease which causes them to produce too much blood. Drugs don't work on them, so the only way they can reduce their blood pressure is by siphoning some of it off. They are a highly altruistic species, so they get rid of the excess by donating it to the people of other planets. All they ask is a small gratuity to cover expenses.'

'Very noble of them,' Peace said. 'But what am I going to do with two litres of blood? I'm not a vampire.'

Amanda smiled tolerantly. 'As it happens, Poopler blood makes an excellent feed for all kinds of vegetables.'

'But I'm not a gardener, either. And I'm not going to walk around with a bucket of alien blood, looking for some thirsty cabbage to throw it over.'

'You don't have to do that, Sebastian,' Amanda said. 'You can donate the blood to the inhabitants of the planet Gronnik. Their world is rather infertile, and they desperately need all the plant food they can get. They have a stand right here in the store and will be glad to relieve you of any Poopler blood you have no use for. All they ask for the service is a small gratuity to cover expenses.'

'This might sound like a dumb question,' Peace said, his brain in danger of overload, 'but wouldn't it make more sense for the Pooplers to cut out the middle man and send all their spare corpuscles direct to Gronnik?'

'Yes, but that would deprive so many people of the Giving Pleasure.' Amanda directed another look of adoration towards Jeeves. 'Jarvie says the Giving Pleasure is the most ennobling of all the human emotions, and that, instead of *taking* all the time, people should prefer to *give*.'

'Yes, but how could you give stuff away if there wasn't anybody prepared to take it off your . . .?'

'What?'

'Never mind,' Peace said, sensing a conversational precipice. 'Where's this blood donor stand?'

He was taken farther back in the store to a small structure which was covered in striped canvas like a funfair booth. There an apoplectic-looking humanoid gave him a plastic jar of a revolting, slightly frothy purple fluid and deprived him of ten monits. Amanda then took him to a similar stand across the aisle where a suitably undernourished humanoid relieved him of the jar and a further ten monits.

'Jarvie will be pleased to see you now,' Amanda said as they returned to the front of the store. 'His diary is very full at present, but he should be able to give you fifteen or twenty minutes.'

Peace nodded. 'And when can I see him this afternoon?'

'You can't. Jarvie is very busy, as always, and twenty minutes is tops for any interview.'

'All right. How about tomorrow?'

'Nothing tomorrow, or any other day. Twenty minutes this morning is all you get.'

'But I need at least a week with him,' Peace said, alarmed by the threat to his plans. 'Look, if it's a matter of buying . . . I mean *donating* . . . a few more jars of gore . . .'

'I'm sorry, Sebastian, but you don't seem to appreciate just how generous Jarvie has already been in allocating you a full twenty minutes.' A reverential look appeared in Amanda's eyes as she contemplated her employer's beneficence. 'He has a packed schedule this week, and on top of that there are all the preparations for President Nuttall's visit to the damask museum. Personally I just don't know how Jarvie copes.'

It might help if he spent less time doling out tooth-rot to gangs of brats, Peace thought gloomily as he came in sight of Jeeves, who was still at work distributing confectionery. The success of the mission was hanging in the balance and he would never again be able to face his Oscar comrades unless he came up with a good idea there and then. He tried to goad his brain into action, but it seemed to have petrified.

'Jarvie, I'd like you to meet Sebastian Graves,' Amanda said as they reached the counter. 'He's the writer I told you about.'

'It's a great pleasure to meet you, Seb.' Jeeves twinkled with his blue eyes, then looked pensive. 'Haven't I seen you before somewhere?'

'No, sir,' Peace said hastily, thinking of the one occasion when they had met face to face by way of television, when Jeeves had been gloating over his impending annihilation. Was it possible that hatred so intense could penetrate the barrier between Jeeves's opposing personalities? Had there been some kind of emotional osmosis?

'That's strange. I could have *sworn* . . . but let's not waste valuable time on the dotings of a silly old geezer like me.' Jeeves's pink features brightened. 'Now, young man, I understand you want to feature me in a book. Correct?'

'No, sir. That's not why I'm here at all.' Peace listened in dismay to the words his mouth was issuing of its own accord. 'I haven't even the slightest interest in you as a person.'

'But . . .' Jeeves looked hurt, disconcerted and puzzled. 'Would you mind telling me why you *are* here?'

'I'd like to hear that as well,' Amanda said.

So would I, Peace thought, striving not to panic as he waited for his mouth to answer the query. 'To me, Mr Jeeves, your sole importance in the great scheme of things is as an instrument of the powers of goodness. To me, personalities are irrelevant. To me, it is the achievement that matters, the part one has played in the ultimate conflict – the one between the forces of Good and Evil. To me, there—'

'To me,' Amanda cut in, 'you're talking a load of—'

Jeeves silenced her with a gesture. 'Let the young man have his say, Mandy.'

'I have something for you, Mr Jeeves,' Peace continued, taking a plastic card out of his pocket. 'It's a Cosmobank draft for ten thousand monits – the entire advance from my publisher for my present commission. I'm going to endorse it in favour of one of your charities. I don't want any thanks for this donation, because *I* am the one who stands to gain. I will be repaid many times over in the only currency I value – the Giving Pleasure. To me, the Giving Pleasure is the most ennobling of all the human emotions.'

Peace thought he heard Amanda give a faint gasp as he completed the final sentence, but his attention was concentrated on Jeeves and his reactions.

'You know, that could have been *me* talking,' Jeeves said in tones of pleasurable wonderment. 'I can't tell you how happy it makes me to meet a genuine altruist.'

Peace lowered his gaze and smiled modestly. 'Thank you, Mr Jeeves.'

'Call me Jarvie.'

'Thank you, Jarvie.'

Jeeves beckoned for a nearby sales assistant to take over from him. The children, seeing he was about to depart, emitted cries of disappointment.

'I'm sorry, boys and girls,' he said warmly. 'I love you all . . .'

'And we love *you*, Jarvie,' they chorused.

'. . . but I have to leave you for just a little while.' Jeeves came out from behind the counter and draped a fatherly arm around Peace's shoulders. 'Seb, my boy, I'd love to spend a lot of time with you and listen to all your ideas. Is there any chance of your staying here for a week or two – as my guest, of course – so that we could talk?'

'Well . . .' Peace tried to ignore the speculative stare that was being directed at him by Amanda. 'I don't know about being your guest, Jarvie – I like to pay my way everywhere I go – but perhaps I could do some unpaid work for you here in the store for a little while. That way we could talk all we want, and I could research your charitable work for my book.'

'Splendid!' Jeeves beamed, clapping his hands in delight. 'And perhaps I'll be able to remember where I saw you before.'

As Peace had begun to realize early on, Happiness Incorporated's premises were much larger than they appeared from the Lancaster Avenue entrance. At ground level they extended all the way through the block, merging into another of Jeeves's pet sideline projects, the Fractal Damask Museum, which had its entrance on Wendover Avenue. On the floor above were some office suites and the unpretentious living quarters which Jeeves the Good used when he was in town. It was there that Peace was installed in a small apartment within two hours of meeting Jeeves.

He was in the bathroom, freshening up to rejoin Jeeves in the store, when his communications tooth gave a preliminary buzz and Brown Owl's voice sounded inside his mouth.

'Warren, I'm really pleased with your work,' the commander said without preamble. 'I should only contact you when it's strictly necessary, but I decided to let you you know how we all feel up here. The way you handled the problem with Jeeves and his press secretary was masterly.'

'It was nothing,' Peace subvocalized, trying to disguise his gratification.

'You're too modest, Warren. I know I've said a few harsh things about you in the past, but I take them all back. You had foreseen that Jeeves could be too busy to spend much time with you, and you knew exactly what to say. I have to admit that we nearly died up here when you told Jeeves you had no interest in him as an individual, but you were one step ahead of everybody on that one, weren't you, Warren?'

'Be prepared, that's my motto,' Peace said. 'Think everything out in advance. Plan for every contingency.'

'Good man! If you go on the way you've started the mission is bound to be a total success.'

'Leave it to me, sir.' Pleased with his new image – the wily strategist – Peace whistled jaunty tunes while completing his toiletries. For once in his life there was cause for optimism. His luck was definitely improving, Jeeves had taken a liking to him, and only an idiot could fail to get through the coming week without messing things up.

The days that followed were, indeed, undemanding as far as Peace was concerned. He was not even required to switch the psychostat on and off – it began to function automatically when he came within a few paces of its programmed target. The effects of its subtle influence on the brain chemistry were cumulative, with the result that as the days went by the chances of Jeeves doing a reversal were diminished.

The knowledge that eventually it would take something fairly drastic to conjure up the evil Jeeves boosted Peace's confidence in his dealings with his host. He began to relax in the older man's company and as a result was able to deal more easily with the little accidents which inevitably form part of the daily round.

An instance came on the second morning, during breakfast, when Peace let a slice of toast fall on the carpet. He grew tense, wondering if such a trivial incident could possibly be enough to precipitate disaster, but Jeeves responded with a quizzical smile.

'Isn't it odd,' he said, 'that when you drop a piece of toast it always lands with the buttered side down? You don't *hold* the toast with the buttered side down, do you, young Seb? Does that mean there's an unknown force which turns it over in mid-air?'

'There's scope there for a scientific experiment,' Peace replied, venturing a touch of his own humour. 'We know that a kitten always lands on its feet, so we could try gluing bits of toast on its back and see if they make any difference.'

'That's funny,' Jeeves said, giving what Peace could only describe as a chortle.

Peace had never seen anyone chortle before, especially on hearing one of his jokes, and he realized he was developing a strong affection for Jeeves. He found it difficult to accept that the kindly, cuddly gentleman across the table, with the silver kiss-curl in the centre of his forehead, could ever change into the arch-criminal Jeeves whose infamy had spread across the galaxy. (The only physical distinction between the two, Peace had been told, was that Jeeves the Good brushed his curl to the right, while the evil incarnation favoured sweeping it to the left.) Peace's growing personal sentiment made him more determined than ever to bring the mission to a happy conclusion.

His nominal job consisted mainly of being present while Jeeves handed out sweets and toys, often without charge, but there were frequent forays into the museum. Preparations were under way for an official visit by Richmalia's chief executive, Stanislaw Nuttall, and Jeeves – as is often the case with one who has an obsession – was highly flattered by the president's show of interest.

Peace had feigned a similar enthusiasm when Jeeves had shown him the fractal damasks in their glass display cases, but privately he failed to see what all the fuss was about. To him the damasks were simply very old and rather tatty bits of cloth. The centrepiece of the collection, known as the Shorrock Sampler, had cost Jeeves upwards of ten million and in Peace's eyes was nothing more than a handkerchief which had seen an excessive amount of service. The idea of people paying out fortunes for such things reinforced his opinion that collectors in general were lunatics.

He enjoyed seeing Jeeves derive so much pleasure from them, however, and in turn felt quite flattered by his invitation to the presidential reception.

'It will give you lots to write about,' Jeeves said, his cherubic features aglow. 'I don't want any personal publicity, naturally, but a visit from the president will be a real boost to our fund-raising.'

'I'd like to be there,' Peace said, wishing he was a genuine writer and not deceiving his host, 'but I don't have the right sort of clothes.'

Jeeves shook his pink jowls. 'No need to worry about that, young Seb. I'm giving you the honorary rank of captain in the Happiness Corps . . . no, let's make you a major . . . and you'll have the dress uniform. You'll cut a fine figure in all the ceremonial gear – I'm too tubby for it – so I want you on parade with me next Friday. Do I make myself clear?'

'Yes, *sir*!'

Later, in the quietness of his apartment, Peace smoked a couple of Summer Clouds, all the while staring thoughtfully at his cigarette case. The device concealed within it was not harming Jeeves in any way – in fact, it was doing him nothing but *good* – and yet he was unable to rid himself of a sense of guilt, a feeling that he was a cheat and a betrayer. *I'm not a hit man*, he told himself. *I'm doing the exact opposite of an assassin's work – extending a good man's life instead of shortening it. I should be proud of myself.*

Determined to avoid negative thinking, he concentrated his mind on the undoubted smoothness with which the operation was proceeding. Six days had passed without a hitch, and by now the persona of the saintly Jeeves was well in the ascendancy. It would take something very serious indeed to bring about a reversal, and his relationship with Jeeves was so good that it was hard to envisage anything he could do causing the mission to fail at this late stage. He had always suspected that it was sheer bad luck which had at times got him into scrapes, made him appear a fool in the eyes of others, but all that was behind him. From now on his career was going to go from achievement to achievement . . .

'This is Brown Owl,' his communications tooth said. 'I'm calling to congratulate you again, Warren. Things couldn't have gone better from our point of view.'

Peace saw the timing of the call as a good omen, a ratification of his new manifesto for success. 'Thank you, Brown Owl,' he whispered. 'I was just thinking the same thing.'

'We don't know how many of the evil Jeeves's lieutenants are surrounding you, Warren, so we have to keep your identity secret until you're safely away from Richmalia. I want you to go to the spaceport tomorrow afternoon, without any fuss, and take a flight to—'

'Hold on a minute,' Peace cut in. 'I want to stay until the day *after* tomorrow.'

'That won't be necessary. If Jeeves gets a few hours of exposure to the psychostat in the morning that will complete the seven days we hoped for.'

'Yes, but I promised him I'd be around for a very special event. President Nuttall is coming here on Friday.'

'I don't like the sound of this,' Brown Owl buzzed severely. 'Anyway, you needn't consider yourself bound by a promise made to the worst villain in the galaxy.'

'But he isn't a villain any longer. Remember?'

'Don't split hairs, Warren. An extra day on Richmalia would only increase your chances of being found out.'

'Yes, but . . .' Peace knew that Brown Owl was making sense, but he also knew that Jeeves would be hurt and disappointed if he vanished without any explanations or farewells. In their short time together he had developed a genuine affection for the twinkly, philanthropic old man, and the thought of causing him pain was hard to bear.

'But what, Warren?'

'Brown Owl, you know a lot more about the workings of the psychostat than I do,' Peace said. 'Is there absolutely *no* possibility of Jeeves reverting to his evil self after seven daily sessions? No chance at all?'

There was a pause before the tooth vibrated its reply. 'Well, there might be one in a million.'

'There you are!' Peace said triumphantly. 'One chance in a million is one too many when you consider what's at stake for the people of the galaxy. I'm going to stay the extra day and see the job through.'

'I don't like it,' Brown Owl buzzed, but he was beginning to sound less authoritative. 'It seems to me you're tempting fate.'

'It's *my* life that's on the line,' Peace said, clinching the matter. 'Besides, I'd say that fate is smiling on me right now. For the first time in my life I feel lucky.'

Chapter 13

'You really do look good in uniform, Sebastian,' Amanda Coogan said, with her perfectly symmetrical smile. She and Peace were standing with the official reception group outside the museum's entrance on Wendover Avenue.

'It's really something, isn't it?' Peace glanced downwards, admiring his resplendent white tunic and trousers with all their bright buttons, buckles and Happiness Corps insignia. Feeling fit and trim, he was glad he had shed his excess weight so quickly.

'It's not so much the uniform itself – more the way you wear it.' Amanda's gaze traced a zigzag down his body. 'Most of our executives look a bit silly when they dress up, but you have the right sort of bearing.'

'Thank you, Mandy.' Since his talk with Brown Owl, Peace had been doubly on his guard, and an alarm bell had gone off in his mind as soon as Amanda had turned on the flattery. She had been slightly distant and very correct with him since he had moved into the apartment, but now he was being complimented on his fine soldierly bearing. Sebastian Graves's invented past showed no military connections, so cool, competent Coogan was doing some subtle probing.

There was a time when I might have opened my big mouth and blabbed something about having been in the Space Legion, but those days are over, Peace thought, pleased with his own canniness. *I don't barge headlong into trouble any more.*

'This must be the president's party now,' Amanda said, shading her eyes from the morning sunlight as three elongated limousines angled out of the traffic flow and came to a halt.

There was a flurry of excitement and a group of Happiness Incorporated senior managers, led by Jeeves, went forward to greet President Nuttall and his party. Peace took a vicarious pleasure in watching Jeeves's sheer joy as he was introduced to the president and other notables, and then ushered them into the museum. The normally hushed atmosphere of the place gave way to a buzz of conversation and polite laughter as champagne was dispensed.

Peace, who had never liked snobby functions, was a little surprised to find himself being seduced by the ambience of wealth, prestige and general bonhomie. His enjoyment was enhanced by the realization that he was drawing frequent glances from several of the exquisite women present.

I should wear uniforms like this more often, he thought, being careful not to relax his military bearing as he sipped the champagne. It had never occurred to him before, but one disadvantage of being in service with the Oscars was that, because they wore no clothes, they had no need for uniforms. But there was nothing to stop *him* being given a uniform. It was the least they could do for him after the great success of the Jeeves mission – and he could even design it himself! A white one would be nice, something like the one he had on, but with a touch more fullness in the sleeves, a little bit of extra detail around the lapels, and perhaps a couple of pleats at the back to improve the hang.

Vistas of a brilliant new future opened up in Peace's mind, putting him into a semi-tranced condition as he wandered unseeingly among the knots of people gathered around the glass display cases of the museum. Perhaps he could become some kind of an ambassador for the Oscars, spending most of his time at glittering receptions, hobnobbing with galactic luminaries, consorting with beautiful women.

Newly preoccupied with appearances, Peace smoothed down his hair, and – so lost was he in grandiose dreams – he was quite puzzled when a fingertip encountered a bump behind his right ear. After a moment's thought he identified it as Zorro – but something had changed! This was not the fierce antagonist which had caused him so much agony in the past. In Zorro's place was an innocuous, painless lump which was quite soft and squishy to the touch. Intrigued, Peace gave it a tentative squeeze. There was an immediate detumescent *glug-glugging*

210

sensation and a warm tide poured down the side of his neck in the direction of his gleaming white collar.

'Handkerchief!' he moaned in panic. From the corner of an eye he glimpsed Jeeves holding out a white square. Snatching the object, he clapped it against the side of his head – then became aware that all was not well around him. People were emitting horrified gasps; Jeeves and President Nuttall were staring at him in wide-eyed disbelief; and, worst of all, the lid of the display case beside Jeeves was raised and the case itself was empty. As Peace's ability to perceive his surroundings improved, he realized that Jeeves had taken a fractal damask out of its case to let the president touch it; and that he – Warren Peace, the cool sophisticate who would never again make a boob – had grabbed the precious relic and clamped it over a copiously ejaculating zit.

Not the Shorrock Sampler, he pleaded inwardly. *Please God, not the Shorrock Sampler.* He focused his gaze on a name plate at the front of the empty case. It read: THE SHORROCK SAMPLER.

Time seemed to slow down for Peace.

He lowered the square of delicate fabric from his ear, praying that he would find it relatively unscathed. It had been ripped almost in half, and much of the intricate design had been soused – irretrievably marinated – in what looked like bull's blood flecked with tiny pieces of cheese.

'I'll get it dry cleaned,' Peace said.

Jeeves gave a piteous whimper and sagged into the arms of President Nuttall.

'I'll pay to have it invisibly mended,' Peace said. 'How would that do?'

Jeeves took a deep, shuddering breath and, with surprising power for one in his demoralized condition, shouted, 'Kill him! I hate that man! *Kill him!*'

Peace backed away, shaking his head, as he saw some of the people around Jeeves make threatening movements as though they were considering actually obeying the orders. He threw the fractal damask to the floor and was trying to find refuge behind a souvenir sales counter when his communications tooth buzzed into life.

'What's going on down there?' Hec Magill said. 'What have you done, Warren?'

'Nothing much,' Peace whispered defensively. 'All that fuss over a rotten old hanky . . .'

'But you must have done *something*, Warren,' Magill persisted. 'Was that Jeeves I heard shouting a minute ago? And who does he want killed?'

'It *was* Jeeves . . . and I guess I did upset him a bit.'

'My God,' Magill quavered. 'He can't have reverted, can he? It isn't possible at this stage, is it? You haven't made him flip, have you?'

'How would *I* know if he has flipped or not?'

'Look at his curl, you idiot! Does it go to the left or the right?'

'I don't know,' Peace mumbled, belatedly appreciating the seriousness of what he had done. 'I'm afraid to look.'

'Then open your cake-hole and let the camera see him.'

Peace, still unable to look Jeeves in the face, partially exposed his front teeth.

'The curl still goes to the right,' Magill said after a brief pause. 'He hasn't flipped.'

'Make absolutely sure, Hec.' Needing assurance that all was not lost as far as the mission was concerned, Peace bared his teeth even further.

Jeeves emitted a strangulated scream and pointed at Peace with a quivering finger. 'Look at the monster! He's grinning at me! Not only does he vandalize my lovely, lovely damask – he stands there and *gloats* over it! Aaarrgghhh!'

'Hold on a minute,' Peace said anxiously. 'I wasn't . . .'

His voice faded as he saw that something was beginning to happen to the portly, pink-faced figure. Jeeves straightened up and disengaged himself from the president's arms. He looked all about him with eyes that had gone hard, then his hand came up and, with a very slow and oddly mechanical motion, brushed the curl from the right side of his forehead to the left.

'What is this place?' he said coldly. 'What am I doing here?'

The people nearest him stepped back in instinctive alarm, but Amanda Coogan went to Jeeves's side and gripped his arm. 'It's all right, Jarvie,' she soothed. 'You've had a little too much excitement, that's all. I'll take you up to your suite and you can have some rest.'

'Thank you, Mandy,' Jeeves said.

'There's nothing to worry about,' Amanda assured the onlookers as she began to lead Jeeves away. 'Jarvie has been working too hard, as always, but he'll be fine in a little while. What he really needs is a long vacation.'

Peace, too shocked to take in the central enormity of what had happened, found himself preoccupied with peripheral details. Jeeves had reverted, there was no doubt about that, but in his villainous personality he still knew who Amanda was. That was proof of what Peace had suspected: she was a caretaker on behalf of the criminal organization. As press secretary she would probably announce that Jeeves was now going to take his much-needed long vacation, which was a nice cover story for . . .

Jeeves has reverted! The realization exploded in Peace's brain. *Oh God, Jeeves has reverted – and it's all my fault!*

'You've really done it this time, Warren,' Magill said from his dental podium.

'It wasn't my fault,' Peace whispered.

'I don't see who else you can blame. Why did you have to go and grin at the man? That's what pushed him over the edge.'

'I wasn't grinning. Whose nutty idea was it to put the camera in my tooth in the first place?'

'Brown Owl thought of that one, but don't try shoving the blame on to him, Warren. When he gets back from his coffee break and hears about this he's going to be mad enough with you as it is. I wouldn't like to be in your shoes.'

'Don't keep harping on about it.'

'But you've made yourself the only person in the galaxy that Jeeves hates in *both* his incarnations. Nobody else could have done it, Warren. You're unique!'

'I told you not to go on and on about it,' Peace said, becoming irritated. 'The main thing now is for me to sneak out of this place without being noticed. As soon as I've done that I'll be able to . . .'

He allowed the sentence to tail off as an alarming new development forced itself on his attention. Jeeves, while being escorted away by Amanda Coogan, had been gazing around the room as though he had never seen it before. But now his gaze had ceased its meanderings, and was directed straight at Peace. There was a taut moment – during which Peace wanted to drop down behind the souvenir desk, but was too petrified with dread – then Jeeves's eyes dilated.

'Warren Peace!' he cried. 'You're Warren Peace and you work for the Oscars!'

'Never heard of the guy,' Peace said, making for the main door in a kind of speeded-up shuffle which he hoped would look casual while at the same time allowing him to cover a lot of ground. Seeing Amanda whisper something into her wristophone, he abandoned all subterfuge and made a run for it. Several men moved across the exit, blocking his escape route. Peace swerved, sprinted to the rear of the room and darted behind a screen where there was a staff door which led into the candy and toy store. He wrenched the door open and plunged headlong into a mass of shoppers, some of whom emitted bleats of alarm.

'Stop that man!' somebody shouted behind him. 'He's done something to Jarvie!'

As Peace bolted along the store's central aisle he heard others take up the cry. The spindly figure of the Gronnik humanoid stepped out in front of him with arms widespread to bar his way. Peace side-swiped him into his stall and the being fell backwards among stacked jars of Poopler blood, one of which popped its lid and spewed purple liquid all over him.

'Sprinkle that on your radishes, you ungrateful scarecrow,' Peace snarled as he ran on.

Groups of children near the store's front entrance watched his approach with only passive interest until one of them, seemingly a born agitator with a gift for picking up ugly undercurrents, cupped his hands to his mouth and shouted, 'He killed Jarvie!'

'That's a dirty lie,' Peace tried to retort, but he was at once caught in an implosion of small bodies, all of them kicking and punching and gouging like frenzied demons. Only the fact that the assault came from all sides at once enabled him to stay upright. He burst out of the mêlée by sheer force of panic, shot out through the door on to the avenue and ran blindly along the pavement. Behind him was a pursuing horde of men, women and little children who were baying for his life like avenging hounds.

'I just hope you're proud of yourself, Warren,' Brown Owl said from the vibrant tooth. 'I just hope you're proud of yourself, that's all I can say.' As if to demonstrate this conversational handicap, he added, 'I just hope you're proud of yourself.'

'You've got to get me out of here,' Peace gasped through the bellowing of his lungs.

'I *told* you not to stay the extra day.'

'I know you did, Brown Owl, and I should have listened to you.'

'It's all very well saying things like that *now*, Warren, but it's too late, isn't it? If only you'd listened to me at the proper time we wouldn't be in all this trouble.'

'*We?*' Peace glanced over his shoulder and his mouth went dry as he saw that casual shoppers, obeying mob instinct, were throwing down their parcels and joining in the hunt. 'They're going to tear me limb from limb down here, Brown Owl. You've got to send a ship for me – right now!'

'If I do that,' Brown Owl said, 'you'll have to promise to do what you're told in future.'

'I promise, I promise,' Peace sobbed. 'I swear to you I'll never step out of line again.'

Chapter 14

Peace was standing at a window of the Oscar headquarters ship on Mildor IV. It was unusual for him to gaze outside – the airless plain was truly uninspiring – but an event in which he had some interest was taking place. A spaceship had just landed about a kilometre away and a lone Oscar, Joby Lorenz, was walking towards the HQ vessel. Joby was carrying some miscellaneous supplies, and among them was a replacement direction finder for one of the Oscar command radios. Peace cared nothing about the component itself, but he was very much interested in the tough plastic bag which enclosed it.

He left the window while Joby was still some way off and sat down at the communications desk, pretending to be absorbed in his work. With most other Oscars such a deception would have been impossible, but Joby had been none too bright as a human being and becoming a symbiont had not increased his IQ to any noticeable extent. His telepathic facility was also somewhat deficient, and as a consequence Peace usually had little difficulty in pulling the wool over his ruby-red eyes.

'Hi, Warren!' Joby gave Peace a friendly wave as he came into the communications room and set the direction finder down on a table. 'Keeping busy?'

Peace nodded. 'You know me – never happy unless I'm hard at work.'

'That's great, Warren. I'm glad you're not all bored and restless and such, the way you were before you went off to do that job on Golborne.'

'I've learned my lesson,' Peace said earnestly. 'I know when I'm well off.'

'Glad to hear it.' Joby took the direction finder out of its bag, went with it to the non-functioning subspace radio and plugged the new component in. 'I hope this gizmo holds up a bit longer

216

than the last one. It's funny the way we've had so many failures recently.'

'Yes, indeed.' Peace concentrated his mind on the green salad he would be having for lunch, using the thought-damping technique to prevent Joby from divining exactly why electronics units had been failing so frequently. Peace had been assisting in their demise by pouring water into the casings.

'I'm going out for a run round the planet, but I'll tidy up in here first,' Joby said, moving towards the empty plastic bag.

Peace got to it first and picked it up. 'I'll throw this in the atomizer for you,' he said. 'You go on out and have your bit of fun.'

'Thanks, Warren.' Joby tilted his brazen head and looked closely at Peace. 'Are you sure you're not even a little bit bored in here? I mean, it's been ten or eleven days.'

'I love it here.' Peace thought steadfastly about lettuce leaves until Joby had left the ship and bounded off into the rock-strewn wilderness.

He was all alone in the Oscar headquarters, but his guardians knew there was no risk of his escaping, even though there were several spare spaceships always parked in the vicinity. The fact that Mildor IV was devoid of an atmosphere made it impossible for Peace to get to any of the ships without a spacesuit.

Humming cheerfully to himself, Peace carried the plastic bag to his bedroom at the opposite end of the ship. He folded it neatly and put it away in a drawer along with some personal possessions and all the other pieces of heavy-duty plastic he had collected.

Let's see, he thought. *Plastic sheeting ... scissors ... glue ... What else do I need to make a spacesuit?*

CRITICAL WAVE

THE EUROPEAN SCIENCE FICTION & FANTASY REVIEW

"CRITICAL WAVE is the most consistently interesting and intelligent review on the sf scene."
- Michael Moorcock.

"One of the best of the business journals... I never miss a copy..." - Bruce Sterling.

"Intelligent and informative, one of my key sources of news, reviews and comments." - Stephen Baxter.

"I don't feel informed until I've read it."
- Ramsey Campbell.

"Don't waver - get WAVE!" - Brian W Aldiss.

CRITICAL WAVE is published six times per year and has established a reputation for hard-hitting news coverage, perceptive essays on the state of the genre and incisive reviews of the latest books, comics and movies. Regular features include publishing news, portfolios by Europe's leading sf and fantasy artists, extensive club, comic mart and convention listings, interviews with prominent authors and editors, fiction market reports, fanzine and magazine reviews and convention reports.

Previous contributors have included: MICHAEL MOORCOCK, IAIN BANKS, CLIVE BARKER, LISA TUTTLE, BOB SHAW, COLIN GREENLAND, DAVID LANGFORD, ROBERT HOLDSTOCK, GARRY KILWORTH, SHAUN HUTSON, DAVID WINGROVE, TERRY PRATCHETT, RAMSEY CAMPBELL, LARRY NIVEN, BRIAN W ALDISS, ANNE GAY, STEPHEN BAXTER, RAYMOND FEIST, CHRIS CLAREMONT and STORM CONSTANTINE.

A six issue subscription costs only eight pounds and fifty pence or a sample copy one pound and ninety-five pence; these rates only apply to the UK, overseas readers should contact the address below for further details. Cheques or postal orders should be made payable to "Critical Wave Publications" and sent to: M Tudor, 845 Alum Rock Road, Birmingham, B8 2AG. Please allow 30 days for delivery.

Who Goes Here?

BOB SHAW

War was one game Warren Peace didn't want to play. So why had he joined the Space Legion? Warren knew he'd got to escape, but to do so meant a hair-raising and hilarious journey into the forgotten past . . .

£3.99   0 575 05678 9

Terminal Velocity

BOB SHAW

Near anarchy reigns in the skies with the advent of the cheap and easy to use anti-gravity harness. As people are free to take to the air in their millions, the authority's control of the sky has begun to falter – with devastating consequences.

£3.99   0 575 05314 3

Merlin and the Last Trump

COLLIN WEBBER

Sir Griswold wasn't sorry about bumping off Lancelot. After all, the sanctimonious prat had asked for it. But he couldn't fathom all the fuss Merlin was making about it.

The demise of one vainglorious knight couldn't be that important, could it?

Evidently it could. And it was to throw Griswold into an adventure involving walking castles, talking boxes, demons that lived in 'cans', and the deadliest enemy humanity had ever had to face. Not to mention the band who were about to play the Last Trump.

'Goes at a cracking pace. Recommended for anyone with a warped sense of humour' – Mary Gentle

'Some delightfully quirky twists, punchlines and dramatic effects, [that] often brought a smile even to my notoriously cruel and thin lips. Watch for what he does next!' – Dave Langford

£4.99   0 575 05718 1

Bill, the Galactic Hero

HARRY HARRISON

Acclaimed as science fiction's answer to *Catch-22*, *Bill, the Galactic Hero* is a hilariously satirical sf novel that explodes sf clichés by the shuttle-load.

'Simply *the* funniest science fiction book ever written' – Terry Pratchett

£3.99   0 575 04701 1

Bill, the Galactic Hero on the Planet of the Hippies from Hell

HARRY HARRISON
DAVID BISCHOFF

The penultimate episode of the bestselling series finds Bill, the Galactic Hero, on Barworld, home planet of the finest beverages in the universe. Can he survive an entire planet of blondes, booze and bathtubs of champagne? Will he quell the assassin-hippies? If he does, he has to find a time portal and stop an evil conspiracy from taking over the world of comics.

£3.99   0 575 05526 X

The Weird Colonial Boy

PAUL VOERMANS

Nigel is a drongo – a wittering, spot-faced pillock whose only, lonely passions are music (it's 1978 and the Sex Pistols are riding high), sex (unconsummated) and tropical fish.

Then one of his fish finds its way into another dimension (don't ask) and Nigel follows it.

It's still 1978 and he's still in Australia. But in this Australia there's no punk music, no Clearasil. What there *is*, is prison camps, floggings, public executions and chain gangs. And understanding it all could mean the death penalty for a drongo like Nigel . . .

'A wild comic romp' – *New Statesman*

'Exhilarating. through pain and slapstick to enlightenment – yay!' – *Locus*

By the author of *And Disregards the Rest*: 'Vigorous and confident and richly authentic . . . the debut of a powerful and distinctive new voice' – Paul J. McAuley, *Interzone*

£4.99   0 575 05715 7

And Disregards the Rest

PAUL VOERMANS

A critically acclaimed debut novel from a young
Australian writer:

'Vigorous and confident, and richly authentic...
powerfully strange and apocalyptic and elegant
...the debut of a powerful and distinctive new
voice' – Paul J. McAuley, *Interzone*

'An interesting and ambitious first novel...so
different from everything else around these days
that it deserves attention' – *Time Out*

'Enjoyable, sometimes poignant, and far better
written than most standard SF' – *Locus*

£4.99   ISBN 0 575 05282 1